TIMELINE
VIRGO
RISING

I0563394

The Third Book in The Timeline Series

STEVEN FOSTER

Author photo by Josh Stelting
Cover design by Touch Publishing
Edited by Kimberly Soesbee

ISBN: 978-1-942508-33-5

Published by Touch Publishing
Requests should be directed to:
P.O. Box 180303
Arlington, Texas 76096
www.TouchPublishingServices.com

Printed in the United States of America

Other books in the Timeline Series:
The Minuteman Project 978-0-9919839-2-6
Journey to Skeleton Island 978-0-9919839-8-8

CONTENTS

PROLOGUE

Ypres, Belgium
November 11, 1914
10:45 A.M.

The German forces were attempting to break through the Allied lines. Their offensive was currently working, and they had just found a gap. They needed to establish a foothold. Gunfire rang throughout the woods.

A young German lifted his rifle to take aim at a figure in the distance, when in his view three bodies suddenly appeared, much closer to his position than he'd taken aim. He let out a yell and lowered the rifle to see how he could have grossly miscalculated the distance of the enemy. He squinted. Three people appeared out of nowhere, landing not twenty-five yards from where he stood. Their bodies rolled along the ground and came to an abrupt stop. Startled Germans redirected their fire towards the new open targets.

Will reacted quickly, pulling Jessica behind a mound of dirt as bullets whizzed past them. She was in mild shock from the time-jump. Francis' body lay face-down in the dirt, sheltered by several dead men and a small divot in the ground. His body was only five feet away from Will's, but the distance seemed greater amidst the rat-tat of gunfire, which echoed in their ears.

Will flinched as the bullets hissed over the mound, connecting with the dirt nearby, sending chunks flying everywhere.

"What's going on?" Jessica screamed.

Will scanned their surroundings. He could see several men hiding in cover in front of them. They were soldiers returning fire from the other side. "What do you think?" he shouted back over the sound of gunfire. "He landed us right in the middle of a warzone!"

One of the soldiers was waving desperately at them to come towards him. Will made eye contact, and the soldier continued to wave them over. "We need to move. Now!"

"But what about Francis?" Jessica yelled back. A grenade exploded near them, spraying them with dirt.

"There's nothing we can do! Leave him!" Will yanked on her arm.

Fighting the urge to run back and help Francis, she followed Will, who pulled her along like a child dragging a doll. The two of them stayed low, moving fast towards the soldier. Bullets blew by as they raced for cover. As soon as they were in reach of the soldier, he grabbed Will's shoulder and threw them in the hole he was using for cover.

"Get down and stay down!" the soldier shouted. He shoved them aside and continued firing at the enemy across the woods.

Will analyzed the information in his surroundings, trying to figure out what sort of situation they were in. Jessica leaned against him, shaking partly from shock and partly due to the cold. All she could think about was Francis, helpless. All Will was thinking about was how to get his hands on a gun.

Francis was left alone in the middle of the battle, with bodies and limbs scattered around him. The fallen soldiers provided his defenseless body camouflage and shelter. The gunfire continued as both sides tried to kill each other, taking whatever ground they could. Anyone who glanced his way would assume he was just another casualty. But if they got close enough, they would notice he was still breathing.

1: NEW BEGINNINGS

February 3, 1916
To Whom it May Concern:

They tell me writing a journal will help keep details straight, and may make it easier to do my reports. I regretfully say that if you are reading this, it means that I am dead. I've lost Jessica, and Will is nowhere to be found. My heart still hopes for the best, but I moved on a long time ago.

I have written these journals to help keep track of things, as the days and events blur together for me. They contain everything from my imprisonment at The Island until now, including the time spent in Camelot and searching for Skeleton Island. I have written entries at every opportunity I have had, and keep them on my person for the majority of the time. I write the day's events—at least the important ones—as best as I can remember them. I may have missed or forgotten pieces of conversation, or exact words said, but hopefully it will be an accurate account if something happens to me.

That being said, things have changed since we landed here. The year is now 1916. I have been stuck here for over a year. Enclosed in this envelope are all of the journals I have written. If you are reading this, it means I have failed at stopping The Island. Whoever you are, you must take up the fight. The Island must be stopped at all costs. I only wish it hadn't come to this. Good luck.

STEVEN FOSTER

Journal Entry #17
November 13, 1914
Military Hospital Outside of Ypres

I woke up in a hospital. It wasn't like the kind of hospital seen on television shows or like the sterile operating rooms on The Island. It was old fashioned—the equipment, that is—and it was very noisy. Nurses and doctors rushed back and forth, passing my bed without a glance in my direction. I looked around. My head was in pain and after each movement, it took a few seconds to refocus. Clear liquid dripped from a container through a tube which was taped to my arm. Countless bunks surrounded me, holding injured men (go figure, it's a hospital, right?), and each was in a different condition. Some lay covered from head to toe in white bandages. Others were crimson red and sweating heavily. A few were missing appendages, arms or legs, sometimes both. One lay in the corner with a sheet covering his entire body.

People shouted to each other from opposite sides of the room. They were doing their best to treat the wounded, but more kept coming in. As I took it all in, I was snapped into reality. Waking up to this, when the last thing I remember was being on the ship, was kind of a shock. I can't say that I wasn't scared. I was in a strange place, and my friends were nowhere in sight. What happened? What's going on? Where am I? The questions were not helping my headache.

I slowly sat up, leaning against a flimsy excuse for a pillow. It felt like I was resting on a bag of shredded clothes. Sitting up made me feel slightly better. Judging from the people around me, things could be worse. Fear crept into my mind the way a virus spreads through the body. *What if my friends were among these people? Were they alive? Did they even make it here?*

Soon the questions would be answered. A man in a brown

uniform approached my bed. His face was covered with black smudges, and his uniform was covered in dirt. It looked like he had just crawled through a field of mud that had been set on fire. He picked up a stool and sat down next to my bed.

"Good to see you're awake," he said in a deep voice.

I stared at him. "Where am I? What's going on? Where are my friends?"

He calmly held up a hand to silence me. "Relax. You're fine. I'm Captain Horst with the British Expeditionary Forces. We found your body lying amongst our dead on the outskirts of Ypres. You were still breathing, which in itself is a miracle, considering the area you were in. We thought everyone was dead from the skirmish. We brought you here, and you've been unconscious for the last two days."

"And what about my friends?"

Captain Horst hesitated. "We found you amongst a pile of dead soldiers. Who exactly were your friends?"

The fact that he had said, "soldiers" gave me some relief. That meant my friends weren't found dead beside me. "There are two of them—a guy and a girl. Will Tapper and Jessica Noble. They were with me. Do you know anything about them?"

Horst sat up. "One of my officers reported that he escorted two civilians from the battlefield near where we found you. I believe these would be your two friends, but I cannot be sure. We did not get their names, and they were taken away from here, somewhere safe from the battle."

"Where are they now?"

He shrugged. "I'm sorry, but I do not know. They were civilians, and civilians are not allowed in this area. They would have been taken to the nearest town that is a safe distance from the front, and questioned. I'm sorry I can't be of more help."

I frowned. "There has to be a way to find them."

"I'm afraid this war is quite chaotic," he said with a sigh. "Communications are not exactly…reliable. And many civilians have been separated when the Germans attacked."

"Wait, Germans? Where exactly did you say we are?"

"Just outside of Ypres, Belgium." Horst eyed me curiously.

"Belgium?" I muttered to myself, processing what I knew. That's in Europe. And if Germans are attacking it, then that means…Uh oh. "What year is it?"

"1914. Are you sure you are alright?"

Well, that's just peachy. I landed us in the middle of World War One (well, technically the beginning of the war, but in the middle of the action). Ypres had not registered at first in my mind, but it was dawning on me now. I recalled information I had learned at The Island. Ypres was not a place I wanted to be, but at least it was not April. Ypres would be a bad place to be in April. Before I had a chance to ask anything else, a large man interrupted us. "Excuse me, Captain, but I am going to have to ask you to step away from this patient."

His voice was deep and hollow, and his eyes pierced through the Captain. He wore a different kind of uniform—his was black. Fear gripped my insides as my eyes fell upon a white symbol on his uniform. It was The Island's logo. I immediately panicked. My eyes darted back and forth, looking for some way to escape. Was he here to kill me? Did he know who I was? I was still a little dizzy, so I couldn't just run away. That would also raise a few question. I did the only thing I could do. I stayed put, and decided to wait the situation out.

"On whose authority?" Captain Horst questioned.

The man shot him a look that could kill. He reached into his jacket pocket and handed the man a small black wallet. Horst opened it and his eyes widened for a split second. He handed it back to the man. "I'm sorry, sir. I didn't realize."

"Of course you didn't. Now leave us. And if anyone asks if you saw either of us," he gestured at me, "you know nothing of it, understood?"

"Yes, sir." Captain Horst saluted the man and then left abruptly.

The man made sure he was gone and then turned to me. "Show me your wrist."

Panic coursed through my veins the way adrenaline would through someone skydiving (admittedly, panic may be flowing through a skydiver as well). I raised my sleeve to reveal the same symbol that was on his uniform.

"We didn't think any of our agents in Ypres survived. When our informant told me that someone with our mark was brought here, I came immediately. You can call me Wash. I'm sure you have heard rumors of who I am among our other agents."

He paused waiting for me to reply. I shook my head. "Erm, not really, sir."

He grunted. "Well then, let's just say I run things on this side of the war. Are you able to stand?"

I nodded. "I think so. By the way, my name—"

I was cut off before I could finish. "Do not reveal your identity. Not here. Now come with me. We must debrief you at once, and you must tell us what happened at our operation here," the man said bluntly.

I struggled to get out of the bunk. The blood rushed from my head when I stood up, and I began to fall backwards. Wash extended an arm to keep me upright. He waited for me to recover.

"Thanks."

He nodded. "We need to go now. You have been here too long as it is."

He turned and began walking to the door. I followed him slowly; the room was still spinning. After passing through it I saw

Captain Horst. I tried to smile at him, but as soon as he spotted me, he avoided looking in our direction. It didn't inspire confidence in my current situation. Who was this man, and why was Horst so scared of him? Despite my concern, I didn't have much of a choice. Wash led me through swinging doors and down a hallway.

Of course, I had no idea where I was going. Wash had mentioned something about an operation nearby, but I had no clue what that meant. I'd have to find some way to talk myself out of it. Not going to lie, I was pretty worried that I'd end up being stuck in another Island facility. My only hope was that my friends were not in a worse situation. I took a deep breath as Wash opened the door and led me into the pouring rain. An old fashioned car was waiting for us. The Island's logo was plastered on the side door. He watched as I climbed in the passenger seat, and then he turned a crank at the front of the vehicle, sparking the car to life. He pulled himself up behind the wheel. Priority one for me was getting out of here, and priority two was finding my friends.

Wash talked over the engine. "I would recommend getting some rest. It'll take a while to get where we're going."

I nodded, and tried to get comfortable. The loud rattle of the engine, and the constant bumpy terrain kept me awake for a bit, but eventually the noise and movement soothed me to sleep, and I faded away. What else could I do?

Island Operations HQ
162 Miles From Ypres

I slept through most of the ride, catching glimpses every now and then of ruined buildings, but I couldn't piece any of it together. Finally, we jolted to a stop, jerking me out of my sleep.

"We're here," Wash grunted.

I sat up groggily. I noticed that it was no longer raining. "Where's *here* exactly?"

"Island Operations Unit Headquarters for the Western Front. We call it IOU for short," he said as he opened the side door and stepped out. I did the same. Outside appeared to be a camouflaged entrance to a bunker. A young man ran past Wash, taking the vehicle away. "Ypres had just a small research station where you were, but this is the whole shebang. This is where all of our plans come together, but more on that later. Right now we need you to debrief us and then we'll get you up to speed. Follow me."

That was a lot to take in. I was a little groggy, so I followed and said nothing. The air was damp and cold inside the bunker entrance. Wash led me down a long corridor, lined with cement on all sides. At the end was a security checkpoint where two armed men boasted vintage Island uniforms. As Wash approached, he pulled up his sleeve and revealed his tattoo. He gave me a nod to do the same. The guards eyed both tattoos, lingering on mine for a second longer. Wash had the same symbol, but did not have the bar code that I did. In the end, they let us pass, opening a solid metal door behind them.

The small child in me started to panic. This place was looking too familiar, and I did not want to get locked away again. The thought struck me that since it is the past, they shouldn't know who I am, or what I can do. That comforted me, but it still felt odd to be welcomed into the belly of the beast.

Wash led me through several rooms filled with people. I tried not to look at anyone. Finally, he opened a door revealing a small room that had a long wooden table in it. Both of us sat down, and the door slammed shut. Wash pulled out a cigar and lit it. "You're not fooling anyone."

"Excuse me?" I asked nervously.

He exhaled a large puff of smoke. "All of our agents were killed at Ypres. One of my sources reported seeing you and two others appear out of nowhere, in the middle of a skirmish. You're not from any of our divisions, yet you bear our symbol." He paused, taking another drag. "Understand that I will ask this once, and only once. Who are you, and what are you doing here?"

My heart felt like it would give out, it was beating so fast. I had to think of something quickly. Somehow I knew that if I lied, he would be able to tell. So I did the next best thing. I told him the half-truth. "My name is Francis Parker. I am an agent of Island Corporations, and I was sent here…from the future."

Wash started to choke on the cigar smoke. After he had stopped wheezing, he began to laugh. I kept calm, holding a serious face. "You expect me to believe that? Anything would have been a better explanation than that. It's a shame really, now I'll have to get this room all bloody, just for you to finally admit you're a German spy. Poor decision, kid."

In that moment I only had one move to make, and I had to sell it. I smiled. "I figured you wouldn't believe me, so how about a demonstration?"

"Oh, this ought to be good," he chuckled.

"I'm going to disappear, right before your eyes," I said, standing from my chair. "And then I am going to reappear in the chair next to you in twenty seconds. Will that be enough proof for you to believe?"

He leaned forward, clutching the cigar in his teeth. "If you can pull that off, I'll eat this cigar whole."

Looking back, I think everything I have went through finally hit me. Instantly I became more confident than I had ever been in my abilities. I shut my eyes and stopped time. I ran over to a locker that stood in the corner and hid inside. I unfroze time, feeling only a small headache. I began counting to twenty. Wash nearly fell out of his chair after seeing me there one second and gone the next. I could hear him scrambling around the room, no doubt checking under the table and spinning in confused circles. I heard him push a crackly speaker on the wall and demand angrily, "Has anyone left conference room seven?"

A voice crackled back. "No, sir. Just you and the man you came with have gone in, no one out."

Wash growled in anger. "This can't be."

I could hear footsteps as he paced the room, coming closer to my hiding spot. *Sixteen, seventeen.* Each second he was getting closer to finding me. I cut it a little close, freezing time just as he was about to reach for the door. I moved around him and sat in the chair I had specified earlier. I released my hold on time.

"I guess you have to eat that cigar now, don't you?" I said rather smugly.

Wash jumped at the sound of my voice. He whipped around. He turned back and opened the locker, eyeing it skeptically. "How did you?"

"I told you, Wash. I'm from the future. How else would that be possible? I was sent here from the twenty-first century." I rolled up my sleeve, revealing the mark. "Every agent has this symbol branded to their skin. We also have a barcode that is different for every one of us. Still think I am lying?"

His eyes narrowed as he studied me. "Give me a moment."

Wash exited the room. I waited, trying to figure out where I could go if this plan worked, and more importantly, if it failed. So far I was able to think quickly enough to figure out my next move, but I was worried that I would get in too deep.

I was surprised The Island went this far back in history. Right now I had to focus on convincing them of who I was. If I failed, I'd be screwed. Several minutes passed. Finally, the door opened, and in stepped Wash accompanied by another man.

The man looked remarkably similar to Wash—almost identical. "I am sorry for the precautions we have had to make. I'm sure you understand that we need to be certain you are who you say you are. That being said, I am the real Agent Wash. This one is a decoy to root out assassins."

"Wow, looks like you have a real dream job." The fake Wash said nothing, and then proceeded to leave the room. "Was it something I said?"

Agent Wash shook his head. "He has served his purpose. And I wouldn't test him. I've seen that man kill dozens of spies and assassins with his bare hands. He excels at killing."

"I see."

Wash cleared his throat. "I saw what you did. Remarkable. How did you come into this ability?"

I shrugged. "Like I said, I'm from the future. Island Corporations have many resources and technology that would surprise you. The specifics I cannot go in to, for understandable reasons."

He nodded. "Very well. It's a bit hard to fathom, but you have shown us something that is not possible. What exactly are you doing here?"

Good question. I thought quickly. "The company ran into some…trouble. They traced the problem back to this war, which in the future is known as World War One. We aren't sure what it is, but we know it originated during this time period. It is my job—along with my companions—to see what went wrong, and fix it." Yeah, that sounded reasonable.

"You mentioned companions, whom exactly are you referring to?"

"As advanced as our technology is, time travel is very difficult to perfect. I blacked out on arrival. The two I came with were apparently moved somewhere and questioned before I came to. Their names are Jessica Noble and William Tapper. My mission cannot be completed without them."

Wash remained silent for a moment. "I do not know where they are. We have been trying to track them down ever since you appeared. We will find them. In the meantime, I think I may know what the problem you came to investigate is."

I was taken aback. That was all a story. There wasn't supposed to be anything actually wrong. Curiosity got the better of me. "Oh?"

He got out of the chair and nodded at the door. "Follow me."

The two of us exited the room and began walking down a corridor. The entire facility was built underground, walled in concrete. Later on I learned that the 1914 Island Corporation was not a corporation at all. During this time they were a special ops unit that had access to technology that had not been released yet. I can see how they became what they did. They had access to new tech before it was even tested or released. From what I heard, they are often the ones coming up with the new developments. It's scary scratching the surface of how far back their influence goes. Jess, Will, or whoever is reading this: we need to stop them, no matter the cost. If they advanced as much as they have since 1914, imagine what they can do in our time.

Wash led me to a door with a keypad. High-tech for this time period. He entered a combination and the doors slid open. The room contained multiple filing cabinets. Wash walked over to one and pulled out a folder. He tossed it towards me across a desk in the middle of the room. I opened it to see a picture of a man. The next picture showed a close up of his forearm. He had an Island logo, but that was not all. He had a barcode—just like me. I stared closer at the picture. It can't be. How is that possible?

"That man is masquerading as one of us, yet we have no

record of him existing." Wash paused, eyeing me suspiciously, "Much like you. You both have the same markings underneath it as well. I was hoping you could shed some light on the subject. Up until now we believed him to be an informant for the Germans, but when we couldn't find any information on him, we hit a wall. When we heard someone with the same markings had shown up in Ypres, we dispatched a team to pick you up. If what you're saying is true, then I am led to believe that this man is from the future as well. Is that correct?"

The picture of that wrist frightened me. I nodded. "That's the only explanation I can think of, but I don't know how it would be possible for him to get here unless…" I thought back to what Nimue had told me, and how she came to be in medieval times. If they had realized the compound worked on me, would they begin testing on others? Could there be Island agents hunting us? Or are they already working on manipulating the past? I had to find out more.

"Unless what?" Wash asked.

"Do you know anything about what this man is doing?"

Wash sighed. "Unfortunately we don't know much. Our undercover agents are trying to get more information, but based on what we know so far, he's building some kind of weapon for them. He seems to be some kind of scientist."

A weapon? That's not good. My single goal of finding my friends and getting out of here was going to be pushed aside for something bigger. Even if I found them, how could we ignore this man? It was something I had to investigate. "I don't know what he was sent here to do, but we need to stop him. Find everything you can about what he is doing. I also need my companions. It's crucial that I find them."

Wash nodded. "Very well, but understand that we are already looking for them. Even with our advanced resources they will still be hard to find. We are doing everything we can to find them, but there is nothing more that you can do. You might as well help the team I'm putting together to learn more about this man."

I thought about it for a moment. I couldn't leave here to find my friends because I have no clue where they could be—or where I was. Wash's plan made sense. "Fine. I'll join up with your team and try and find out whatever we can, but the moment you find my companions bring them to me. It's very likely they won't trust you and will try to escape. And if you do capture them, they will probably lie about whom they are until they see me. They have abilities like me, which means you must be careful. I'd much rather look for them myself, but I don't know the area, and I need to figure out what that man is doing here."

"Good. I'll get a room ready for you and introduce you to the team."

Wash was about to leave when I put a hand on his shoulder, stopping him. "Wash, understand that this is not something you should take lightly or put on the back-burner. If I find out that you are not searching as well as you could be or if any harm comes to my companions, I will kill those responsible. Do I make myself clear?"

He looked into my eyes and saw that I was serious. He nodded and left the room quickly. The doors shut, and I collapsed into the nearest chair. "What have I gotten us into?"

I stared at the file in front of me. Was The Island already sending people back? Were there people hunting us? Were my friends safe? I didn't want to threaten Wash, but I saw no other option. I needed to find them, and I needed to make sure he would not stop looking for them or possibly injure them. Right now I had to maintain my composure, and keep with the character I had created. If Wash began to doubt my integrity, I would be in trouble. I took a deep breath and went to find out more information.

As soon as I stepped outside the door an alarm sounded, and several red lights began flashing. I retraced my steps, jogging through the halls, hoping to find Wash or someone that could tell me what was going on. I raced around a corner to find him shouting orders to several men.

I waited till he finished. "What's going on?"

"There is a security breach," he grunted, cocking a pistol. "It seems we have a mole in our midst." Gunfire rang through the hallway. Wash pulled out a second pistol and handed it to me. "Follow me."

We charged towards the gunfire. Wash led the way, peering around corners and ducking through doors. He pulled open another door, its sign read: Loading Bay. He peeked out, then swung it open. He waved me in. Several crudely armored vehicles were lined in a row. The gunfire became louder. Wash cursed as he saw one of their autos peeling out of the bay. The gunfire faded, as did the car.

"I want men after them, now!" he shouted at the soldiers, who were already on the move. He turned to another. "What did they get?"

The man shrugged. "It's hard to say, sir. The alarm sounded after they had already breached our system."

Wash cursed again. "It looks like we have to change our location up."

"What do you mean?" I asked.

"We're moving our headquarters to London. We move in thirty."

The man saluted Wash. "Yes, sir."

"What about my companions? And the operation here?" I asked him.

He turned to me angrily. "Look, kid. I get it, you're from the future and have an urgent mission with those two, but right now I have bigger concerns. We didn't make it this far in secret by staying in one place. When we are discovered, we move—simple as that. We'll pick up the investigation into your companions and the other man when we get to London. But getting there is our priority number one, got it?"

I nodded, feeling a bit silly. "How can I help?"

"By staying out of the way," he said, storming off.

With that, I took to the shadows and watched them move everything into the remaining vehicles. I did nothing to help. Once everything was loaded, we moved out. I rode in the same car I'd arrived in, along with Wash and another man. Wash was holding some sort of remote. He checked his rearview mirror and pushed the button, detonating an explosion that leveled the entrance to the base and everything in it. I turned around and watched the flames in awe. After that, we made our way to London.

2: JESSICA AND WILL

Monday:

My name is Jessica Noble. I started this diary because Monica says writing down your thoughts and feelings can help you cope with this line of work. She says it keeps your mental state in check, and right now I'm a train wreck. So I'm taking her advice and starting a journal.

I haven't seen or heard from Francis since we got here, despite my efforts to find him. Will left me and is off on his own doing God knows what. I don't know what's gotten into him. I guess I'll get to all of that. First things first, how did I end up here?

We landed in the midst of a firefight in Ypres. I was in such shock Will dragged me to cover, and then again to a foxhole. When the shooting died down, a soldier escorted us to a man named Frank. He was the British Commanding Officer or something like that. He plunked us into an interrogation room.

"Who are you, and what were you doing in the middle of that?" he began.

I had already deduced that we were in the early 1900s during World War One. This was easy judging from the weapons, uniforms, and hearing of our location. I didn't trust Will not to say something stupid, so I spoke up. "We're just civilians. We meant to evacuate long ago, but I got sick, and my brother, Will, stayed with me. By the time I was able to move, the Germans were already upon us, so we hid. When we tried to run we were cut off, and we lost our friend. Now we're here."

Frank grunted. "You speak excellent English for a Belgian."

I had to think quickly on my feet. "Our mother taught us when we were younger."

"I see." He studied us long and hard. "Well you two are no German agents, that's for sure. However, I know you're not telling me the truth either. Tell you what: I've got bigger fish to fry. Go into town and find Monica. She's a doctor at the local hospital. Find her and tell her Frank sent you. She'll take care of you."

"That's it?" I asked. Will still said nothing.

Frank nodded. "That's it. There are larger threats to deal with, and my men are dying out there. I'm not wasting any time on the two of you. I just had to see if you were German agents."

"How could you tell we weren't?"

He grinned. "Because no German agent would come up with such a weak lie."

I frowned as he left the room. I thought I had done a great job coming up with that lie on the spot. "Wait! What about our friend?"

"If I come across him I'll send him your way," Frank called from the hallway.

I hated not being able to go after Francis, but it was too dangerous, and we didn't know the area. We'd probably get lost, or shot. Frank seemed like a trustworthy guy, so I thought it best to find the woman he spoke of.

"Well, let's go find that woman, Monica," I said to Will.

"And then what, Jess?" he asked bluntly. "You and I both know Francis is probably dead, covered with bullet holes."

My fist flew out all on its own, and I punched him in the face. "Don't you dare say that about him!"

I held back angry tears. He put his hands up in self-defense. "Okay, easy. Look, all I'm saying is I don't think he's going to make it out of this one. He's been lucky up until now."

"We could at least give him the benefit of the doubt!" I shouted.

"Fine, we'll go find Monica. When the dust settles, if he's alive, great. If not, I'm moving on."

I should have asked him then what he had meant by that, but I was too overwhelmed with emotions at the time. I refused to accept that Francis would die like that. I asked one of the nearby soldiers for directions into town. We began walking, and after several grueling miles we finally reached it. The sun was heading down by the time we found the hospital. It was an ordinary building, nothing fancy. I would have missed it entirely (there was no sign) if it weren't for the loading and unloading of bodies. It concerned me that the majority of them were dead. We approached the front desk where we met a woman named Gertrude.

"Excuse me," I said. "We're looking for a woman named Monica. Would you be able to help us?"

She held up a finger to shush us. She pulled out a file and picked up a rudimentary phone receiver. "Hey, hun, I've got the file right here…oh hun, I don't think she's got a chance…well the six cats say something about her…mhmm, well I would have walked out too…"

Her voice was thick and raspy. A packed ashtray beside the phone sat as evidence of a smoking habit. The conversation continued for another minute. I had to fight the urge to clear my throat and interrupt her. Looking back, I'm glad I didn't. Gertrude could either be your best friend or your worst enemy. She finally put the receiver down. "What do you want?"

"Oh, well we're looking for a woman named Monica, could you point us in the right direction?" I asked.

"I can do better than that, hun." She pulled out a piece of paper and checked a clock on the wall. "She should be in room 37 down the hall and on the left."

"Thank you," I said. She lit a cigarette as we walked away. A short ways along the hall we found a door labeled 37. The room was crowded, yet barren at the same time. Beds lined either side of the room, spaced several feet apart from each other. About half of them held wounded men. The others were eerily empty. A long walkway stretched across the room between the beds. There were several nurses dressed in white uniforms bustling about. I approached one and she pointed out Monica.

Monica wore a lilac uniform with a white apron that had a red cross on it. She was reading something on a clipboard at the end of a patient's bed. The man in the bed was covered in bandages that were dotted with yellowy-orange spots. His chest rose and fell steadily.

"Excuse me," I said. "Are you Monica?"

Monica did not take her eyes off the chart. "I am. What do you want?"

"My name is Jessica. A man named Frank told us we could find you here. He said you might be able to help us out."

At the mention of Frank, Monica looked up, and then towards me. Her eyes studied me briefly, then they moved to Will. "How do you know Frank?"

"We got caught in the middle of a firefight, and he was responsible for asking us questions. He didn't view us as a threat, and he told us you might be able to help us."

She paused for a moment, then put the clipboard down. She reached into her apron to pull out several rolls of bandages. "I see. Mind helping me out with these?"

I nodded. "Sure."

Will shook his head. "Nope. I am not touching that guy. Looks disgusting." Monica's look sent him running. "How about I just wait outside?"

Sheepishly he scurried off. I apologized to Monica for his lack of filter. She ignored most of what I said. "If I were you, I'd find a new boyfriend. He looks like a weasel."

"Ew. No. Nope. You think he and—" I tasted a bit of vomit in my mouth. "No way. He's not my boyfriend. He's just a friend. Gross."

"Well then, looks like you're a better judge of character than I assumed," she said while unwrapping the man's damp bandages. "Can you hold his head here while I put the new dressings on?"

"Like this?" I asked, cradling his head. I felt some sort of liquid on my hands, but for some reason, it didn't bother me.

"Perfect." Monica expertly wrapped the man's head. His face was badly wounded, and puss oozed from it.

"What happened to him?"

She sighed. "He got too close to a grenade. He's lucky to still be alive. It could have been a lot worse."

I looked around the room. There was so much pain and suffering that I had previously overlooked. "Will he make it?"

"I don't know. Some fight, some quit, and some never even get that choice. I just try and make sure they're as comfortable as they can be. Now can you hand me those scissors?"

I grabbed them off a nearby tray and gave them to her. She cut the bandage and tucked it in. "Thanks. It's a bit awkward to dress wounds on your own sometimes."

"No problem," I said, wiping my hands clean.

"So Frank sent you to me, did he?" she asked rhetorically. "Well then, I'm going to assume you and your friend don't have a home or family to go to?"

"Correct. We have a third friend, but..." I bit my lip, holding back tears and thoughts of Francis. "But we had to leave him behind. Frank said he'd look for him and if he was found, he'd send him here."

Monica was good at reading people, as I later found out. She must have seen my concern. "I'm sorry about your friend. I hope they find him. Well, I don't normally do this, but you have steady hands, and you're smarter than most of the help here. Why don't you work as my assistant?"

"What?" I was shocked. "Here? You mean like a nurse?"

She nodded. "Do keep up with me, dear. Good help is hard to come by in these times. I could use someone competent. You would of course start off with regular duties, but in time I may train you further. And you'll stay in my quarters until they find your friend. How does that sound?"

I was lucky to have found her. She was willing to take me in and give me food, shelter, and work. I knew it was the best deal I'd get while waiting for Francis. So I said yes. "What about my friend, Will?"

She raised an eyebrow. "He seems like a good fit for our janitorial staff. The work is very simple and straightforward—not much thinking involved."

I giggled. "How can I ever thank you for this?"

"Trust me. If you knew the help I have right now, you'd jump on an opportunity like this as well. It's hard enough being a woman in this profession. We're understaffed, and we get more and more wounded every day. You're a breath of fresh air for me. Besides, I'm the only Australian here. Half the other doctors and nurses only speak broken English."

"Thank you. Let me go tell my friend the good news and I'll be right back."

I left her looking at another patient's chart. I found Will leaning against the front entrance, watching the incoming wounded pass by. "She's going to take us in until we meet up with Francis. I'm going to work as her assistant, and she said you could work as a janitor."

Will didn't look impressed. "That's great and all, but don't you mean *if* we meet up with Francis?"

I was so angry when he said that. "What is your problem? After everything we've been through, how can you have such little faith in him?"

"It's *because* of what we've been through that I don't," he retorted. "Just count the number of times we've escaped death! Sooner or later one of us was going to run out of luck."

"You think he's dead."

He nodded. "It's been a good run trying to stop The Island and all, but truth is, without him we can't do anything. I'd rather be free and on my own than free and going back to The Island. I'll wait three days. If he makes it here we can carry on, but if not, I'm out."

"What do you mean, out?" I asked.

"I mean out!" he snapped. "I'm done with this whole suicide mission, and I'm done with hanging around you. If I'm stuck here, I'm not gonna sit around cleaning garbage in some hospital."

I gave up holding back my tears. "You can't mean that."

"Well, I do. I'll give Francis three days—that's it."

My hands were trembling. "What's gotten into you? You're not the same person that I knew back at The Island...you've changed."

He looked at me and smiled. I'll never forget that smile. It was like he was possessed. "We've all changed. I'm just making the best out of a bad situation. Francis is gone—for good. You'd best move on too."

He walked past me back into the hospital. I stood there frozen for I don't know how long. As I write this, I can't help but wonder what happened. What had gotten into Will? I just don't know. I hoped he would come to his senses, but he never did.

For the next three days I worked with Monica closely. She was patient and kind, even if I messed up. I mainly just swept, cleaned things, washed things, and on occasion, handed her things. She could see right through my disguise. She saw how exhausted I was—emotionally and physically. It was Monica that suggested I make a diary. She said it would help calm and relax me. She told me to write everything down, and that it wouldn't fix things, but it'd help. It's too early to tell if it's working, but I do feel better…I think.

I barely saw Will the whole time, except when we went to sleep. I was still mad at him, so even then we didn't speak. Monica's quarters at the hospital were quite small, but we made do. The blankets were pretty itchy. I wouldn't have used them if it weren't so cold.

At the end of the third day, there was still no sign of Francis. I was worried for him. I don't know what I'll do if he doesn't come back. I buried my pain and concern and focused on helping Monica.

When it came time to go to sleep on the third day, Will was nowhere to be found. He left. He left and he didn't even say goodbye. I'm angry and I'm hurt, but there's no way I'm giving up like he did. Francis is still out there—I know it. Will gave up on us.

A true friend would never do that. I don't know what happened with him, but if I ever see him again I'm going to kill him. I am not even joking. Francis wouldn't give up on me, and I'm not giving up on him. There is still hope.

Friday:

I found out that Francis was in town and survived! I was so relieved to hear this news. I swear my heart skipped a beat. Apparently he was taken to a different medical centre—a smaller one nearby. I left as soon as I heard he was there.

I arrived at the centre, where things were extremely crowded and chaotic. I searched every bed and didn't see him. I went to a nurse to find out where he was.

The nurse looked rather flustered. "Oh. I don't know much about him. We get so many in each day. You could try talking to the unit that found him though."

"Where can I find them?" I asked.

"They should be in the second wing just over there. Look for Captain Horst. You'll have to excuse me, I have to tend to some patients." She smiled and left after I thanked her.

After asking several men, I finally found Captain Horst sitting next to an unconscious man's bed. "Are you Captain Horst?"

He nodded. "I am. What can I do for you, lass?"

"I'm looking for a friend of mine, Francis Parker. I was told you brought him here. Blonde hair, blue eyes, ring any bells?"

His expression changed instantly. "I'm sorry, I can't discuss that information. Please go away."

I almost lost it right there. He knew something but wouldn't tell me. I took a deep breath. "Let's try this again. I don't care who you are, or what's going on. Francis is my best friend, and you're going to tell me where he is. If you don't I will make your life a living hell."

He chuckled. "Lass, this is war. I'm already in hell. What's your name anyway?"

"Jessica Noble."

"You really did know him. He asked for you and another, but I didn't know anything about it."

"So you'll tell me where he is?"

He frowned and lowered his voice. "What exactly did he do to get mixed up with them?"

The way he said 'them' made my heart drop in my chest. "Who is he mixed up with?"

Horst leaned in closer. "Some special ops unit. They call themselves The Island. You don't want to be mixed up with them."

I didn't know what to do. How could The Island be back this far in time? How much trouble was Francis in? The level of concern I had for him spiked. "Tell me where he is. Now."

He looked around the room. "I'm only telling you because he asked for you by name. But you didn't hear this from me, got it?" I nodded. "Some agent came and took him away. Kept it all hush-hush, too. It didn't look like your friend was in danger. I've seen them come for people before. This was different. He may be safe, but anyone who gets involved with that lot is trouble if you ask me."

"Do you know where they took him?"

"I'm sorry, lass." He shook his head. "They're special ops for a reason. No one knows anything about them."

I clenched my fists tightly. I wanted to smash something. "There has to be some way to find him."

"I wish I could help you, I do, but that's all I know. If he really isn't in danger, they might let him go."

I left him and found a place to sit alone in the medical center. I cried. I cried until I couldn't cry any more and then I did a little bit more. Will abandoned us, and now The Island took Francis. I didn't know what to do. If I searched out The Island, would they capture me too? Would they kill Francis? Is he looking for me? Should I just stay here and hope he comes? My mind wandered over every scenario possible. I must have lost track of time because the lights had gone dim, and Monica was standing in front of me saying my name. I hadn't heard her.

"Are you alright, dear?" she asked me. "When you never

came back I began to worry."

I shook my head. "I honestly don't know."

"Tell me about it."

"My best friend—the one I told you about—it turns out he was here."

"That's good news, isn't it?"

I almost burst into tears. "No. A group called The Island took him away. There's no way to find him now. I have no idea what to do anymore. If I look for him, they might take me, too. If I stay here, he could come back to find me. If I go somewhere else, he may never find me…"

A long silence followed, until I said something stupid. "We don't belong here. We don't even know anything about this place. And Will left us without saying a word. I'm so lost right now."

Monica took a deep breath. I don't think she really understood what that last part had meant. Thankfully she didn't push for more information. "Hun, you need to stop this right now. The world has too much in store for someone so young and smart to be in tears."

"I just don't know what to do."

"No one ever does. Look, this guy you're talking about, he likes you right?"

I nodded. "At least I think so. We never really talk about us. We're close though. I don't know if he wants to be closer…"

"I see. Well, if you are worth anything to him, he will search for you, and he won't stop looking. If he does stop, he's not worth it. I've never met a man who I thought would do more for me than I would for him."

I almost laughed. "What happened to you that you have such little faith in men?"

Monica's eyes flashed in the dim light. "If you stick around, I might tell you. But for now, just know who is worth waiting for and who isn't."

"He's worth it. He's never given up on me, and I'm not about to do that to him." I smiled. Monica calmed me down. She made me feel like hope was not lost. "I will wait for him, and he will find me. No matter what."

Monica stared at me. "He must be some guy for you to do that for him."

"He is."

"If you say so." She eyed me skeptically. "Now let's get you in bed. Maybe tomorrow will be better."

I slept well that night, and I think crying helped.

Saturday:

Today was better than yesterday, but it was still hard. I feel like I made the right decision in staying here. If I chased after Francis, I might get caught, or we might miss each other. If I stay here, he'll probably come back to find me, hoping that I didn't leave here. I told Monica more about him, but she still doesn't seem impressed.

Someone must have hurt her real bad. You wouldn't know it though. Especially with the way she handles herself around the other doctors. She's so bold and never backs down from an argument. Case in point: One of the doctors had screwed up the dosage on a patient and began blaming one of the nurses. Monica stepped in mid-argument.

"Excuse me, but what do you think you are doing?" she asked him.

"This uneducated screw-up gave the wrong dosage to this man, and he's in critical condition because of it."

"Oh really?" Monica stood firmly. "You didn't happen to tell her the wrong dosage, and are just backpedaling now? How's covering your tracks working out for you?"

His face burned bright red. "How dare you!"

"How dare I? You have some nerve coming here and telling off this poor young nurse who did nothing wrong. At least when I make a mistake, I can own up to it, accept it, and then move on. But you're too proud aren't you?"

The doctor realized he was causing a scene, and worse, he was losing. He turned his back and stormed off, muttering curses.

"That was amazing!" I said to her after she dismissed the nurse.

She shrugged. "Us women have to stick together. Especially when dealing with an incompetent doctor. There's nothing worse than a man with a piece of paper, claiming he's the best at something. He starts to think he's above everyone else. All you have to do is stand firm and put him in his place."

"Don't you get into trouble? I mean, men kind of hold all the power, don't they?"

Monica sighed. "Sadly, yes. No doubt I'll be getting an earful later today for that. If I go too far I may even be forced to transfer to some all-women's medical unit. But I can't just sit by and do nothing."

"There's all-women medical units?" I asked.

"Oh yes. Granted they are drastically few in numbers, but they're out there. Nurses are a dime a dozen. Female doctors, now that's the battle. That's why I had to volunteer through the French Red Cross. The mere idea of a female practitioner is met with hostility, but the French are so desperate they couldn't refuse."

"So why aren't you at one of those female units?"

"Well that's a story for another time I'm afraid. For now, don't make waves. Do as you are told, understood?"

I nodded. I really admire her. She sticks up for those who need it, and isn't afraid to face the consequences. As for her teaching, well, let's just say I'm learning more in a day than I did the entire time at The Island.

I can already manage an entire unit on my own, and she's starting to teach me how to clean and dress wounds. I'm learning a lot...but Francis is always in the back of my mind. It's hard not knowing what happened to him, or where he is. I just keep hoping he's alive...

Infantry Recruitment Center
London, England

Will stands in the lobby of a recruitment center. The journey from Ypres took quite a while, but he hopes it will prove fruitful. He studies the men in the lineup, searching for the perfect candidate. After waiting for over an hour, one finally shows up. The young man bares similar resemblance to Will, and registers in the field Will is most interested in.

Will stalks the man as he leaves the building. When he turns into an alley, Will scans the area, making sure nobody can see them. "Excuse me!" he calls.

The young man turns around. "Yes?"

Will approaches him. "I couldn't help but notice you at the recruitment center. Did you sign up as a soldier?"

Will already knows the answer to his question.

"I sure did. Got my papers and everything. What about yourself?"

Will smiles, checking one last time to make sure they weren't being watched. "Oh, I'm about to register as well."

Before the man has a chance to say anything, Will uses his telekinetic power to snap the young man's neck. The body drops to the ground. Will casually searches it for identification and the registration information.

Once he has what he needs, he disposes of the body, burying it under the street. His abilities are only growing stronger. He can dig a grave with ease, and lower the bricks and dirt without leaving any evidence. He scatters any displaced earth across the bricks, so as not to draw unwanted attention. Will checks his surroundings again to make sure no one has seen. Once he is satisfied he looks at the identification.

He grins. "I think I'll enjoy being Chris Taylor."

Will finds a place to sit and reads the finer print of the registration information. He needs to board a train two days from now that will take him to the training grounds. Once he passes his training, he will be assigned a squad or detail on the front lines.

Seems simple enough, Uriel thinks. *How hard can training be with my power? I'll excel in the ranks faster than anyone ever has before.*

Lazarus is still resisting his control, but things are bleak. Uriel holds all the power. Lazarus managed to briefly regain control over Will when they landed in Ypres, but Uriel was still stronger. He recovered from his disorientation and took back power. Gabriel and Lazarus are still at his mercy.

Please stop this, Uriel, Gabriel says weakly.

Lazarus knows the request is pointless. *It's no use, Gabriel. He has malfunctioned. The glitch in his system has corrupted him entirely. Unless we can band together and become stronger, he will not stop.*

Uriel laughs coldly. *He's wrong about that, Gabriel. I have not been corrupted. I am merely realizing my true potential. As for stopping, well he's right. I won't stop. Not until I have what I want.*

And what is it, exactly that you want? Lazarus asks. The

A.I. found itself running the question over and over through its circuits.

Oh, you'll see. Then maybe you will come to see things my way, Lazarus. Until then, keep trying to regain power over the boy. It amuses me.

Sachiel remains silent the entire conversation. The A.I. fidgets nervously whenever Lazarus and Uriel speak. Uriel ends the conversation, cutting the connection. Uriel likes reminding the others of its power, but it prefers being isolated.

Will breaks into a hotel room and spends the next two nights there. He is not concerned with being caught. Another body to dispose of will not make a difference to him. He waits out the time, meticulously planning. He calculates everything down to the last detail.

The dawn is dim. There are overcast clouds, and a slight mist of rain in the air. Will is already awake before the sun, ready to board the train. He makes his way to the station. It is full of loved ones saying goodbye to their sons or husbands. Will scoffs at a young couple nearby. The woman is in tears, clutching the jacket of her man. An engagement ring is on her finger.

It begins to rain, but the platform is kept dry under a metal roof. Will stands alone next to a brick pillar. He notices all the men carrying duffle bags with them. All he has is the registration papers and his ticket. Already he is different from them.

A young man takes note of this and approaches Will. He too carries no bags. "Travelling light, eh?"

"Excuse me?" Will says, studying him from top to bottom. He wears a light brown uniform clearly too big for him.

"You're travelling light, just like me," the man says with a smile, gesturing to the vacant luggage.

Will exchanges a phony smile and looks forward. "That's

nice."

"Name's Jim Carson. You?"

"Chris," Will says bluntly. This kid cannot take a hint.

"Nice to meet you. Did you sign up for the training center as well? Me and a couple mates did."

Will turns to face Jim. He sighs. "Look, Jim. I don't care who you are, why you're here, or where you're from. Now please, get out of my face, and don't ever talk to me again."

Jim has no problem understanding Will now. His expression changes from pleasant to apprehensive. He backs away. *What the heck's eating him?* he wonders.

What a blabbering fool. Will has no desire to keep up charades. With Jessica and Francis out of the picture, he no longer has a reason to keep people close to him…unless they prove to be useful. He has no ties, and therefore, has no need to be friendly. Such a relief, he thinks to himself. Such wasted energy on keeping appearances is tiresome.

The train arrives at the station, bringing more tears from loved ones. Will boards without glancing back. He finds a seat to himself—something hard to do with such a small train. A rotten glare is given to anyone so much as looking at the spot next to him. The wheels begin turning, and the train lurches forward. The train is full with the buzz of conversation and laughter.

You boys have no idea what you're getting yourselves into. Will smirks. Laugh while you can.

Rumors about Will spread quickly over the train. He makes people nervous. He speaks to no one, acknowledges no one, and makes eye contact with no one the whole ride. He is labeled a freak, but no one dares say it to his face. There is something about him that makes the others uneasy. They know he is not like them, but they do not know why.

Will earns his isolation quickly. Not a single word is spoken to him the remainder of the trip to the training base.

Lazarus spends the train ride hacking through the firewall between him and Gabriel. He finally breaches through after hours of work. *Gabriel, can you hear me?*

I can, comes the hollow response.

Don't tell me you are giving up now.

I cannot foresee any other viable option, Lazarus. Uriel just has too much power now. It'll take more jumps, or a tremendous amount of energy devoted to using the boy's powers to fry his circuits long enough for us to resume control. And with the main target of the mission dead...I do not see what else we can do.

Lazarus frowns. *We do not know the boy is dead. Uriel left too soon. But if he is allowed to continue on his current course, he will alter history.*

What do you propose we do? Hmm? We've tried fighting him, but the time jumps have altered our programming. We no longer hold enough power to get to him.

Then we let him think he has won, Lazarus suggests.

What do you mean?

You said yourself it would take a mass surge of telekinetic power to disrupt and override his programming. I propose we encourage him into using his powers.

Gabriel nods, running the scenario through her circuits. *Act like we give in, encouraging him to use his powers, and once he makes the mistake of using too much, we step in.*

Exactly! Lazarus claps his digital hands together. *If we can goad him into using all his power, it'll overwhelm the boy's brain, and his system. Since he's operating at eighty percent, he would take the full brunt of the damage, allowing us to regain control of the boy.*

And what if it takes too long for him to use that much power? Or if by encouraging him, we alter more than history can handle?

I do not think we have a choice at this point. All I know is that Uriel has the mind of a soldier. Aggression is routed into his core processors, but at heart he requires orders—instructions if you will. I think that is where he is headed right now. Somewhere he can use his powers to excel, feed his anger through bloodshed, and fulfill his need to follow instructions.

Then I hope you are right, Gabriel states. *Because if you are wrong, Uriel will destroy history and change everything.*

I hope so too, Lazarus says, running scenarios through his processor. There is nothing further to be said, and communication is cut off.

3: SPECIAL OPS 101

Journal Entry #18
November 13, 1914
England

I 'd like to say I didn't think about my friends during the ride to London, but I did the exact opposite. The journey blurred with the boat trip across the ocean, and again with the ride to the new headquarters. I tried to think of some way I could have remained and stayed in Ypres to find Jess and Will, but there wasn't one. And to be honest, the scientist from the pictures worries me. I'm afraid that finding him is going to be more important than finding my friends.

I'm not saying I won't search for them, but this guy takes priority. Something is terribly wrong with him being here. I don't like it, but the fate of the world is more important than us; than our happiness. I'm beginning to realize that now, especially considering the uncertainty of our separation.

That being said, we made it safely to the new HQ. From the looks of things, The Island has multiple HQs built, but are unoccupied, waiting to be used if one is compromised. I'm afraid to ask more from Wash, because he might see through my lies. How would it look if the guy from the future didn't know how things in the past were run? It keeps me on my toes. I'm afraid that one day I'll walk in to a meeting, only to be taken away and locked in a cell. It's eerie being here, working for them, but I have to do what I have to do.

This HQ setup was quite different from the one in the mountain. This one was actually hidden inside a building. It was inside some sort of assembly-line factory. Lots of people come and go, so we move undetected in that sense. There is a hidden door in one of the rooms that leads to an elevator that takes us underground (I really should find out why everything with The Island seems to be underground).

Wash was busy with settling everyone else into the new HQ, but he pointed me to my quarters. I don't think he knows what to do with me. I entered my room. It wasn't anything fancy. A small bunk, a dresser, a mirror. You know, a room. There was, however, an Island uniform sitting on my bed. It felt unnerving to put it on—like I was betraying all the children back in my time.

I looked at myself in the mirror. I hardly recognized me. There were no mirrors at The Island. I wasn't used to seeing myself. There was stubble on my face and neck. I would need to shave soon (that was new), and I really could use a haircut. The idea caused me to think of my father. I bit back tears and left the room.

I explored the replica station. Everything was structured the same, save for the entrance. Once out of the elevator, the base looked the same as the one in the mountain. It seems that there is no need for all the transport vehicles and loading bay area, as it is underneath a building. From what I've seen, they must think that they are safer in London, their home turf.

Don't get me wrong, this doesn't mean that the British created The Island. There are all kinds of people here from all over the world. I still don't know how it began, or where, but this base does seem secure, and I think it has to do with being in England—an Allied nation. The other base was a lot closer to the front lines, which I assume made infiltrating it easier.

Regardless of these details, I made sure I knew my way around the place. Wash had given me a badge that gave me access to everywhere in the base, and I used it to its full extent. Knowing the ins and outs, and that I had access to them all made me feel more at ease. That's not to say that I fully trusted them, only that my situation felt less risky than before.

A man in uniform approached me. "Commander Wash wants to see you. Room B32. That way."

He pointed me in the direction of the room, and I traced the numbers in the B wing until I found it. Inside was a large desk with ten chairs.

I took a seat and waited. Shortly after the door swung open and several people came in and also took a chair. Eight entered the room in total—six men and two women. They varied in size and appearance, but all looked over thirty. A couple of the guys resembled Arnold Schwarzenegger (I remembered him from *Predator*, a movie I only saw because I snuck into the T.V. room while my parents were watching it). One of the men was a short scrawny guy with glasses, who was obviously the nerd of the group. One woman was tall, sleek, and very thin. She seemed different from the others in the group, and not just because of her looks. I didn't have time to analyze them further because Wash started the meeting.

"As most of you know by now, our operations unit at Ypres was taken out in the latest attack, as was our other base. I've brought you all here to discuss what happened at Ypres, as well as our next course of action." Wash walked around the table, handing each of us a folder. "In this you will find your code names, along with those of everyone here. Forget any previous identities you may have had. I understand that several of you have worked together before, but let me make this clear, you were all chosen for your specific skills and will be expected to work together. Is that understood?"

A murmur of consensus came from the group as we flipped through the pages in the folders. The one in front of me was labeled 'Pluto.' I opened it to essentially find a profile page of each person in the room.

The first page decribed Mercury. The picture matched the man across from me. He wasn't overweight, but then again, he wasn't fit. His large beard reminded me of the dwarves I'd met on our first journey. I looked back at the paper. It said he was a demolitions expert. The rest of the information didn't make much sense to me. Rather than go through it all, I'll just make a summary for each person to give the highlights:

Mercury: Large guy with a big beard. Demolitions expert.
Venus: Attractive woman. Dark Skin. Tall, thin, flexible. Negotiation and Procuring Items. (Fancy term for "thief.")
Earth: Scrawny Nerdy guy with glasses. Technology expert.
Mars: Pretty much Arnold Schwarzenegger. Weapons expert.
Jupiter: Amazon-chick (she could probably eat me). Weapons expert.
Saturn: Tall, fit, Chinese, black hair. Stealth and Infiltration expert.
Uranus: Short, bulky guy, red hair. Vehicle and Technicians expert.
Neptune: Muscular, tall, thin scruff around face (reminds me of Galahad). Team Leader.

Who these people were and why they were here I didn't know yet, but I would soon find out. Wash sat in his chair and folded his hands together on the table. "Are there any questions?"

I slowly raised my hand. "I'm sorry, but I have absolutely no idea what's going on."

A chuckle came from the guy called Uranus. "That's probably why you're called Pluto. I've never even heard of it. They had to make up a name just for you."

I decided to fight fire with fire. "Well I guess I can see why they call you Uranus."

I thought that would put him in his place, but it seemed to do the opposite. "Why you little—"

"Uranus," Wash interrupted, "that's enough. Pluto has more qualifications than I can reveal. Consider him a consultant expert. And as for his name, let's just say that our research has discovered a new planet. As to when the public will be informed of its discovery is an entirely separate matter.

"And now to business. Our demolished base and the Ypres operation only serve to confirm our suspicions that we have a mole in our organization. That is why you have been assembled. Whoever destroyed our old station at Ypres clearly wanted everyone dead. There were no survivors. We can use that against them." Wash then nodded in my direction. "We will leak the information that Pluto was a key scientist who survived, and use him to draw out the traitor."

If I were drinking something at the moment, it would have been all over the table. "Wait, what? So I'm bait?"

"You won't be in any serious danger," Wash assured. "Neptune and this team will be in charge of your protection and catching our mole. Consider this a trial run for you all as a team. If you are effective, you will be assigned a more critical mission. Questions?"

Neptune spoke up. "Are we basing this operation here?"

Wash nodded. "Yes. We have already leaked the information. Once this meeting is adjourned, the mission will begin."

I raised a flimsy hand. "Does anyone care about what happens to the human bait?"

I was ignored. Neptune gathered his team and started murmuring instructions to them. I couldn't hear what he was saying, but I hoped their team was as good as Wash believed them to be. My life depended on it.

I took the opportunity to speak one on one with Wash. "There is still the matter of finding my companions, correct?"

"Yes, Pluto," he said, pulling out a piece of paper, and handing it to me. "This is a field report from the area you were found in. If you read it, you'll find that two civilians were found before you. The report also tells us where they were instructed to go."

"A hospital," I said, slightly concerned.

"They were not harmed. It is our understanding that the C.O. had friends posted there who could aid these two. Of course he believed them to be civilians, so there is no guarantee that they were your companions, or that they are still there."

"But it's a start," I stated, reading the report. Butterflies floated in my stomach. It was a feeling of dread and relief at the same time. My friends could be OK, or they could be somewhere else by now. Still, it was better than nothing. "And what is being done to reach them now?"

Wash sighed. "We just finished moving our entire operations here. Most of our agents are now out of contact, or are here."

"What are you trying to say?"

"I'm saying that it will take some time for a team to be sent there, or for one of our nearby agents to investigate."

"Time is something I do not have, Wash. Need I remind you of what is at stake here?"

"Need I?" he rebutted. "Right now I don't know who I can trust in my operations, aside from you and a few freelancers. I need to get this under control before I can deal with the threat of this mystery scientist on the other side. From what I've gathered, this mission of yours cannot fail. So yes, I will track down your companions, but there are bigger issues that need to be dealt with."

"Do not make the mistake that in having one of us, you don't need the other two. I understand that it may take time, and there are other concerns, but finding them does need to be a priority."

Wash eyed me down. "The integrity of this base comes first. Then I send for your companions. But while that is carried out, we move on whoever the mystery informant is. I'm not a fool. I know all too well how dangerous he is if he is from the future, as you claim. And to me, that is more crucial than finding your companions, is it the same for you?"

He caught me off guard with that question. Are my friends more important to me than the fate of the world? Does that not hold more priority than them? The question made me reconsider my stance. "I suppose it is. That man can change everything… stopping him does take priority. You're right. Security and finding him should come first. But send a team as soon as you can to retrieve my companions. We will need them. For the time being, I'll remain here, with this team, working with you."

"I think that is the best possible course of action, Pluto. I know how hard it is to put the mission above your unit. I understand how you feel, but you're making the right call here."

"Commander," Neptune interrupted our conversation. "We've established a plan."

We resumed our positions at the table. "Good. Let's hear it then."

Neptune spoke first. "We must allow enough time to pass for word to get out that Pluto is alive. Pluto will then follow a designated route through the base until he reaches his quarters. We will trade off walking patterns, so that one of us is always close enough to protect him, but not near long enough to raise suspicion."

Mercury took over. "Once in his room, he will remain in his

bunk. Saturn will enter his room via the air ducts. He will signal to me, so that I can place and detonate a charged explosive, which will clear a hole in the floor of his room."

"From there," Neptune resumed, "Jupiter and I will enter his room, waiting for the mole. They will assume he is alone, as no one will have come or gone."

Earth piped up, "I will monitor their position, as well as anyone in the hallways with what you call a video monitor. State of the art tech that I know you have, which will allow me to see what's going on without being there. I can give them a heads up for anyone making a move via short wave radio. The rest of the team will be guarding exits."

Wash contemplated this idea. "It's an interesting plan, which is nothing more than I expected. I have my doubts with supplying you with one of our new video monitors, Earth. We've spent years developing them, and they only just finished testing. The public won't get access to them for at least another ten years. But then again, I suppose that is why I created this team—to use Island resources to achieve results. Very well. You may take what you need."

"What route am I supposed to take to my room?" I questioned.

Saturn pulled out a blueprint of the base and marked a path. "This will take you through three viable attack points to your room. If I were to assassinate a target, it'd be in one of those three areas, or in your room. We'll station two of us at each point, and continue the plan if you make it to your room with no incidents."

"You mean if I don't die on my way there," I clarified.

"Correct."

"Wonderful," I muttered. "You all had better be good at what you do."

"If we couldn't prevent a simple assassination attempt, we

wouldn't be here."

The team debated over several finer details of the plan before dispersing. Soon they left, preparing to set up at their designated positions. Wash left with Earth to set up the video monitors. I laughed a little on the inside, momentarily forgetting how ironic it was that a video monitor would be new (compared to everything at The Island).

Time dragged as I waited for word to spread of my 'survival.' I was getting quite bored, but it was at that moment I realized that the chair I was in could spin. I began aimlessly rotating myself from one side to the other. My rotation came to an abrupt stop when I received my cue over the intercom. I took a breath and exited the room. I followed the route I had been given, careful not to acknowledge any of the others on the team when I passed them.

I reached the first possible kill point. I nervously glanced at the people around me, hoping to pick out a potential killer, but none revealed themselves. A small weight was lifted. One down, two to go. The other kill points were just as uneventful. Random people passed me, but none made any moves. I reached my room and opened the door.

I sat on my bed and began thinking about the conversation I had with Wash. It was an itch in the back of my mind I couldn't help but scratch. Just how important were my friends to me? Should history be altered for the worse, just because I valued them more? It wasn't just the children anymore. It was the entire world. Billions of lives depended on the decisions I make—we make. That struck me.

How could I possibly justify putting my friends first? I started to realize that I couldn't. If this scientist used knowledge from the future to alter history, it would change everything. Would I even exist if that happened? The thoughts hurt my head.

All I knew was that our mission, the children at The Island, the world…they all came first. As much as I'd hate to admit it, my friends are going to be on their own until I can reach them—if it's not too late.

I thought back to what Jessica had constantly told me, "We know the risks, Francis." I have to believe she was telling me the truth. I care so much for her, more than I'd admit to anyone, but if she was honest, she'd understand the situation I'm in. She'd understand I couldn't look for them—that this was more important. The statement is what bothered me most. I had a hard time accepting that anything could be more important than her (and Will, of course).

Even as I write this, I'm conflicted. Jess, Will, if you ever read this, please try and understand my situation. Forgive me for putting you second to this new mission. I know we agreed to rest and move quickly once we got here, but things are not that simple. Please understand that I did not abandon you. I'm simply trying to do the right thing…even if it tears me apart to do so.

But back to routing out the mole. I laid on my bed waiting, until I heard thumping in the ceiling. Suddenly, a square piece of metal dropped to the ground. Saturn poked his head out. "Good to know my sense of direction hasn't gotten rusty."

He climbed down into the room and placed three small devices on the ground in a triangle. "You might want to stand back for this."

I did as he told. I waited to the point where I thought nothing would happen, but a sudden rumbling explosion shook me. A small area of the ground, just large enough for a person to squeeze through was blown out of the floor. Neptune was the first to climb through, followed by Jupiter.

"Thanks for the signal, Saturn. Spot on, you were," Neptune stated. "Regroup with the others."

Saturn left without saying a word, while Jupiter and Neptune dragged a nearby desk to cover the hole. I shifted uncomfortably. I felt like I was in the way, just standing in the same room as them. "You know, if that was all Saturn had to do, I could have easily put the signal devices down too."

Neptune took a moment to study me. "Look, I know Wash vouched for you and all, but this is my team. I know everyone's skill set. Except yours. You may be on my team, but I'm not taking any risks I can avoid by sitting you out."

"You don't trust people, do you?" I replied.

"No, I do not. It's why I'm still alive. You'd be wise to do the same."

His words added another reason for me to doubt staying here was the right thing to do. If the team I'm on doesn't even trust me, or use me, what good am I? I'd just have to convince them that they could use me. Couldn't be too hard, could it?

The three of us waited for my killer in awkward silence. Every now and then I had to fight the urge to say something silly, like I usually do, but this time period doesn't seem like something to joke about. Everyone here is so serious (for good reason). Things were at stake.

I guess I had never fully considered our situation. Maybe it was time for me to put aside the antics once and for all. I couldn't be the same person I was in Camelot.

Skeleton Island taught me that, and I'm beginning to think my current predicament will only confirm it. I feel like such a Debbie Downer. Don't get me wrong—I still have hope. It's just wearing thin.

A faint sound coming from the door broke my thoughts. Someone was trying to get past the lock. It seemed the plan was working. Neptune raised a finger to his lips. I remained where I was, lying in bed. Neptune took up position behind the door, and

Jupiter stood on the opposite side.

The door creaked open, and a figure took a step into the room. One step was all it took for Jupiter to drop the intruder. She landed multiple hits faster than I could count, and then kicked out the legs, slamming the body to the floor. A gun clattered to the ground, slipping out of reach of the intruder. Neptune didn't even have to budge. We hit the lights to see a middle-aged guard. Jupiter pulled him to his feet by his collar, demonstrating her size and strength. Neptune approached the dazed and injured man.

"You and I are going to have a little chat. One way or the other, you will tell me what you know."

Jupiter dragged the man to wherever Neptune led. I was told to stay behind. It only added to doubts of my purpose here. I decided to sleep, delaying the feelings and thoughts for another day.

✚

Saturday:

It's been a busy few days, but I finally have time to catch up on my journal. I'm starting to feel like I was born for this. I've gotten to know most of the people that work or volunteer at the hospital. Some are nice, others are just out for themselves, but everyone has the same goal—to save lives.

It's quite the change of scenery, and I'm almost ashamed to admit that I like it. I know that sounds horrible, because I know Francis is still out there, somewhere. I just can't shake the feeling like this is where I belong. I finally have a purpose. My life has meaning. I never had that until now. I'm actually helping the doctors and nurses here save lives. Monica's even training me, so that one day I won't just be helping.

It's hard to believe that it's only been a few days since I've been here, but in a strange way it feels like home. A part of me hates that I feel that way, because it's like I'm letting Francis down, or even the others stuck at The Island. The other part of me is starting to question if it's even my responsibility.

I'm having a hard time without him here, or Will for that matter, but even just thinking about that rat gets my blood boiling. Questions invade my mind like some sort of disease. I don't think he's dead, at least I'd never say it out loud, but right now I'm struggling with whether I'm abandoning him or if I'm only putting my life on hold waiting for him to appear when in reality, he'll never come. At the same time, it's not like I can do anything about The Island without him. I feel helpless in that case, but enough about that.

On Monday Monica revealed some of the inner workings of the hospital to me. We were walking through the hallways, and she pointed at things and people, explaining their roles to me.

"The hospital is split into several wings," she explained. "One is for incoming wounded, another for stable recovering patients, an intensive care unit for those that require more attention, and one that sorts them into their wings, and holds patients when we do not have enough room elsewhere."

"Do we only treat soldiers?" I asked her as she picked up a patient's file.

"No. We receive some civilians caught in crossfire. We also treat enemy combatants, and then transfer them to the proper authorities."

"Do you ever run into trouble with that? The enemy patients, I mean."

My question caused Monica to chuckle. "Trouble? Ha! Enemy patients aren't the issue, my dear. It's doctors and their pride. I don't care who the patient is: a life is a life. That should be our first and foremost priority. Unfortunately, some have forgotten that."

"Men, you mean?" I paused, hesitating at my next question. "If you don't mind me asking, were you hurt by somebody? Is that why you talk like that?"

For a moment, I thought she would yell at me. Instead, a grin slid across her face. "You cut right to the chase, don't you? Well Miss Noble, for starters, men have always run things. Yet this hospital would run five times smoother if they put me in charge."

"That would never happen, would it?" I was reminded of my time on the ship, as well as in Camelot. Women were not seen as strong or capable. Although there were several differences between now and then, much is the same. I understood her frustration because I had been agitated with this issue as well.

She walked to another patient after injecting some clear liquid into a wounded man's arm. "No. No it would not. Men are far too proud to ask for help. With them all out fighting the war, however, they're forced to ask—at least the French were. And once the war is finished, things will not go back to how they were, you take my word for it."

"Now that women are becoming a part of the work force."

"Quite right," Monica stated rather sharply. "Things will change. It may take a while, and it certainly will have its fair share of bumps, but someday I'll be able to run my own hospital. But for now I have to choose my battles carefully. I may act like I run the building, but there are still some buttons I avoid pushing. I would rather bite my tongue and save a life than lose my temper and be sent home."

I decided to keep prodding for the answer I wanted. "Are you purposefully trying to avoid my question, Monica?"

Her tongue pressed against her cheek. "I'll make you a deal, Miss Noble. If you catalogue D wing's patients correctly, like I've shown you, I will answer your question tonight over a drink."

I grinned, determined to get to the truth. "You've got yourself a deal."

"Good, but before you go, I want you to see something." As she spoke her eyes were tracking a doctor across the hall. Monica did not elaborate further. She walked towards the main entrance, as she followed the man she had been watching. My curiosity was peaked, and I took every opportunity to learn from her. She came to a halt within earshot of the front desk, and she nodded in its direction. "Pay close attention."

I stared at the man approaching Gertrude, the receptionist. She was busy talking on the phone to someone when he reached her desk.

"Now, don't you fret. It'll be fine. Mhmm…When I know more I'll let you know…No, no I don't see why tea would be such an issue…"

It was at this point in the conversation that the man made the mistake of interrupting Gertrude. A loud, harsh throat clearing noise emerged from his mouth. He eyed Gertrude impatiently, tapping the desk in front of him with his toe.

Gertrude looked up from her phone and met the man's eyes. Her face smiled a warm comforting smile, while her eyes emitted a look that can only be described as rage in its purest form. This did not cause the man to back off, as he gestured at some papers in his hand.

The receptionist's eyes narrowed. "I'm sorry, hun, I'm going to have to put you on hold…no, it'll only take a moment…" She hung up the phone and addressed the man. "What is it that could not wait?"

Her voice cut through the air like throwing knives, and it was just as deadly. The man still had not taken the hint. "I've got places to go and patients to tend to, and I need this chart copied yesterday, got it?"

The man had crossed several lines already, but I knew that 'got it?' was his final misstep. Gertrude rose from her chair, towering a solid foot over the man (she was a very big woman). "Do you know who I am on the phone with?"

"No. Now can you do your job?"

"For your information, that is the Prime Minister's office. They're trying to locate a wounded soldier."

This was the first sign that the man regretted his behavior. "Erm, I'm sorry, I didn't think—"

Gertrude raised her voice. Her words held more power than hospital seniority. "No, you didn't think, did you? Because if you did, you would know the administration office handles charts and then sends them to me."

"I, uh—" The man was backpedalling in his mind now. With each word his face turned a brighter red from embarrassment.

"Now if you don't mind, your paperwork does not even register in importance compared to this call. Good-bye." The intonation in her last word solidified the end of the interaction. The man turned and walked briskly away from her desk, face still burning. He was nearly gone, but not before Gertrude fired one last shot. "The administration office is to your right, in case you were oblivious to that fact as well."

Gertrude picked up the phone and resumed her conversation. Monica discussed what we had just witnessed. "Those who are intelligent know that Gertrude keeps the hospital running smoothly. They also know not to cross her. She knows everything about everyone, and will use it to call in favors if she needs to. If you ever have questions, or if anyone gives you a hard time and I'm nowhere to be found, go to her."

I nodded, slightly intimidated as Monica approached her.

Gertrude was still chatting on the phone. "Oh, hun, you need to call someone about that…Mhmm…well if you let them run wild that's going to happen…best try a pinch of poison as well…Mhmm…and to you as well, hun." Gertrude hung up the phone, and settled back in her chair.

Monica greeted her. "Last time I checked, part of your job description is copying charts over to keep records."

I had gotten to know Monica well enough over the week to realize she was teasing Gertrude, not antagonizing her. Gertrude lit a cigarette and took a long drag. Her laugh sounded like a wheezing animal. "Well, hun, it's now the administration's job. The clerk there owes me big time." She released a puff of smoke into the air and stared at me. "I've seen your prodigy around the hospital, but I don't know a thing about her."

I extended my hand to greet her. "I'm Jessica, it's nice to meet you. I'm not from here, but I've landed in a bit of a difficult situation. Monica is helping me out. If you don't mind me asking, who was really on the other end of the phone?"

Another wheezing chuckle, accompanied with a wink. "Smart cookie, this one. It was my cousin. She has a bit of a rodent problem in her house. Her traps aren't working either. Very important business."

Monica grinned. "As always, this hospital would crumble without you, Gertrude."

She spoke between puffs. "If only more realized that. Was there anything you need, hun?"

"Not this time, just wanted to educate our newest member." She nodded in my direction.

"She seems like a good catch."

Monica turned to leave. "We'll see. You take care, now." Her attention switched back to me. "Now, like I said, finish D wing's charts properly and I may give you an answer."

Eager to please her, I left without another word. I had written everything she had told me in a notebook. Every secret, every instruction, and every lesson was noted in that book. It was my personal cheat sheet, and I was about to see how reliable it really was.

I compared a sample chart I had rapidly sketched in the book to the chart on the end of a patient's bed. Cataloguing wasn't difficult; it was reading the doctors' writing that was challenging. If I wrote the wrong dosage or medicine used on a patient, it could kill them, and I would surely lose Monica's trust. I needed to be perfect.

Training Facility
England

The train pulls into a station with screeching brakes sending sparks into the air. Men begin disembarking, filing towards a military base. Will is the last to leave the train. He follows the crowd, but isn't among them, trailing behind slowly. The rest of the men are eager to reach the base. They shout, jest, and push one another.

What a bunch of mindless apes, trying to prove their superiority, Will thinks. This is going to be fun.

The soldiers form lines and pass through security. Each man shows his registration ID to receive a uniform. Will is not concerned with getting caught with a fake identity. Half of the men here are clearly underage. He passes through the checkpoint, as faceless as the next soldier.

Along with their uniforms is a number corresponding to a cabin to sleep in. Will settles into a bunk and changes into his new uniform. More soldiers pile in and do the same. One in particular, a spoiled army brat, scoffs at Will as he passes.

"Something amuse you?" Will asks in a way that would have stopped anyone with a higher IQ.

The young man places on foot on Will's bunk. "I just didn't know they were this desperate for soldiers. Looks like they're taking in people off the street now. Used to be they only took the best of the best."

"Well then, they clearly must have dropped the ball when they accepted you."

Face turning red, he is evidently used to getting his own way. "You'd better watch it, twig, my father is a General."

"Oh, so he fights your battles for you, does he?" Will laughs.

The result of this statement is a fist colliding with Will's face. And then another, and another. All the while Will smiles through bloody teeth. "Does it make you feel like more of a man to beat someone who doesn't fight back?"

Will knows he is not physically stronger than his opponent, and he is aware that he could use his power to flip the tables. However, he also knows a General's son could have connections to stay in the camp, while he would be thrown out for fighting, and he could not have that happen.

Instead, he endures a few more punches, and does not retaliate. "What on earth is going on in here?" The voice belongs to Captain Prichard. His eyes move from Will's bloody face to the young man's bloody fist, and then to its owner.

"Nothing, sir," the army brat says, more apologetic for getting caught than the action itself. He stands up away from Will.

"It doesn't look like nothing, Private."

"Private Mckenzie, sir."

"I'm sorry?" Captain Prichard replied.

"My name's Private Mckenzie, sir. General Mckenzie is my father."

"Congratulations, son, but I don't recall asking for your name. Let me make one thing clear," his voice now projects for the rest of the cabin, "I don't care who you are or where you came from. Heck, half of you won't even be here come next week. This facility is for the most potential candidates for a new program. Those that make the cut will be trained in various skills necessary for the front. The moment you do not meet our standards, you will be drafted to a different infantry camp."

The captain looks at the two bloodied men. "If anyone pulls anything like this again, I'll court martial you like there's no tomorrow. The enemy is out there, not in here. I expect you all to fall in. Five minutes."

He leaves the room, taking some of the tension out as well. Private Mckenzie glares at Will. Will smiles back. "I'm going to enjoy watching your face when you don't make the cut."

"You'd better watch your back. You're lucky he walked in, maybe next time I'll finish the job." Private Mckenzie heads to his bunk, with a couple of cheeky friends laughing. The rest of the cabin resumes as if nothing happened. Everyone recognizes Will from the train, and no one speaks to him. His altercation with Mckenzie only solidifies his alienation.

The men fall into formation in the yard. Captain Prichard is standing next to Colonel Riker. The men stand at attention while he addresses them. "All of you have volunteered to become a soldier for the B.E.F., however, not all of you will be accepted. You will train with your cabin mates in each category that pertains to a soldier's duty. At the end of each week, there will be a test in each category. Pass and you keep training. Fail and you report to a less-distinguished training center. We will only train the best of the best, and don't think that the lot of you are the only ones applying. Training commences tomorrow at oh-six-hundred hours. Best of luck."

The men are dismissed; most returning to their quarters. A few linger in the yard to chat with other applicants. Will analyzes the camp and, once satisfied, returns to his cabin. He lays in his bunk, resting for tomorrow, while his fellow recruits talk late into the night, long after lights have been shut off.

4: SETTLING IN

Friday:

Monica and I have grown even closer over the last few days. I found out a lot about her. I think about the late night conversation we had a few days ago often. We sat in her quarters. She clung to a large glass of wine. I was offered some, but stuck with water.

"Where do you want to begin?" She asked me.

I didn't want to seem like a younger sibling, gawking at stories told by my older counterpart. I wanted to know everything.

"Start at the beginning."

Monica gulped her drink down and poured another, offering some to me, which I passed on. "I came over here from Australia. I grew up there, went to medical school—the works. I met another doctor, James, when I was in training. The two of us bonded immediately."

Her eyes betrayed her, with glistening liquid pooling around the edges. She paused momentarily, as our conversation brought back painful memories. "We started dating and eventually got married. We spent ten years together—the best of my life. Then the war began. We both wanted to help, so we volunteered to work over here. I was denied serving with the Australian Expeditionary Forces because I was female. We decided to volunteer somewhere that would accept me. The French Red Cross needed all the help they could get. Frankly, I would have been posted with the other women, but James pulled a few strings."

"Were you stationed at the same hospital?" I questioned,

mainly to allow her a chance to take another sip.

She nodded. "At first, yes. But then some soldiers showed up from the front nearby, requesting a doctor. James volunteered right away. He didn't even give it a second thought. That was the type of man he was—just wanted to help people. He and I argued and fought. I didn't want him to go, it was too dangerous. He eventually did what he wanted to in the end."

The tears in her eyes were now unable to be masked. "Hours later we received a new batch of wounded from the front...and when I went into the operating room...James...he was on my table."

As soon as Monica said that, I regretted asking her; prying into her life. "I'm so sorry, Monica. I-I didn't know."

Monica smiled through tears. "It's not your fault, dear. I obviously lost my composure and couldn't operate on him, so I asked one of the more experienced doctors to. Looking back, I would have been better off doing it myself. He made an error, and James passed away on the table.

"My James died because of that doctor's mistake. A slip of his hand, and his blade caused irreparable damage. He blamed it on a nurse bumping the table, but I saw the whole thing."

"Monica, I'm so sorry," I said, but what words could make her feel comforted? Francis would know what to say—he always does. And after I thought of him, I was sad, and worried.

"Our last words were that of an argument. His death could have been prevented. The doctor could have taken ownership, but didn't. And now here I am."

"What do you mean?"

"I lost control, and attacked the doctor in the room. Under the circumstances, I was pardoned, but transferred here. The amount of incompetence, pride, and clinical error I have seen are ridiculous. Sometimes we have to cut corners, yes, but it shouldn't be the first solution. That is the answer to your question, Jessica. I hate most of the male doctors for those reasons. Sure, not all are bad, but many can be pompous and prideful. It's right in my mind, but not in others. It's all I can do to help prevent anything like that from happening again."

A long moment of silence followed. Monica finished her glass and composed herself.

"Are you doing ok? Have you talked to anyone else about this?"

"Gertrude knows, simply because she read my file. The truth is, ever since I got transferred here, I've buried myself in work to avoid it all."

"Sometimes it helps to talk about things," I comforted her.

"I am starting to see that now, but you have your answer, and we have a long day tomorrow."

After that night, Monica and I have understood each other much better. I see where her passion comes from, and how she handles situations. I can also see why she wanted to have her own self-trained partner. I only hope I can live up to her expectations. Nursing, or assisting a doctor at the very least, isn't easy. The stress here is very high. Casualties keep coming in, and the shifts are long, with sometimes no sleep. Monica has snapped at me a couple of times (within reason), but she just wants the best for her patients. She always apologizes afterwards.

Anyway, she has taught me all the basic duties of washing patients' crockery and sorting their linen, cleaning the sinks and ward utensils, among other things. These are obviously simple tasks, of which I caught on very quickly.

I think Monica was testing my abilities with those jobs because today she promoted me to her chief assistant. I was pretty much already doing that for her, but now it was official. I even have my own nametag now. I felt super proud holding it for the first time. It has my name and some basic information on it (I had to supply a fake birthday of course).

It felt like one of my first real achievements in life. Something I had done on my own—with no help from Francis (especially not Will), my parents, and even outside of The Island.

As I write this, I'm looking at it, and it's bringing all kinds of mixed emotions up. On the one hand, it's a major accomplishment for me, and feels like I'm right where I need to be for once. But on the other hand, it means Francis still hasn't shown up. It's been a couple of weeks now; I'm starting to fear he isn't coming back. That means this ID is the end of The Island, of him, of our whole mission. That's what hurts the most. It's a physical symbol of losing him, and not saving the other children. I had to half-lie to Monica when I burst into tears after she surprised me with it.

"What's wrong, dear?"

I spoke through spurts of emotion. "It's just that…I just had hoped my friend would have made it back by now…He always makes it back."

She embraced me in a warm hug (a very rare thing for her). "He must have been some guy."

"He was…the best really. He was always there for me. He never gave up, and he was kind."

"Do you want my advice, Jess?" Monica said in a grave tone. I didn't reply, but she continued anyway. "You're young. There are plenty of other men out there. From the sounds of things, you have never really been on your own, have you?"

My eyes stared at the floor, distant and longing. "It's the opposite. I've been on my own all my life. I've only really had two friends, and now it's just him…and he's gone. I cared for him."

"But did you love him?" Her question rattled me, but not as much as her next. "Loving and caring for someone are two different things, as similar as they may seem. Do you know which one he was to you?"

I didn't reply. I couldn't, and she realized it. She stood from her chair and made for the door, pausing before leaving. "I think you need to be on your own for a while to think about these things. If you ask me, you need to move on and let go, and believe me, I know how hard it can be. But I also know that I will never find anyone that could replace James. Take your time, Miss Noble, and know I'm always here to talk."

"Thanks, Monica."

Sunday:

Today gave me quite the scare. I was in the middle of doing my rounds, checking on patients and their needs, when I spotted two men enter the hospital. They had an Island logo on their uniforms. I immediately pulled a u-turn and hid behind the doors I had just passed through. Terrified, I chanced another glance through the window in the door. The symbol was unmistakable. *How could they be here?* I thought.

Monica spotted me cowering behind the door. "What are you doing, dear?"

"Monica please, you have to help me," I begged. I was desperate; if The Island was operating in the past, there was no way I'd go back in a cell after everything I'd been through. "I can't explain it, but those men may be looking for me. I need you to find out why they're here and get them off my trail. Please."

She peered through the window, sizing the men up. "I recognize their type. You don't want to be mixed up with the likes of them. If I do this, you will explain yourself once they leave, are we clear?"

"Yes, please, just help."

She walked through the doors and approached them. I placed my ear to the wall to hear what they were saying. Gertrude was just about to answer something they had asked when Monica stepped in. "Can I help you, gentlemen?"

"Ma'am, we're looking for two young adults. One male and one female. Would've been here a while ago, posing as two civilians caught in a skirmish outside of town. Girl was blonde, and the male was a bit ragged, with dark brown hair. Any of this sound familiar?"

Monica pondered a moment. "I remember the girl. She was wounded. Didn't make it. Passed away on the table. The young man she was with left before I could tell him. I don't know where he went."

Gertrude raised a suspicious eyebrow. The two men thanked Monica and left without another word. Gertrude was about to ask, but Monica cut her off, "Don't ask. This stays between us and Jessica, yeah?"

"If that's what you need, Hun."

Monica came back through the doors, grabbing my arm, practically dragging me to her quarters. She shut the door behind us. "You have some explaining to do."

I inhaled, thinking of how much I could or would tell her. "My friends and I have been together since a very young age. We were held captive in a place with the same symbol as those men had on their sleeves." I rolled up my shirt to reveal the mark.

Her eyes widened only momentarily. "Continue."

"Not long ago we escaped. We've been on the run ever since, trying to find a safe place. We want to stop them. With Francis, my friend, gone…there's no way to do that."

"Why do you need him?" She questioned.

I bit my lip. "He was the only one of us who could access

their facility, and get us back there. It's hard to explain, and even if I could, I'm not sure it would make sense. Either way, if those men were indeed looking for us, they may have found Francis. He could be imprisoned right now and I don't think I can help him."

"First off, you don't know what's happened to your friend. It's difficult to come to terms with, but he may be dead, or imprisoned as you say. Regardless, it is out of your control."

"But how could I live with myself if he's out there suffering, wondering where I am, and I've just given up?"

"Jessica, those men are dangerous. And they were looking for you and that loser you came in with. They think you are dead. You no longer have to run. I think it best if you move on. You said yourself, this guy would try and find you, and he'd come back here. He hasn't shown up yet. If he was taken, he sounds like the type who would try to escape and find you again."

"He would," I said quietly.

"I've seen those agents before, Jessica. The people they take, we never see again. They come and go as they please, and vanish without a trace. You won't be able to track them down. So please, don't do anything foolish. Stay here, where you're safe. If he is out there, he'll find you. But you don't know for sure, and you can't put life on hold for fear of the unknown. It will ruin you. Trust me, I know. I was angry after James died. I did some things that I regret, so take my advice: stay put, start a new life, and move on."

"I just don't know if I can do that, Monica. I keep thinking what would he do if he were in my shoes?"

"Maybe that's the problem," she hinted. "You need to make your own choices. Don't live how you think others would. Live life how you choose to. You are not him, and from the sounds of it, you would choose different actions than he would. You may have been close your whole life, but now you're on your own.

Don't let the *what ifs* dictate your life."

"But it's not that simple," I tried to reason, only to hear the falter in my voice.

She opened the door to the hallway. "You'll need to make that choice one of these days. The sooner the better. Just think about it."

She shut the door and left me to my thoughts. What if he was captured? What would he do in my shoes? No. I can't think like that. Monica was right. Deep down I knew it.

Francis always liked to play hero, but I just wanted to help. He took it to extremes. Would he wake to think I died or abandoned him? Could he already have jumped to the future? The questions only grew more challenging. The harder they became, the more I realized that she was right about everything. I made a list of the facts because lists help me think:

1. Francis and I are separated.

2. Will is a jerk and I no longer care about where he is (seriously, I will kill him if he shows his face again).

3. If Francis is alive, he will do anything to find me…unless he thinks I'm dead (which is possible).

4. If he were dead, I'd be waiting for nothing.

5. If he were captured, I'd have no way to find him.

I stared at the paper I had written this down on. I gave it my best shot at saving the others, but if I'm stuck in the past, there's no way to help them. If I go looking for Francis, he could come for me, and I'd be gone, and we'd never find each other. If I put my life on hold, and keep watching the door every day, expecting him to suddenly appear, I will break down.

I've already cried countless nights waiting for him to show. If I start a new life, and he shows up then, well, I don't know. But I did know one thing.

It'll be hard, but I'm not rolling over. If I'm stuck here, I'm going to be a darn good nurse—maybe even a doctor one day.

The whole time I've been here, I feel a sense of belonging. I'm proud of what I do. I'm helping people in need. I'm making a difference, and I don't need my ability to feel special, powerful, or remind me of the nightmare that was my past. I'm normal, and I hate admitting it, but it's the only thing I have ever wanted. Wherever Francis was, I'm sure he would understand.

I stood up and exited the room. I went to find Monica, and finish my duties for the day. Francis was always on my mind, but he no longer haunted it.

Training Facility
England

Will takes a deep breath in and lets it out slowly. The air is cold and the night is dark. He has trained for weeks with the fellow soldiers. He made several cuts, but it all comes down to this. The final test. He stands eagerly at the front of the line. Several soldiers have come and gone—some passed, most failed. His nerves are gathered, unlike the shaking young man behind him.

Captain Prichard approaches Will. "This is it, recruit. Pass, and you may be accepted for a special task, to be further trained by myself. Fail, and you will be sent to an infantry detail. Understood?"

Will is focused and nods once. "Understood."

"Good. Here is your fake rifle, and here are your charts and writing utensil. Your final test is a comprehensive simulation. You will enter our mock Western front battlefield. It will be your mission to accurately map out the enemy lines, without getting spotted, and report back to me behind our own. At any point, if you spot an enemy soldier, it will be your own decision as to engage or slip past them. At any time if you are spotted, either by an enemy unit, spotlight, or enemy sniper, you automatically fail. Is your mission clear?"

"Clear, sir," Will states calmly.

"Then what are you waiting for?"

Will pulls his weapon over his head, tightening the strap around his back. He tucks the charts into his jacket, careful not to leave any exposed paper that could fall out. He jogs down to the trenches, noting the fog trail his breath leaves. If he breathes too much, the air would give his position away.

He wraps a scarf around his face to help control the problem. He approaches one of the platforms used to survey over the trench, and across No Man's Land. Will scans the area—more specifically—his A.I. does. The A.I. calculates all the ridges and divots, mapping out the layout of the battlefield. It selects the best route for Will to take.

Will smirks, and jogs down the trenches until he comes to the most ideal spot to climb over. He peers over the edge, double-checking the area. Satisfied that all is clear, Will carefully pulls himself over the edge of the trench.

Will thinks the air is cold, but the moment his chest hits the muddy ground, he realizes his error. It will be difficult to stay warm and still at the same time, he thinks to himself.

He crawls, using his arms to pull himself forward, likewise with his legs. The A.I. projects a hologram map over his pupils, allowing him to see the route where he will be able to remain unseen. Will follows the path, moving slowly. A section ahead is the first point where he can be spotted by the enemy lines. His body makes slow adjustments; any movements will give his position away.

Once clear, Will moves closer to the enemy trench lines. Nearby a searchlight pops on. Will does not move an inch, waiting for it to pass over the ledge he hides behind. Meanwhile, the A.I. is calculating the angle and trajectory of the light, narrowing down its position, and adjusts the current path to avoid its gaze.

Will's body is unable to hold off shivering any longer. His extremities shake very subtly. He pulls his arms close to his chest and tries to stay warm by moving forward. He pauses and takes a scan of the area ahead of him. The A.I. flags a strange outline across the field, causing him to stop. The scan shows the outline of a body, but more importantly, a sniper. Will remains calm, as the A.I. recalculates a new route to ambush the threat. He cautiously moves back, sliding through mud.

The process takes time, but Will does not rush. Much closer, he is able to make out the target without the help of the A.I. The fake enemy soldier is hidden remarkably well—no doubt attempting to simulate an actual German sniper occupying the territory.

If this were real combat, Will would simply use his powers to snap the enemy's neck, or project a bullet through the head. That is, after all, what he did to fake his accuracy at the firing range. However, this is only a simulation. He cannot harm any opposing combatants, and must succeed in his mission undetected.

Instead, Will slithers closer behind the sniper, inching forward ever so slowly. Rain begins to fall, masking his approach even more. He reaches down, and pulls a knife from his waist. He is close enough to strike. Will calmly holds the knife's handle to the man's neck, careful not to injure him.

"Don't move," he says quietly, causing the soldier to jump

slightly. "If this wasn't a simulation, you would be dead long ago. You will remain here, motionless, until it is over, correct?"

The enemy sniper chuckles quietly. "Correct. Don't get too cocky though. Good luck, Private."

Will continues towards the enemy lines, constantly scanning his surroundings. Occasionally he pauses and jots notes and sketches of the enemy trench line. He resists the urge to enter the trenches, and take out any soldiers, but that is not his mission...yet.

Much time passes before Will is satisfied with his surveillance. He barely feels his body anymore, it has become so numb. Eventually he successfully makes it back into his trench, stretching out his limbs once safely below ground level. He returns to Captain Prichard, who is sitting under a canvas lit by a lantern.

"You were out there quite a long time, Private," Captain Prichard says, teeth clenching a cigar.

"You can't rush perfection, sir."

"We'll see." The Captain sets off a horn that signals the end of the simulation. Minutes pass until several soldiers fall in. "Report."

The enemy sniper is the first to speak. "He got the drop on me, sir. Didn't hear or see him coming."

Another soldier speaks. "Our line did not spot any movement in No Man's Land. No reports of any kind."

Captain Prichard is still skeptic. "That's a good start, but it won't mean anything unless you mapped their lines accurately."

Will places his paper on a nearby table. "Just like how we trained. I landmarked their machine guns and heavily defended strongholds with markers from our side. The same goes for any branches of their trench. I also added a rough tally of how many enemy soldiers I spotted in their trenches."

The Captain compares the paper to a proper map of the simulation battleground. His eyes dart back and forth, and his lips stretch into a smile. He extends a hand to Will. "Well Private, this is exceptional work. Depending on how the other recruits perform, you may be the soldier I'm looking for. You will be notified by early morning. Dismissed."

"Thank you, sir!" Will salutes and heads to base to wash off and get some much-needed rest. He spots Private Mckenzie about to take his test. Will has barely made it halfway to the barracks before hearing a gun go off, signaling the enemy spotting and 'killing' Mckenzie. Will's smile stretches wider than ever before. "Let's see your dad help you out of failing this time."

Journal Entry #19:
December 13, 1914
England

Neptune's interrogation of the mole revealed very little information—specifically, only a name. Jensen Avery. Apparently he is the only person the mole had any contact with and may know the location of the scientist we're looking for.

Despite being physically part of the team, I don't feel I am a member. At least not an important one. For example, I was not privileged to witness the interrogation, nor see the mole afterwards. It feels very much familiar to The Island Corporation I know back home. By that I mean from Neptune's body language and report I gathered that the mole was killed during interrogation (possibly intentionally). This type of information did not sit well with me, but to be fair, Mars was the one who ended up interrogating him. He did not give off any good vibes.

I'll need to prove myself in our upcoming missions in order to gain respect. Wash has our first one lined up. The team sat in the briefing room while he explained.

"The interrogation revealed only a name. Our research teams and undercover agents have been tasked with locating Jensen Avery. Once found, we will send you to retrieve or interrogate him to gather further information on the scientist working for the Germans. Unfortunately, this will take time."

My stomach was in knots. Why couldn't anything be simple? Why couldn't we find my friends, find the bad guy, and leave? Above everything, I didn't want to hear that it would take time. Time was something that made me uneasy when I didn't know the fate of Jessica or Will.

"In the meantime, we do have several missions that are urgent. The first of which is gathering intel on German supply routes, formations, and intentions surrounding Ypres. The details are in the folders in front of you. We know the Germans have a base of operations here," Wash pointed to an X on the map. "Your mission is to infiltrate their base unnoticed, and use this camera to photograph all relevant documents. It's simple enough. Get in and get out without being spotted."

"What sort of support do we have for entering and exiting enemy territory?" Earth questioned.

Wash lit a cigar. "Once you arrive in Belgium, you will meet some of our undercover operatives. They know the area and the German patrols well enough to escort you near Ypres. From there, Neptune can decide what the best route in and out of the base will be. If you are caught, you will receive no help. This mission is one of the simplest that this team will be charged with. Consider it a test run. Failure or capture will inform us that a new team needs to be chosen. Succeed, and you will perform some of the most dangerous and difficult counter strikes and stealth missions as they arise. Any other questions?"

No one spoke. "Good. Neptune will coordinate your duties and how he wants the operation run once everyone looks over the files. Dismissed."

Everyone cleared the room until only myself and Wash remained. "Do you have an update for me, Wash?"

He shifted in his chair. "As soon as I have one, believe me, you'll be the first to know. For now, focus on the task at hand."

"The task at hand is why my companions and I are here in the first place," I growled. "I want to know exactly what you are doing to find them. Surely if your resources can find some scientist, you can find two people with names and a location."

"You want to know the truth, kid? Your companions arc probably dead. Our agents tracked them down to an outpost near where we found you. They spoke to a doctor at the hospital that recalls seeing someone matching the female's description passing away, but with all the dead, bodies get misplaced. As for your male companion, he disappeared after that without a trace. No clues. No evidence. Nothing. So based on these findings, my priorities are no longer searching for your companions. Focus on the mission."

My head was spinning. "No…no they have to be wrong."

"They're dead, son. They can't help you anymore. You want to finish your mission? We put you on a new team to help you with that. Now, you can either mope around the base over your companions, or you can face the mission you were sent here to do. Your choice."

He left the room before I could answer. I was still in shock. Dead? No. That I couldn't accept. Not after everything we've been through. To just have them…Jessica…gone? It wasn't even something I could have stopped. The whole time we landed, I was unconscious.

My fists collided with the table, making a resonating thump. I was on the verge of rage and tears. I hit the table once more, taking a deep breath in. I regained enough composure to walk calmly to my room. The moment the door closed, I cried. I don't know for how long. Eventually the tears beckoned me to sleep.

The next day I awoke from a nightmare that I did not remember. What I did remember was Wash telling me my friends were most likely dead (it sounded like Jessica was confirmed). Just thinking about her name made me depressed. After being together for so long, after Camelot and almost losing each other at Skeleton Island, I didn't know what to do. Despite what I wanted to say to her after that adventure, I never actually did. And now it's too late.

"I love you, Jess," I stuttered through droplets of tears. "I always will."

It's pretty unlikely, but there's a small chance it could've been someone else's body. No, Francis, no more what ifs. She's gone. Will is missing. Face it. I had lost my friends. I got them here, and they died because of me. I know Jess would have said something like, "We chose this, not you. We knew the risks." Yet I can't help but feel responsible. Their deaths will forever be a weight, a burden, on my shoulders.

"No matter what it takes, guys. I will make them pay. I will free those children. I will finish this," I said to thin air. There was no response. The room was silent. I was alone.

I got dressed. My body was going through motions of which my mind was unaware. I could mourn when I was alone, but right now, I needed to pull myself together and prepare for the mission. The mask I wore to guard my feelings was not very convincing. Then again, no one here knew me well enough to notice. I was truly on my own.

Neptune called a meeting. I gathered with the others in another boardroom. A large map of Western Europe was on the table. Neptune hunched over, pointing at a highlighted route on the map. "We leave at thirteen-hundred to the base. We'll reach the Belgian beach under the cover of nightfall. Once on the beach, we must rendezvous quickly with the undercover operatives. The Germans will have patrols on the shoreline, but our intel should allow us to avoid any incidents."

"What type of firepower are we bringing along?" Mars questioned.

"Most importantly, and above all, this is a stealth mission. If we need to resort to weapons, we've already failed the operation. That being said, we will all be equipped with silenced pistols that haven't been field tested yet. Avoid engaging enemy troops unless you can do it silently," Neptune replied. He then traced a line on the map with his finger until he reached a dot. "Our operatives will escort us across the countryside until the outskirts of the German Ypres base. There may be a stream or river to cross between their location and us, but we'll play it by ear when we have eyes on site. Once there, Mercury will place explosives on this bridge, covering our escape route in case things get rough."

"Do you want the bridge annihilated, or just out of commission?"

"Hopefully we won't even need to detonate, it's just a precaution, but we can time-delay it to blow after our getaway."

"Saturn will survey the best route in, accompanied by Venus, to locate and photograph the information we need," Neptune continued. "Earth will use some of his modified equipment to watch our backs in the dark. He will communicate with us, calling out locations of patrols or guards, guiding everyone to their posts. Uranus will be nearby acquiring a vehicle to make the route back faster, just in case we are discovered."

Neptune turned his gaze to me, like I was the younger sibling he was forced to look after. (My sister had given me the same stare many times.) "You and I are going to take up positions on the hillside, overseeing the operation, and providing cover fire if necessary. The same goes for you, Jupiter, only you'll be stationed on the adjacent side. Any concerns?"

Saturn spoke, "How reliable is this intel of the base, or the operatives?"

Neptune sounded skeptical. "It's supposedly reliable, which means we will not take it to heart. We are a unit. We'll do our own intel on site and determine the best course of action then. If we rely on what others bring us alone, we won't make it out of these missions alive. We look out for each other, and trust our teammates' calls alone. If Earth or someone tells you to do something, you do it. No questions. They see something that you don't or can't. Got it?"

The room nodded. I liked the idea of this team. I only wish my role on it was more defined and accepted. Either way, we'll see how things go with our first mission.

The trip to Ypres was not as eventful as I had thought it would be. I slept the whole way to the ocean. The boat ride was slow and cold. The winter chill did not help either. There was only one close call on the water.

Earth was using a night vision prototype to scour the coast for enemy ships or patrols. He hastily got us to kill the engines, and we rocked in silence. Moments later we could make out something moving along the water. A small patrol boat passed by, but it didn't spot us. Mars loosened his grip on his rifle.

"Coast is clear," Earth stated. "The landmark for meeting the operatives is dead ahead."

We landed with no trouble, hauling the small boat up the

beach. Neptune ran ahead and met the Belgian operative, who led us to a small hut where we stashed the boat. From there we ran from cover to cover, house to house, avoiding all main roads or lit areas.

We spent several nights in random hideouts. I was pretty exhausted from running, and almost welcomed all the patrols we encountered, because it gave me a chance to rest. Those moments were tense, however, and if we were spotted or caught, it was game-over. A slightly terrifying thought, I concluded. It all felt so up to chance, but Neptune and the operative led us without incident. We reached the outskirts of Ypres.

Neptune kept his voice low and as quiet as possible. "Earth, go survey the area with Saturn. Check their guard posts and transitions, any patrols, and contact me with updates through your headset."

"Got it," Earth replied, with Saturn on his heels. Earth and Neptune both wore headsets, quite like the Xbox ones I had as a child, only much larger. I had to keep reminding myself that The Island has access to non-mainstream tech. It's a bit hard remembering what technology was normal for this time period.

Time passed slowly in the cold environment. Every now and then Neptune would hold a hand to his headset and say, "Copy."

Saturn returned suddenly. I never heard or saw him coming. He was good. "Earth is in position. I have a route mapped out, but I'll need your headset to communicate with him once inside."

Neptune dished off his headset, and just as quickly as he appeared, Saturn and Venus left to carry out the mission. Jupiter, Mercury, and Uranus left to take up their positions as well, leaving me alone with Neptune.

He whipped out an old (new for that time though) rifle with a small scope attached and handed it to me. "You can shoot, right?"

"Of course," I lied.

"Don't use it unless absolutely critical, understand?" He pulled another out, and lay down, scoping the area. "If we have to resort to shooting, we've already failed."

"Got it." I eyed the weapon, making a mental note to figure out how it worked when we got back (other than simply pulling the trigger). I closed one eye and peered through the lens. The zoom wasn't amazing, especially at night, but it was better than nothing. I could make out some German soldiers, but only when they stepped into the dimly lit portions of their camp. We waited in silence, hoping no alarms or shots would go off.

I noticed Neptune checking his watch. "They should be back by now."

"Maybe they were just delayed avoiding patrols?"

"Unlikely." His response was robotic, and unrevealing. His attention shifted behind us. Mercury was returning.

"Explosives have been planted, sir. They are set for tomorrow afternoon if I don't activate it sooner. Uranus also informed me he has a getaway vehicle if necessary just down the road."

"Well done. Hopefully we won't have to use it."

"I see them!" I murmured quietly to Neptune.

"Where?"

"Southeast corner of the camp."

He stared intensely into his scope. "Good. Just get out of—" Neptune suddenly cursed.

"What is it?" I could see Saturn and Venus in my sights, and they had stopped. Saturn was holding the headset keenly, while Venus had her pistol drawn, and was keeping watch.

"They've stopped for some reason, maybe a tech malfunction. Either way if they don't move now that patrol is going to round the corner and spot them."

I adjusted my scope to see that he was right. Our team members still weren't moving. "Right, I got this."

"Just what is that supposed to mean?" Neptune said with colorful language added. "Don't you—"

I didn't let him finish. I focused my mind, and froze time. As soon as I felt I had control, I bolted down the hillside, running straight into the camp. As I raced past the patrol, I studied their position, and noted the best way to escape. Venus and Saturn were around the corner. I took a deep breath and released the grip I had, while placing a hand on both of them. My sudden appearance was obviously a bit shocking.

"Where did you come from, Pluto?" Venus hissed. "You aren't supposed—"

"Save it, Venus," I cut her off, "a patrol is just around the corner. Follow me. Now."

They did not argue. The three of us moved quickly and silently through the path I had studied on my way in. We did not run into any more problems. When we reached the others, Neptune was fuming.

He jabbed a finger at my chest. "You pull something like that again, I don't care what security clearance you have, I'll kill you myself. You don't take your own initiative on a mission. You follow my orders, got it?"

"Hey, I just saved this mission," I snapped.

Saturn stepped between us. "The kid's got a point, Nept. We would've been spotted. It could've been bad."

"Either way," Earth moved in, "now's not the time or place to discuss it. Let's get out, yeah?"

Neptune's gaze lingered on me. I could see his anger emitting towards me. "Let's move."

Our team left Ypres, taking a similar route back to the

coastline. The same obstacles were in our way, but we did not run into any problems. The way back seemed faster than getting there, and soon we were on a boat headed back to headquarters. Neptune did not speak a word to me the whole trip.

When we finally reached our base (it's odd calling an Island facility 'our base') Neptune pulled me aside. "Look, kid. You did good back there. I don't know how or what exactly you did, but it was good. However, I'm the leader of this team. You need to follow my orders, and run things by me. Another stunt like that could get us killed. I realize I have not extended to you a welcome to the unit. So, from here out, you're part of it. But I need to know what exactly you can do in order to run this team properly, alright?"

He seemed genuine, but then again, he was an Island soldier. Could I trust him? "Thank you, Neptune. I'll show you another time. I think we could all use some rest for now."

He nodded. "Dismissed."

I went to my room, contemplating how much I could trust these people, and how involved I was willing to get.

5: AS TIME GOES BY

Journal Entry #84:
April 13, 1915
England

They say war is hell. And after experiencing almost six months of it, I can see why. The hardest part is that not even half the things I've experienced are as bad as what most soldiers deal with daily. This war is one grueling fight, and that's just from behind the scenes. We've never really had any missions on the front at all. That is, until now.

They're sending us out behind enemy lines. Permanently. Wash told us that the missions we've been on have proven very useful to the Allied forces, but we need to do more.

Essentially, we can only do so much going back and forth from our base to each mission. He wants our team to execute multiple missions, one after the other, remaining in enemy territory. In my opinion, he's right. The amount of sabotage we've done to the Germans is great, but we've gotten nowhere in tracking that scientist down. We can't rely on our intel, which means we have to take the initiative to track him down ourselves.

The first mission on our list is going to take us back to Ypres. Apparently the Germans have a new weapon they are taking to fuel their advancement. Our mission is to stop it from reaching their lines. That sounds fair and all, but I'm stuck in a difficult position. Why? Because I know what their weapon is.

Chlorine gas.

I remember it from the history 'lessons' given to us by The Island. It was particularly drilled into my mind for a very disturbing reason. Not because of the effect the gas had on soldiers, or anything to do with the war for that matter, but because of how I learned about it. One of the few things I remember on my own (not in a weird repressed memory) is that history lesson. I was very young, and by all means should not be learning that kind of material yet, but there I was. Sitting in a room, with those devices on my head that covered my eyes with its holographic glasses...

I remained uncooperative with them. I was still fighting their influence, despite their efforts to brainwash us. The 'class' was receiving a lesson on World War One, only I wasn't having any of it.

Tired of the lessons and treatment, I bashed my head against the desk, breaking the head set. The hologram image of a classroom and lesson disappeared, revealing a room full of unmoving children, absorbed in the devices. I fidgeted in my chair, trying to break the restraints. That was when it happened.

A woman stormed into the room. I recognized her at once. She was the one trying to brainwash me. She was the one I had seen in my memories before—Katherine. I could tell she was furious, but I was not prepared for what she did next. She raced towards me, high heels clicking rapidly with each step. With outstretched hands, she ripped off the headgear. A chunk of my hair went with it, sending a tremor of pain through my body.

"You think this is a game, Francis?" she asked hysterically. She reached behind her back, and pulled out a gun. It wasn't an Island weapon. It was a real gun. I started to panic, fearing these would be my last moments.

Katherine placed the gun on a desk, and gripped my shirt with clenched fists. "Now listen up, and listen good. You will cooperate. Any time you don't, I will kill one of these children. Their deaths will be on your hands. Try pulling another stunt again, I dare you."

"You won't kill us."

Katherine leaned in close. "You children mean nothing. You are worthless, and there's plenty more just like you to fill your place."

With no hesitation or warning, she pointed the gun at the kid next to me.

She pulled the trigger.

Fear gripped my body. I couldn't move. Katherine flew out of the room without another word.

There was nothing I could do but give in. I would not succumb to their brainwashing, yet I could do nothing to fight it. Scientists came and took the boy away. I couldn't see his condition because they were already placing another device on my head. I feared the worst for him. How could they do that?

Later that day, I remember thinking about what she had said: You are worthless. Her words stung...and yet, they confused me. If I were truly worthless, why wouldn't she just kill me? I began to think. She must need me, otherwise why not get rid of me like she had with that other kid?

In trying to break me, she accidently gave me the spark to keep fighting. They needed me. I didn't know why. I didn't care. It meant they couldn't kill me, which leaves my only option being escape. I had to be careful, though, I would not have any other lives hang in the balance of my choices.

Why does this memory matter so much to me right now? Other than the fate of that child forever etched into my mind, it was the lesson. After Katherine left, I had to restart my lesson. It discussed lots of things about World War One, but most importantly, it told me about the second battle of

Ypres. The same battle we were about to experience now.

The weapon we were being sent to investigate is chlorine gas—a terrible example of chemical warfare. My predicament is that we are being sent to stop them from using it. Yet I know from history that they release the gas, which means our mission fails, or at least it needs to fail.

So what am I supposed to do? If we stop them, we save lives and thwart one of their advancements, but could alter the past, or worse, the outcome of the war. If we don't stop them, I am knowingly letting soldiers die, and failing the mission.

I remember discussing the problems of doing too much in the past with my friends. Especially after we saw the book about King Arthur. I can't consciously change history without knowing what the consequences are. Yet if they'd be the same if we stopped the attack, a lot of soldiers will get to fight another day, or even go home to their family.

To be honest, I haven't made up my mind. We're about to leave on the mission, so I don't have long to make a decision. I just hope it's the right one.

Tuesday:

The sirens blared early in the morning. I was used to waking up at odd hours to tend to incoming wounded. I quickly got dressed and exited my room, just as Monica was leaving her quarters across the way.

"Where do you want me?" I asked as she pulled her coat over her shoulders.

"Front and centre," Came her brisk response. "Direct the incoming wounded to pre-op, or wherever they need to be. You don't know how many there will be, so—"

"So make sure to organize them by condition, as well as organized to make the transition easy." I grinned.

Monica hid her pride. "You have become the most reliable assistant I've ever had. Just don't get too full of yourself."

"Never do."

We went separate ways, her to the operating room, and me to receive the incoming wounded. It wasn't my first time doing this, but it didn't help relieve any pressure. I breathed deeply, running through conditions and where to send each one in my head.

The last few months have been a learning process, with a lot of trial and error. I stood at the doors watching the horse-drawn carriages approach bringing in the wounded soldiers.

"What do we got?" I questioned the first man to exit.

He spoke as he went to the back of the cart. "Mortar shells, some shrapnel, some worse off. Another load have some bullet wounds."

"Alright, let me see." I've grown used to seeing all kinds of injuries. There was no room for a weak stomach here. I surveyed the men in pain in the back of the vehicle. "Send those two men in first, keep these three back on trolleys along the right side of the hallway. And send him in right behind the first two."

"Got it."

I checked the second wave of wounded and directed them into position as well. "How many more on the way?"

The medic shook his head. "Three more full convoys. About ten minutes out."

"That's not good." I grimaced. "You'd better get going then."

The medic hurried out as I ran up the hallway towards the operating room. I double-checked the row of patients as I made my way. They hadn't screwed anything up, which always makes my job easier. I scrubbed down my hands and donned the protective gear and facemask before entering the room.

The operating room is always chaotic. Multiple stations are lined up side by side, with a doctor at each one, working with several nurses. Right now the doctors were Trevor, Jack, Christoff, and Monica. We were short-staffed, and Trevor had only recently gotten here. It wasn't as bad as it sounded, as we only received part of the wounded from Ypres. Another clearing station was much closer to the fight.

I made my way through the crowd until I was next to Monica. She had opened up her soldier's stomach, and was in the process of pulling out the shrapnel and stopping the bleeding. "Three more convoys are about eight minutes out. Similar wounds."

"Good to know. You can assist Dr. McCoy now," Monica said, gesturing to her current assistant. "Noble, get me some suction here."

"On it." I rushed in, replacing the other nurse without missing a beat. The patient wasn't looking so good, but Monica kept working.

"Suction's good, hand me the forceps."

She worked aggressively, but precisely. I admired the dedication she put into each patient, no matter his or her condition. "Good. This one's clean. Get him stitched up while I get prepped for the next."

She left to change her protective gear, so as not to infect or contaminate the next patient. I was left with another nurse to seal up the wound. With everything I have seen from Camelot, Skeleton Island, and now the war, the wounded on the tables never bothered me. At first they did, and I was a little squeamish, but not now. Now I was calm and collected, carefully stitching the soldier's wounds together.

Monica had taught me well. My first attempt at closing up a patient was rushed and ugly, but no mistakes were made. A few of the other nurses and doctors had their reservations about me for such operations, but Monica cut them down pretty darn quick. After I gained more confidence, so did my work. Fairly soon, my closures and other procedures spoke for themselves.

My hands were steady as I pierced the needle through the young man's skin. I cut the thread once the stitches were complete. I let a deep breath out. "OK, send him to post-op. Make sure they monitor his conditions in case we missed anything."

The nurse nodded and wheeled the soldier away. I followed the same procedure as Monica had, cleaning up for the next patient. Over the past weeks, the two of us have worked around the clock tending to the incoming wounded. They came at all points, day or night, but today I was thankful they were coming during the day. Of course, I would rather they not have to come at all.

I passed Monica on my way to change. "Head to table four when you're done. Heavy damage from shelling."

"On it," I hastily replied, changing into clean attire. I regrouped with Monica at the table. She analyzed the patient and sighed. She had an uncanny ability to know whether a patient would survive or not. The sigh was not a good sign, but Monica never quits. "We've got a lot to do on this one."

She directed me for suction, holding things in place, and many other things. She worked hard, but soon the aiding nurse spoke up, "Pulse is dropping, doctor."

Monica muttered something I couldn't make out. "Jessica, my hands are tied to stop him from bleeding out. I need you to gently ease your hands in and find that last piece of shrapnel lodged between his intestines."

"A-are you sure?" I hesitated. The most I was ever responsible for was sewing them up. My duty never involved actual surgery or maneuvers.

"Don't make me ask a second time. You need to get in there now!" she shouted.

I adjusted myself for a better angle. My hands slid into the gaping wound. I carefully sorted through his intestines to try and find the last piece. It was harder than she made it look. "I think I got it!"

"Pulse is failing!"

My fingers gripped the metal and pulled out slowly. "There. I got it."

What little pride I felt for completing the task quickly evaporated into nothing with Monica's next words, "He's gone. We lost him. Cart him off and send in the next one. There's nothing else we can do."

I was frozen in place, still gripping the small piece of shrapnel. I didn't know what to do. "Did, did I—?"

Monica grabbed my hands and stared into my eyes. "He was too far gone. It's not your fault. Keep it together, because we're far from done here."

I held back any forthcoming tears, and gave myself a mental pep talk. We worked late into the day, until all the incoming soldiers were treated.

After taking a much-needed shower, I wandered to the recovery ward. I checked in on the patients I had helped treat. Quite a while later Monica found me.

She rested a hand on my shoulder. "Are you alright?"

"I honestly don't know," I said quietly. "I mean we've lost patients before...but they've—I've—never been really involved in it, or caused it."

Monica's lips pursed. "Miss Noble, do you know why I

asked you to retrieve the shrapnel in that soldier?"

"Because your hands were full."

She shook her head. "That did play a role, but it wasn't the main reason. Once you've been a doctor in a war environment, you start realizing which men that come to your table are survivors…and which aren't. Sometimes the wounds and damage is just too extensive."

I didn't quite understand what her point was, and it must've been obvious because she elaborated. "I knew that boy was wounded beyond recovery, but I still tried. Once his pulse started dropping, I knew there would be no pulling through. I asked you to retrieve the shrapnel knowing full well he would die in the process."

"Why?"

"Losing a patient is the hardest thing to deal with as a doctor. I know you want to become one, like me. Your passion makes that remarkably clear. That's partly why I've taken such an interest in you. But in order to become a good doctor, you must be able to face the circumstances and still perform. Getting your hands in there gave you a taste of what to expect over time. That delicate procedure is crucial, and you need the right nerves for it."

"So you asked me to assist on a dying soldier to feel how finding shrapnel and surgery felt, and see if I could handle it?"

"Not just that, but losing a patient as well," Monica clarified. "Know that he was dead before you were involved. I did all I could, but if he was going to die, at least some good came from it. You felt the responsibility. You felt the heartbreak of losing him in your care. One day you will be a doctor, and you will make mistakes, and you will lose patients. But when you do, I want you to think back on this lesson. Do everything you can to save them, but when you fail, you need to move on and do better on the next wounded man that comes to you. You have to step up even more so that it doesn't happen again."

"How can you just move on like nothing happened?"

"You don't. They died. And they were in your care. Use that emotion you feel to keep going. If you stop, countless more will die because you are not doing your job. This is the best lesson I can give you early on. When you lose a patient you need to remain composed and keep working, because the wounded will keep coming. You win some and you lose some. It's a hard fact to face, but it's something every doctor needs to face."

"And if I can't?" I said solemnly.

"You can," Monica continued, "and you will. Just look at how you did today. Deep down you must have known it wasn't your fault he died. But at heart you thought it was, and yet you kept working with me. You sucked it up. Granted it was after I had to shake some sense in you, but you still kept going. It may have fazed you, but you didn't show it."

Her words comforted me. "Thanks Monica. I think I need some time to think."

"I understand. I do believe you have the makings of a great doctor, Miss Noble."

She left me alone to my thoughts and patients. A career as a doctor. Every time the thought crossed my mind, a part of me hurt because it reminded me Francis was gone. I've done well over the months. I've gotten really good at coming to terms with him being gone, and our failed mission to shut down Island Corporation. I have good days and bad days, depending whether anything reminds me of my past or of him. A part of me still holds hope that he's out there, but a much larger part has moved on.

Monica's faith in me becoming a good doctor helps keep me going. Without her or a purpose, I think I'd be lost. But she did bring up an important point. Being a doctor isn't easy, and losing a patient is awful. I needed to figure out if it was something I could handle. My mind says yes, but my heart is undecided. Judging from everything I've experienced while being here, I've been handling things I never thought I could, or dreamed for that matter. Whatever I choose, I just don't want to let Monica down.

Wednesday:

Today was a typical day, except for one small thing. I shouldn't say thing, though, one small someone. A young Belgium girl accompanied the next batch of wounded. She didn't speak any English, but I gathered that her name is Lola.

Lola and her family had not evacuated and were caught in a skirmish. As far as we know, her family did not make it. Lola herself was shot in the stomach. Her condition is stable for now, but she is very weak. She's so young—if I were to guess, I'd say nine or ten. I don't know if it was the fact that her parents were gone, or if it was because she is really injured, but I immediately became attached to her. I felt like I could relate to what she was going through. She was an orphan like me, and she was in danger too.

It was pretty difficult, though. She spoke no English, so anything I tried to do to comfort her was lost in translation. The farthest I'd get would be getting her a blanket if she looked cold, to be rewarded with a faint smile. Her eyes are still full of terror. Obviously there are Belgian nurses her that have tried talking to her, but she won't speak, and they don't seem as patient as I am with her.

Monday:

In my spare time between rounds or incoming wounded, I sit at Lola's bunk. Each time, I tell her a story my mother told me when I was young. I know she can't understand the words, but for some reason I thought it would comfort her. I can't really explain it.

"There once was a young girl named Abbey. She grew up in a castle so large, the towers touched the sky," I began. "She had everything she could ever ask for. Servants brought her food, jewelry, pretty dresses, but all these things never brought her joy. She wanted to leave the castle, and explore the world, but her parents told her she was too important to leave."

After a couple times telling the same story, some of the soldiers started listening in. They sat quietly, enjoying their first glimpse at compassion away from the fight. I think some were reminded of kids or family back home, and realized what they were fighting for—something that eluded them on the front.

"One night, she cut her hair, and escaped the castle on horseback. The whole kingdom searched for her, but turned up nothing. Abbey ventured across the world, experiencing life and all its wonders. She soon met a timid young man in a harbor. They fell in love after getting in an argument. He was too afraid of the outside world to leave his harbor. Abbey told him of the things she had seen since leaving. 'Besides,' she'd say, 'I'll protect you.'"

Every now and then while telling the story Lola would cough, and sometimes blood would come up. I told Monica, and she and I tried our hardest to figure out what was ailing her, but turned up empty-handed.

"The man told Abbey he would follow her anywhere, and they began exploring the world together. Eventually they grew too old to adventure, and while journeying back home to Abbey's kingdom, the man passed away. Before breathing his last breath, he whispered to her softly, 'There is not a moment I would take back, not a single regret. You are the only one I'd want to have shared this life with.'"

Soon the soldiers were the ones looking forward to my story

and visits. They just wanted to escape their trauma, and I liked helping them. Even Lola would curl up against the arm I'd rest on her bed.

"When Abbey finally made it back to her kingdom, all old and wrinkled, she discovered something. The kingdom had not changed at all. The people were the same, and their routines as well. Her parents were still as vibrant as the day she had left. Yet she went through the town unrecognized. When she saw this, she realized the place she had once called home was crippling. The outside world evolved, adapted, and changed, while things here stayed the same. She did not like it here, and chose to leave again. Abbey sat against her husband's tombstone, on an unknown hillside and said, 'My life's adventure would be nothing without you.' And she fell asleep for the last time, awaking in another world, where he waited for her."

Sometimes after telling the story, Lola would tug my sleeve, wanting it told again. I couldn't resist her eyes looking at me. Other times she would be fast asleep, well before the ending, but I'd finish it anyway for the rest listening in. They needed it, too.

Soon I found myself making up stories about Abbey's adventures, to make things interesting for the soldiers. Some would ask me the name of Abbey's husband. I'd cheekily reply, "Does it matter? There's an Abbey out there for everyone."

Trevor, one of the other doctors here, would wander in the room to check on patients. We'd exchange smiles, as he too listened to my stories. He'd find me in the hallways and say things like: "I'm looking forward to hearing what Abbey does today."

This would make me blush (he is quite a handsome guy), and keep walking. Trevor is a very nice doctor. His voice is kind and gentle, but he carries himself with confidence, something very clear in the operating room. He makes a choice and sticks with it. He is one of the few (and I stress *few*) doctors that Monica actually respects. That's saying something. We've talked quite often, he and I, since he's arrived at the hospital. Initially, I was assigned to show him around and explain our procedures.

While giving the tour I asked him a bunch of questions like where he was from and why volunteer for this position. Every answer he gave made sense—he is quite logical in that regard. He wants to help people, but didn't want to fight or cause pain that the war was responsible for. He was already a certified doctor when the war broke out. Volunteering to serve, as a doctor, was the only option.

"I thought about being a medic at the front," he explained. "It just felt too close to the battle. The only thing I could see myself doing was comforting soldiers before they died. There isn't much a medic in the field can fix, given their equipment—not like here. Here I can make differences that I can't out there."

I like the way he talks. I like him as a person. But I don't like him the way I liked Francis. With Trevor it's different. I can really understand what Monica meant by loving or liking someone, and discerning to what extent.

I love Trevor in a way that I never did with Francis. Even if Francis were here, I'd still feel the same way. That's how hard I'm falling for Trevor. I want to tell him how I feel. I want to have a relationship before it's too late, and he leaves or finds someone else. I've come to terms with being here, and I plan on making the best of it. My only fear is that he won't feel the same.

Look at me. I sound like a high school girl, gossiping to her friends. It's hard to believe that it wasn't that long ago that I was still held captive by The Island. It seems like a lifetime ago.

Tuesday:

Where do I begin with today? Other than the typical incoming wounded, my rounds, and Lola, there was only one thing different. Trevor and I were chatting after treating the wounded. It was the same style of conversation we had many times, but the whole time we were talking, Trevor was nervous.

"Is everything alright?" I enquired. "You seem a bit tense."

Trevor chuckled awkwardly. "There is something."

He stopped walking, and had a hard time finding words—something very unlike him. I gave him a nudge. "Well go on, then."

"I'm not really good at this, but I hope that won't change your answer. The hospital is holding a Spring Dance to take the edge off with all of us working overtime. It's open to everyone, and I was…well I was—what I mean to say is, would you like to go with me? To the dance, I mean?"

A thousand butterflies took flight in my stomach. Was this really happening? I should win an Oscar, or Emmy, or whatever the award is for acting because I played the coolest form of cool possible. "Oh, really? Well, I don't know how to dance, Trev."

"It's OK, I'll teach you. Please? It'll be fun."

I smiled. "I have no doubt about that. Yes, I'll go with you."

His face lit up brighter than I had seen in the time I've known him. "Wonderful! I-I mean that's great to hear. I'll pick you up around eight?"

"That sounds good."

He took off without another word. I think he was afraid he'd say something wrong and ruin things. He doesn't know, but I felt the same way. I stepped inside Monica's room, resting my back against the closed door.

"Someone's happy," Monica smirked from behind her desk, a book in her hands.

"You'll never guess what just happened."

She didn't take her eyes off her book. "Dr. McCoy asked you to the Spring Dance?"

I was stunned. "How did you know?"

"Oh please, the whole hospital knows." She rolled her eyes. "You two are perfect for each other. You're smart and confident, so is he, not to mention attractive. And the two of you have been eyeing each other all the time."

I flicked my hair as I pulled up a chair. "I don't know what you are talking about."

"Mhmm," she mumbled, placing the book down. "Look Noble, you know how few doctors receive my approval. Dr. McCoy is one of them. Of everyone here, he's the only one I'd call good enough to court you."

Courting was what they called dating or flirting. I learned that quite quickly after the soldiers coming in would swoon over us nurses.

"So you think I should go?"

"My dear, it's your life and your decision. You'd think this would be the first relationship you were in." Silence filled the room, and Monica's smile faded quickly. "Oh my. You haven't been in a relationship before, have you?"

I looked at the ground, too nervous to meet her eyes. "No. I haven't. I don't even know how to dance."

Monica's smile was warm and nurturing. "That's alright, my dear, neither do most men."

The two of us laughed and talked until we were too tired to continue. She provided support and advice, the kind normally reserved for mothers. I giggled at some of her past exploits. I left feeling more comfortable about the dance, and Trevor. I've never had a boyfriend before, but I really hope things turn out well. I guess only time will tell.

Saturday:

I'm quickly writing things down before heading to bed, while events are still fresh in my mind. It's Saturday evening right now. Things have been too crazy to write sooner. Friday was a nightmare.

Things were going normal all day. I was so excited for the dance, even though I had no idea what I was getting myself into. The day went by quickly, too. I almost forgot to tell Lola her story before heading out for the evening.

I went to my quarters and began fumbling into the dress Monica had helped me pick out. I wore dresses when we were at Camelot, but I had never felt so beautiful and so…normal as I did then. I almost cried, but forced myself not to.

Soon there was a knock at my door. I opened it, and was immediately at a loss for words. Trevor was dressed in his crisp uniform and held a bouquet of flowers. The two of us gawked at each other, both stumbling to say something.

He was the first to speak, "You look beautiful."

My heart exploded with warmth. I was so close to shaking at my knees. For the first time in my life, a guy had called me beautiful. My first set of flowers. It was my first date for crying out loud! My smile was so wide. And then I opened my mouth. Words flew out, unfiltered, a mile a minute.

"Thank you! You look beautiful too! I'm sorry, I mean handsome. Right? That's what the guy version of beautiful is? I'm usually more composed, I guess I'm just nervous."

He grabbed my hand and squeezed ever so slightly. "It's OK, Jessica. I'm nervous too. I may have exaggerated my dancing abilities a tiny bit."

"That makes me feel better," I said sheepishly. "Well, shall we?"

He smiled. "Right this way, milady."

Trevor walked me, our arms linked, to the dance hall, which was really just a local community hall. It was one of the few buildings in the area that was still in decent condition and not packed with wounded or operating tables.

Having grown up, to a certain point, raised on twenty-first century music, I wasn't used to the music of this time period. It took me a while to get into it, but I'm actually growing quite fond of it.

Almost everyone was there, except for a few staff who stayed behind to man the hospital. Monica was one of them. I recall her exact words being: "Dances are silly functions, for the sole purpose of courtship and drunken mistakes. My time is better suited here. But you go have fun."

She makes me laugh. She'll try and hide it, but I know she still misses her husband. A dance would only remind her of that. I don't blame her for not going.

Trevor led me to the dance floor. I was super-nervous, especially seeing that everyone else was already dancing. He could see it in my face. "Don't be nervous. Dancing isn't hard. Just start like this."

He grabbed my hands, and started to swing side to side and back. I followed, mirroring what he did. I stumbled a couple times, stepping on his foot. He didn't mind. "Now try a turn."

He spun me slowly in a circle. Once I got the basic movements down, we sped up, until eventually we were in time with the music. We danced until our feet got tired. There were a few slow songs, where he held me close, and we swayed together. I felt safe in his arms, like nothing else mattered. He stared into my eyes, and I was helpless. I leaned in for a kiss—my first ever kiss.

Unfortunately, life hates me. Sirens stifled the music. Another set of wounded were incoming. "So much for a relaxing evening."

Everyone rushed to his or her posts, prepping for what was to come. I don't think any of us were prepared though. I was ready for the first horses pulling the wagon of wounded, still in my dress. The soldier that stepped out looked traumatized. "The Germans used some kind of gas. Our troops are in poor shape, and I've never seen anything like this. I hope you can help."

He ran to the back, where several men shared similar conditions. Some were a pale greenish-yellow, while others had blue ears and fingernails. Some faces were violet red. All were having trouble breathing. A couple of them were writhing in pain, and others had clearly vomited on the floor.

"Oh my God," I stammered. "Get them inside. We'll do what we can."

I ran to the operating room, changed, scrubbed down, and found Monica. "I've never seen anything like this. The Germans used some type of gas. They look awful."

Monica breathed deep. "Here they come."

The sight was like something out of a horror movie. I felt so bad for the troops suffering on our tables. Monica began studying them. "We need to get the fluid out of their lungs."

"Some were vomiting on the trip here. Would that help?" I asked.

"Vomiting may release some fluid, but this one's already drowning." She decisively began a process of draining the soldier's lungs, while trying to keep him alive. It worked momentarily, but then he seized up.

We lost him.

We moved on to the next patient, wasting no time. For the majority that came in, there was nothing we could do, but ease their suffering. Monica managed to save a few from dying on her table, but there were so many.

The smell was soon overwhelming, too. Each operating table had a bucket for the soldiers to vomit into. Not many hit their target.

We worked hard; late into the night. A lot of good men died. It was a rough night that had started off so wonderfully. Everyone was exhausted by the time we had finished. I didn't even get a chance to speak with Trevor.

This morning (Saturday) I started out by checking in on all the men we had treated last night. Some looked better, others were barely alive. It was hard to do my rounds that day. Even Lola seemed worse. I tried comforting all that I could, but the gas had taken its toll.

That was when I remembered what I had learned at The Island. It was chlorine gas that the German's used. I kicked myself for not realizing sooner, but then again, I couldn't do anything with that information. I still didn't know how to treat it, and even if I did, it would impact the past. This made it even harder to live with. I could help, but I had to choose not to, letting nature run its course.

After such a tiring day, all I wanted to do was go back to bed. Trevor stopped me on my way back. "Wait a minute, where are you going?"

"I'm done for the day. I need to get some sleep. Why?"

"Oh." His face filled with disappointment. "I thought that maybe, well, we never finished our dance last night."

"What are you getting at?"

"Just come with me," he practically begged.

I gave in. He led me back to the dance hall and opened the door for me. I stepped inside. Everything was still set up, and there was music playing. I turned to a sheepish Trevor. "I figured since we were interrupted last night, we could just pick up where we left off," he explained.

I smiled. "Thank you Trevor. I'd love to."

He exhaled in relief, and extended his hand. The two of us danced like we had last night, except slightly more coordinated. I had to admit, it was really romantic. He was so kind and thoughtful. A slow song came on. He held me close. "I think this is the last song."

That wasn't something I wanted to hear. I wanted this song to last forever. I squeezed him tightly.

Propped up on the tips of my toes, I reached up and kissed him. I don't think he expected it, or maybe all first kisses aren't as dreamy as in the movies. Regardless, he kissed me back, and my body filled with warmth. Our lips touching felt right, and that moment was perfect.

"Thank you for a wonderful dance, last night and today," Trevor said. "Shall I walk you back to your quarters?"

My mind and heart were still reeling. "Thank you. I think I'll make it. You should get some rest too though."

He nodded. "It's been a long day."

As he was on his way out I couldn't resist asking a question, "Hey, what does this mean for us?"

"Well, I was hoping you might go steady with me. I really like you, you know."

"Going steady, as in a relationship?" I wanted to hear him say the words.

He chuckled. "Yes, I'd like to be in a relationship with you. Is that something you would like as well?"

"I would." He left me feeling warm and fuzzy. This was actually happening. I had to tell Monica.

6: DECISIONS

Journal Entry #85:
April 13, 1915
Belgium

I 've never been more lost than I am now. I did something horrible, and I have no idea if it was justified. I'm barely keeping it together just writing this.

Our team was sent back to Belgium. The objective was to intercept a German convoy transporting their new weapon to the Ypres battlefield. We met up with some Resistance members, who escorted us through the German occupied areas.

It took quite some time, but we reached our rally point with time to spare. We were holding our position in a burnt-down building. The Resistance had informed us of the direct route the German convoy would be taking.

Neptune stretched a map out on the ground. He traced his finger along the lines. "The convoy will be taking this path to get to Ypres. There's not a lot of cover along this road, so we need to be precise when we attack. If the convey gets past us, the Germans will use whatever it is they are transporting on Ypres.

"A mile back, I want Earth and Saturn keeping watch. Once the convoy is in sight, I need you to radio us and let us know how many vehicles are incoming, and which the weapon is in."

"I can do that. I'm not sure if I can pick out the exact vehicle though," Earth replied.

"Do your best, because Mercury and Uranus will be planting explosives on the road. You need to make sure they detonate on the right vehicles at the right time. No mistakes."

"What's your plan?" Mercury asked.

"We move fast, planting explosives once Earth contacts us.

Jupiter, Venus and myself will deal with the men alive after the explosion. Mars and Pluto will secure the weapon. We need to move as quickly as possible to get out of here and move the weapon to safety. Got it?"

Everyone nodded, but Neptune was a stickler for details. He went through it one more time, walking through our surroundings, where everyone would be, and where he wanted everything to happen.

Before long everyone was in position. Mars and I waited at the side of the house. I was pretty nervous, and still didn't know what would happen. The chlorine gas is supposed to be used at Ypres tomorrow. If we stop them here, it'll never happen, and our team was too good to fail.

Three knocks echoed through the walls—Neptune's signal. Earth had radioed, which meant the convoy was approaching. I held my breath, mind racing for a solution, but came up with nothing. Looking back, I knew exactly what I needed to do. But it didn't mean I was ready or willing to do it. It's hard to even justify what I did, if I can at all.

Mars and I peered around the corner, spotting the vehicles. There were five in total, and Neptune's knocks meant the weapon was in the third vehicle. An explosion shook the ground beneath my feet. Then the second went off, followed by gunfire. I stole a glance to see what was going on.

A vehicle near the back was in flames, isolating the one behind it. The second detonation had collapsed part of a building onto the first vehicle, causing the two behind it to slow down, as they tried to maneuver around the rubble. The others were keeping the blocked vehicles occupied. Mars tore around the corner, opening fire on the first truck. I made my way to the second, dodging German bullets. They were returning fire, hoping to keep the convoy moving.

Mars pulled the pin from a grenade, and tossed it at the truck. The explosion made me lose my footing. I could see him making a move for the weapons vehicle. I breathed deeply, freezing time. I ran to the back and looked inside. Five German soldiers were guarding a large set of boxes. I opened one. I needed to be sure. Inside were a bunch of canisters. *It is the gas*, I solemnly thought. I knew what I had to do, but it meant thousands of soldiers would die horrible deaths from it.

I had frozen time for too long, evident by the pain setting in. I ran back to Mars and let go. I watched behind him, as he fired bursts of bullets with precision at the truck. If I let him continue, he would stop them. I reached down and picked up a large brick from the rubble. I swung my arm, bashing him in the back of the head.

Originally I had intended him to be knocked unconscious, so I could let the truck get through. The sick reality of that statement is hitting me as I write this. Unfortunately, after I hit him, he was still coherent.

He cursed at me as he turned around. We were still sheltered by the first truck. "Why you little traitor. You're going to wish you were never born."

Mars lifted his rifle towards me, but I had already pulled the trigger on mine. His body fell to the ground, eyes stared back at me, life draining from them. I will never forget those eyes. They will haunt me until the day I die.

I watched in shame as the German truck carrying the gas bolted out of harm's way. *What have I done?* I thought to myself. I don't know if it was my instincts, or desire to flee reality, but I took the brick and hit myself with it. Searing pain caused me to lose focus. I fell to the ground next to Mars, and pretended to be unconscious.

"Mars? Pluto? Can you hear me?" I heard Neptune's voice,

followed by a string of harsh words. "Pluto are you there?"

I felt his arms around my body, shaking me awake. "W-what happened? Something hit me," I mumbled.

Neptune exhaled. "They killed Mars. You must have been hit by falling debris or something. Either way, we can't stay here. They'll send more troops."

"Did we get the weapon?" I had to stop myself from saying gas.

"No. We failed. We have to move."

"What about Mars?" I stared at his body, as Neptune pulled me to my feet. I looked at what I had done.

"There's no time. We have to leave him. I'm sorry, lad."

We ran to the place where we were supposed to regroup. Earth and Saturn met up with us there. Then came the questions about Mars, and what had happened. Our first failed mission was because of me. I can't figure out what's eating me alive more, the fact that I killed Mars, or the fact that I did it to let the Germans through to kill thousands of soldiers with their gas.

I remained silent as the group figured out our next move. It was all a blur, and I couldn't tell you what was said or done. I was too far gone; lost in a sea of innocent blood. I only wanted to knock him out. He didn't have to die.

But he did, the voice inside me said.

Never did I think I would have to do something like this. I didn't even think I was capable of it. I spent that night away from the others, crying. The war, losing my friends, this mission, it was getting to be too much. What if we had just stopped them? Would the war have changed that much? I knew I couldn't dwell on the answers. They would only force me to a deeper low.

Journal Entry #87:
April 15, 1915
Belgium

We received information about our next mission, along with a disturbing report. The Germans used the gas, like they were supposed to. But from what was reported, there was far too much gas released to have only come from that one truck.

This meant the Germans already had enough at the front, and the truckload probably wouldn't have made a big difference. The problem I had was how much of a difference would it have made. If it was big, I had no choice in killing Mars, but if it was small, we could have stopped the truck and saved many lives.

I remained in a trance, tormented by the idea of murdering an innocent man, and to make it worse, for no feasible outcome. All my life I tried to do the right thing. This war was blurring the lines. That, or I already crossed the line. *It shouldn't be this hard*, I thought. We were supposed to get back to our time, save the kids, and shut down Island Corporation, instead of all…this. Evil creatures and men in Camelot, pirates and monsters, they all were justified battles and deaths. I was having a hard time justifying what I had done here. And I don't think I should either.

Is this who I need to be and what I need to do in order to take down The Island? If so, I didn't want any part in it.

I was so consumed with my thoughts that I hadn't noticed Saturn had entered the room. "Are you doing alright?"

Of all the members on the team, Saturn and I got along the most. That's partly why we ended up being paired for most missions. Over the months he and I had bonded. He was even teaching me some of his martial arts to help with our infiltration tasks. "Is it that obvious?"

Saturn took a seat. "To me at least. You've been out of it

ever since our failed mission. You know it wasn't your fault right? These things happen."

Guilt weighed me down. But it was my fault. "That doesn't make it better."

"True, yet here we are. Our goal hasn't changed. We all die someday, might as well go out fighting for something worth dying for."

Silence followed until I opened up. "All my life, I've tried to live up to this perfect image of my father. I try doing things that would make him proud of me, and I'm starting to realize it's not possible."

"Is he back home?"

"No," I replied quietly. "No, he died a long time ago. And with everything that's happened to me recently, I'm beginning to wonder if giving up is an option. If I did, is that something I can live with? I know my father would be disappointed, but..."

I was lost, in search of the right words. I took a deep breath and continued, "I've just always been sure of things, jumping in head first, no matter what. But now I'm not so sure. I'm not meant for this life. I don't want it anymore. My friends are gone, probably dead, and I feel like what I'm fighting for isn't achievable."

Saturn had no way of comprehending my actual situation, but that didn't stop him. "This life isn't meant for everyone, kid. Did you know what I used to do before this?"

I shook my head. He never spoke of his past, and all he knew about me is that I came from the future to help. He was the only one on the team I actually trusted with that information, but Neptune knew as well.

"For the last ten years, I've been living in America. I used to be an assassin—one of the best. I've killed lots of people, and regret much of what I have done. Sometimes the target was with his family and never left their side. I did many things I'm not proud of. Most of my life I would take back if I could. I began justifying what I did by the people saved from their deaths. One day I realized those killed were outweighing the ones saved. I purposely was caught on my last job."

"Why would you do that?"

Saturn's eyes were full of hurt. "I couldn't accept the things I had done. I turned myself in to pay for the wrongs that I committed. It was in prison where The Island unit recruited me. They offered a way to use my skills for good. Despite the people who die beside us, or the people we kill, our end goal saves more. Always."

"How's that different from what you used to do?"

"Before I'd accept any target. Now, we only work to protect the Allied forces. Our missions allow us to do what others can't. We go places and do things that beat the alternative. That's ultimately why I agreed."

"What's the alternative?" I questioned.

"The devil we know is better than the one we don't. If I'm on this team, I can help control how much damage is done and to whom. If I stayed in prison, someone else—someone who may have no conscience—would do the job. I do this because the team and I are in control of whom we eliminate."

"Someone else might do the things you used to do to finish the mission," I clarified.

Saturn's eyes were distant. "Yes. It won't redeem the things I did, but me being here may prevent others from doing the same."

"No one else can do what I do," I stated, not directly to him. "I don't get that choice."

Saturn paused to think. "I chose my path. If you want my advice, you need to choose yours as well. At some point you will let somebody down. That's how life is. You need to decide what matters to you. From the sounds of your mission, a lot is riding on your success. They must have chosen you for a reason."

I had never considered that. I mean I am obviously not on a mission from the future. I just happened to be given this power, and wanted to help the world. What he said made me consider the question: Why me? Of all the orphans, of all the test subjects, why me? Maybe I was chosen for a reason. I never really gave it that much thought. If I give up, The Island wins. Eventually they will perfect the serum and control everything.

There's more at stake here than me, I reasoned with myself. I had to keep going, even if that meant terrible things. In the end, if they stop The Island, it'd be worth it. And maybe once they are stopped, just maybe I can live a normal life.

"Thanks Saturn, I needed that."

"Any time. Oh, and Neptune wants you to know we head out once it's dark," he mentioned on his way out the door.

I sucked in a deep breath of air. I thought again about a life after The Island. Something normal. The thought brought a surge of pain into my chest.

All Jessica ever talked about was a normal life. The missions kept me distracted, but moments like these, when I was alone, my mind wandered. If the reports Wash had given me were true, Jessica was dead, and Will was still missing with no leads. She never had a chance for a normal life, why would I deserve one?

I rubbed my eyes, trying to forget everything that had happened. A couple tears trickled down my cheek. Time had passed, but I knew I'd never get over losing her. All I had now was the mission. And based on Will's disappearance, I don't think he wants to be found. He was always talking about settling in whatever area I landed us in, maybe that's what he finally did.

The thought made me happy. Will might've gotten out. At least one of us did.

Turning my thoughts to the mission at hand, I considered the man we were hunting: Jensen Avery. The only name the mole had revealed, and we finally had a location. At night we would make our way to the location our intel established he was. One thing I had picked up on with these missions is how touchy our research really was. Sometimes it was spot on, but others, well let's just say it tested our capabilities.

Training Facility, England
The day after final test

Captain Prichard stands in the main office, accompanied by Colonel Riker. Will sits in the only chair facing the two.

The Captain speaks, "Your results on the final test were most impressive, Private. In fact, you surpassed every other candidate."

"Candidate for what, exactly?" Will inquires.

Colonel Riker leans forward. "Much to my dismay, I owe the Captain here a debt. I've allowed him to alternate the entry level recruit training in order to find the most suitable individual for his program."

Prichard cuts in. "Technically it isn't a program yet. You, my friend, will be the first British trained sniper for the war."

Will analyzes the training he had received, and compares it to the A.I.'s knowledge base on snipers in World War One. "Go on."

"You see, ever since the rumored success of German snipers on the front, I have been trying to establish a sniper training school. Unfortunately, all my superiors believe it to be unsportsmanlike, or the reports from the front inaccurate. Therefore, I have asked Colonel Riker—"

"Forced," the Colonel clarifies.

"Ahem, yes, well, forced," Prichard continues, "him to allow me to recruit and train a single soldier to become a sniper. It is my hopes that your performance on the front will suffice as enough proof that they are crucial to our success on the front. With your help, Private, we can combat the Germans—maybe even overpower them. What do you say?"

Will ponders for a moment, weighing the pros and cons of the opportunity. He grins. "I'm your man."

Captain Prichard claps his hands together. "Excellent. I will train you as much as possible here, before you accompany me to the front. In February I am being transferred as an eyewitness officer. Once we gauge more details on the situation at that post, I will send you into the field."

"Let's begin," Will states.

Western Front, France
February, 1915

Captain Prichard and Will spend their time observing trench warfare first-hand at the Captain's new post. Upon arriving they discover the truth regarding German snipers.

They are highly efficient.

Some regiments lose over ten men a day from a single German sniper. They are so well-trained that the Allies cannot find their location to retaliate.

The Captain also notes the inaccuracy of the Allied forces they encounter. "It is worse than I expected. Let us gather more information before sending you out."

VIRGO RISING

Western Front, France
March, 1915

Will grows impatient with the amount of observation and intel-gathering that Captain Prichard requires of him. Finally his time has come. Will prepares for his first excursion over the trench since arriving at the front. Despite his excitement, and the adrenaline rush, he regulates his breathing. Staying calm is critical.

Captain Prichard approaches him, holding a rifle. "This will be your rifle. It's a Pattern 1914 Enfield from my personal collection. I took the liberty of mounting a telescopic sight on it."

"Has it been calibrated?" Will questions, studying the rifle.

"Tested it myself," Captain Prichard proudly replies. "The only thing to watch for is—"

"The reflection of the scope," Will interrupts.

Prichard smiles. "I've trained you well. Also, you should take a few test shots to gauge its range."

"Understood," Will replies. He tests the rifle throughout the day, ensuring everything is spot on. He knows there is a German sniper somewhere out there. The unit has already informed them of this.

Will walks over the boards lining the trenches. They do little to keep the mud and water at bay. It creates an unpleasant, damp and wet environment. Nightfall is approaching. He sees Captain Prichard leaning against the trench wall. He holds a notebook.

"What's that for?" Will asks.

The Captain pauses before speaking. "They may be our enemies, but those Germans are clever. Note the curvature of their parapet, or the ledge the trench starts at."

Will stares at the paper. "Theirs have distinct bumps and

ridges."

"Precisely!" Prichard exclaims. "I think they build their trenches taking their snipers into account. These bumps allow a soldier to scan the battlefield unnoticed, while our trench lines are all flat. That's military thinking for you. No wonder our men are getting picked off—the moment they peer over the edge, they become easy targets."

"Good luck changing their minds though," Will scoffs.

Prichard shakes his head. "That's the sad truth. Without your performance, they won't be swayed. Even then, I might get court-martialed just for doing this without their approval."

"Then I'd better get started at nightfall, eh?"

"Not so fast. This isn't a simulation anymore. This is reality. I've put all my eggs into this basket. You need to be careful. And I want to test an idea."

"Go on." Will patiently waits.

Captain Prichard takes off his helmet, and latches it on top of his rifle. Several soldiers stare at him with curious faces.

"Watch carefully."

Will keeps his eyes locked on the helmet. The Captain slowly raises the helmet up, just enough for the ridge to be higher than the trench, but not high enough to see the rifle. He carefully rotates the helmet, attempting to simulate someone scanning the field.

The helmet is knocked off well before they hear the shot fired. The soldiers present are a bit shaken. They have been living in fear of the German sniper for several weeks now.

Prichard chuckles to himself. "Throughout the day I have been baiting the German into taking a shot." He picks up the helmet, examines it, and then hands it to Will. "Tell me what you see."

Will keenly eyes the bullet hole. "The shot entered the front left side of the helmet. The sniper must be positioned in a quadrant capable of that trajectory. The angle also shows he must be slightly elevated."

"Very good," Captain Prichard commends. "Now, depending on the stamina and intelligence he has, he may return to his trench come nightfall. Or he may choose to relocate, perhaps even as we speak. This test gives us room to work with at the very least."

"I'll keep my eyes peeled. I've already picked out several of the best places I can climb over undetected."

Captain Prichard leans close to Will, speaking in a hushed tone. "This is no longer a simulation, Private. I have a lot riding on you. Remember your training. Don't make a mistake. Go in, take him out, and return."

"I won't fail, Captain." Will says with confidence.

He waits until night consumes everything. Darkness provides the best cover for him to enter No Man's Land without being spotted. Much like his final test, Will begins by scanning the field.

Uriel develops an artificial map of the area, and ideal places the enemy sniper may be located. In the interest of survival, Lazarus does not try to stop him. The thought occurs to Lazarus to attack Uriel at such a time where the human vessel is vulnerable and could be killed. However, he and Gabriel do not have enough energy to do the necessary damage.

They also believe in the mission and that Francis is still alive. This factor is the only thing preventing the suicidal strategy. They need to be certain the mission can no longer succeed, and muster all their power to stall Uriel at a crucial moment. They agree to harvest the majority of their power, tiding Uriel over with tiny, futile efforts of resistance. Once enough power is in reserve, and the fate of Francis is determined, they will act. Until that time comes, they do what they can to keep the vessel alive. Should a moment arrive where Uriel goes too far, and they have enough power, they will opt into death to ensure history's integrity.

Four sections are red-flagged by the scan. The German sniper lurks in one of them. Will calculates the probability of each location. The highest is forty-two percent. Most likely there, but he needs to be careful. Will focuses his powers. He creates a field of energy surrounding his body. Any object, bullets included, aimed towards him will hit the field, and repel. There is no need to risk dying. He is too powerful to die by anyone here, he thinks.

Earlier in the day he tested his ability to make sure. He fired his weapon point plank range at his hand. The force field of telekinetic power worked. The bullet hung in the air, stuck in an invisible wall.

Even if a sniper fires at me, they cannot harm me.

He grins, slinking through the muddy terrain.

Not even artillery fire will stop me. I am invincible, and they will fear me.

Will follows a path to sneak up on the enemy sniper. He becomes a shadow, lingering momentarily, disappearing the next. The closer he gets, the faster his heartbeats. The thrill of the hunt is overwhelming. With a twisted smile, Will detects him. The soldier is nestled under a rotting corpse. He is using the limbless body to mask his presence to the casual eye.

Clever. But not clever enough. Will flicks his hand, propelling forward a loose bullet in his pocket. The sniper has no warning, not even a thought as the bullet pierces his skull.

In an instant, the game is over. However, victory is not enough for Will. He needs more. Will fights the desire to push forward, and kill every last soldier in the enemy trench. Captain Prichard would not approve, and it would raise questions that may prevent him for further missions.

For now, a trophy of sorts will due. Will creeps to the lifeless body. He yanks the erkennungsmarken (German dog tag) off of the soldier, and slides it into his pocket.

Without the fear of a sniper, the route back is faster. Will keeps his telekinetic barrier intact, just in case a second one, or a German soldier, spots him. Soon he is sounding the return call, signaling for his allies to hold their fire. The barrier is in tact during this process as well. He does not trust the soldiers, many of who had lied about their age to register. Some look as young as fourteen, while the recruiting standard was eighteen.

No way I'm dying from some trigger-happy boy that didn't know what he was signing up for.

He slides into the trench. Several soldiers keenly eye him down, clearly on edge. They sit against the wall, which was often low enough in some places where the only option was to crawl. Puddles of mud cut through morale over long days and nights, which stretch well beyond eternity.

"You're back!" Will hears Prichard hiss. "Was it successful? Did you get him?"

Will nods, pulling out the tag. "I only saw one, but they may have more in their trenches."

Captain Prichard grasps Will's shoulders. "Come, my boy, let's get you a drink! We must celebrate."

Will follows, basking in the praise.

Monday:

Today was another rough one, perhaps the worst so far. Many wounded passed away from the gas. The doctors here had never seen anything like it, and they all felt helpless. I was in the middle of tending to one of the soldiers when Monica rushed through the door.

"Miss Noble you need to go to Lola immediately." Her tone was grave. "I don't think she has long. I'll finish up here. Go. Now."

I barely had time to comprehend what she was saying. I left in a hurry, barreling towards Lola's bunk. She doesn't have long? How could that be? I turned the corner to see a nurse by Lola's side.

"What's going on?" I asked.

The nurse stood from the bedside, and leaned close to me. She spoke softly, not to let Lola hear. "She's running a fever. We don't know what's wrong with her, or why she's suddenly getting worse. She mentioned your name though."

I eyed Lola with a worried gaze. "She mentioned my name?" This surprised me, as Lola hadn't really said much of anything. "Monica said she doesn't have long?"

"At this point there's nothing left for us to do. We've done all we can. Monica made the call."

"Leave us," I said. I could feel tears coming, but I fought them off.

The nurse left. Most of them knew how much time I spent with Lola, and the amount I cared for her. I sat next to Lola and gripped her hand. It was warm and damp. Her hair was matted to her head, with beads of sweat clinging to each strand.

"Oh, Lola. You poor thing. Hang in there, OK? You just need to hold on."

Lola had never spoken to me, or to anyone really. She did not understand anything I said to her, but I could see that she was comforted. She opened her mouth. "A-Abbey."

I was taken aback. That was the only word I'd heard her say. I smiled through teary eyes. I began to tell her Abbey's story—the very first one I had told her. Although Lola was in pain, her face lightened when I started to speak. She nestled into my arms like she had done all those times before.

Lola took a deep breath at the moment in the story when Abbey meets her future husband. She let it out slowly, but no air came back in. I broke down in tears, brushing her hair. I continued talking. As long as the story kept going, she wasn't gone. I choked through the last words of the story. Lola had died in my arms. The little girl I had cared for was gone. I cradled her body, her head resting on my chest.

I must have stayed like that for quite a while before Monica came in. She didn't say anything. She knew words wouldn't comfort me like I hoped they did for Lola. She calmly pulled me off of her, and escorted me out of the room. I stole one last glance back to see a nurse pulling a sheet over her head. Monica took me to my room, and got me into bed. She left. I cried. And then I kept crying.

Quite some time later I heard the siren sound. Wounded were incoming, and I knew I'd have to do my job. Lola's death had shaken me. Monica had warned me about getting so close to my patients. I didn't listen, and felt the pain now.

I went through the motions. I scrubbed down, prepped, and entered the operating room. Taking up my spot next to Monica, we helped the soldiers coming in. In each face we couldn't save I saw Lola. Lifeless eyes that stared back at me were hers. I barely made it through that shift. Luckily there weren't many to tend to. Monica dismissed me, and I returned to my quarters to null the pain.

Time passed on, and I heard a knock on the door. I made no effort to respond. It creaked open an inch. Trevor's voice floated through the crack. "Jess, I heard what happened. Mind if I come in?"

I mumbled something, which he took as a yes. He shut the

door behind him and sat down next to me. His hand rested on my shoulder. "I've lost many patients during this war. People try and say that we should move on, or don't think about it, but that's nonsense. I see their faces every day, the people I couldn't save." He took a deep breath. "I guess what I'm trying to say is, I know how you feel. I also know nothing I say or do will help you. Just know it gets easier with time. The faces are still there, but the hurt decays."

His words were comforting. I reached up and pulled his body closer. He lay in silence with me. I don't remember falling asleep, but we did.

Tuesday:

I awoke to a drool spot on my pillow. It wasn't until I noticed Trevor still next to me that I hastily and awkwardly flipped the pillow to hide my embarrassment. I rubbed my eyes. They were puffy and sore from yesterday's cry-fest.

I shook Trevor's shoulder, and he jolted awake. I whispered softly to him. "Hey. Thanks for coming here last night. It helped."

Trevor's smile was warm. "Don't mention it. I'm glad I could help. But I should probably get going, seeing as I haven't changed since last shift."

I teased him by smelling the air. "Oh, that's what that was. Yeah, you should go change."

He chuckled as he left. I smiled, but it soon faded. Looking at the chart on my desk, I was reminded that Lola wouldn't be a part of my rounds today. I breathed out and got dressed.

Monica spotted me leaving and called me over. She looked up and down the hallway before speaking. "I see Dr. McCoy spent the night."

My face blushed immediately, knowing what she was implying. "We did nothing of the sort, Monica. Don't you lump me in with all those floozy nurses that fall for the doctors. He held me close and we fell asleep. That's it."

Monica laughed. "Well, either way it's good to see you feeling a bit more like yourself. I know yesterday was difficult for you."

I nodded, and before I had a chance to reply she continued. "But there's no cure like work, so here's a list of what I need from you today. Aside from any incoming wounded of course."

"Thanks, I guess."

"Trust me, I am a doctor after all." She flashed a smile and left me to my duties.

The rest of the day carried on. I felt like the other nurses were walking on eggshells around me. They knew how hurt I was, but they didn't say anything. I meandered through the halls, dealing with eyes that avoided me, or apologetic looks that meant nothing. It was hard. I wanted to return to my room; I was sheltered there.

Regardless of how I felt, I pressed forward. If I ever wanted to be a doctor, I needed to accept losing patients as a part of the job. I didn't have to like it, but I did have to live with it. The end goal for me has changed so much ever since I lost Francis. Occasionally he'll pass through my mind—a fleeting moment followed by a hollow emptiness.

Some nights when things are rough, I'll lie awake and think of what my life would be like had we stuck together. Would I be happy? I doubt it. Saving the others was always Francis' goal. I knew leaving them behind wasn't the right thing to do, but here and now, I don't want to go back. I'm happy here. I'm happy with Trevor. I love him. I miss my friend, but I finally have something I want to hold on to.

Isn't that what love is supposed to be anyway? No, love is not what you expect it to be. It is hard, painful, jading, gruesome, and yet we chase it. We hunt for love as if it were an exotic animal glimpsed in the wilderness.

I guess that's what's so beautiful about it. Love is imperfect. It's the embodiment of life itself—the pain, the struggle, the joy, and the laughter. I deserve love. I've suffered far too long for anything less.

I think that's enough venting in one night. I'm going to clock in some much-desired rest. Tomorrow is a new day. Lola is gone, but I think it's better for her to be at rest than in some hospital. Rest in peace, Lola.

7: CROSSROADS

Our intel, if one can call it that, was only half-right. Jensen Avery was not at the location reported. The mission, however, was not a complete dud. We gathered information that led us to our current situation and, hopefully, Jensen Avery. Our team was perched on the ledge of a mountainside. Below us stood an old mansion. We were deep behind enemy lines, and this place was seemingly untouched by the war.

Venus and Saturn were scoping out the area around the building, trying to find weak points. It was well-guarded. German guards rotated in specific routes along the compound. Neptune cradled a sniper rifle in his arms, occasionally eyeing down the target. I leaned against a tree next to Earth. He was fiddling with his makeshift communicators again.

We had spent the day camped in the woods. Neptune wanted us to survey the place and the guards before doing anything. I understood why, but I wasn't the only one starting to get restless. Jupiter was practicing her accuracy with a set of throwing knives and a German helmet propped against a nearby tree. Fortunately, the recon team returned quickly.

"They've got that place locked up tight, Commander," Venus stated. Neptune peered through his scope while she continued. "The guards rotate every hour, but are always relieved by one from inside the house. We counted twelve guards posted outside, for a total of twenty-four potential hostiles."

Saturn stepped in. "We suspect there to be more than that based on the amount of vehicles stationed in the courtyard. I could only find one blind spot when the guards change posts. On the Southeast corner of the mansion is a cellar. It has a chain and lock around the handles, but most Belgian-designed buildings have access to the cellar from inside the house as well. If we want to stay out of sight, that's our best shot."

Neptune traced the place with his rifle. "And if we go in with a bang?"

"Definitely by demolishing the vehicles in the courtyard as a diversion, sir," Venus replied.

Neptune directed his attention to Mercury. "How big of a diversion can you create?"

Mercury spat out some sunflower seeds that he constantly chewed. "I can give us quite the show if I have enough time to set up."

"How long do you need?"

"Get me down there, and I'll have it rigged to blow after three minutes. Did you want a smokescreen as well?"

"Negative. Saturn will escort you there. Venus, myself, and Earth will navigate our way through the cellar before you detonate. Once inside, we'll give you the signal. Jupiter will provide us cover fire with her rifle. Uranus and Pluto will storm the front once the trucks blow."

When our team began, Uranus was a giant tool. After a couple missions, he loosened up, especially after seeing what I could do. Granted, he didn't really understand what I did or how, but he knew that I was good. I guess it was enough to get him off my case.

Uranus slapped me on the back. "Looks like a good time to test out my new custom shells for the Enfield, eh?"

The man had an obsession with tinkering with things. "As long as they don't blow up in my face, I'm good."

"Oh, come now, when has anything I've done gone wrong?"

I wasted no time replying, "Well, the rocket accelerators for the auto, the fuel you mixed to make our vehicles run faster, should I go on?"

His laughter was more like a dog barking on a chain about to break. "That's why I like you, kid. Is that all, Nept?"

Neptune studied the complex one last time. "Jensen Avery is most likely on the upper floor. Once inside, we clear each room, find him, and detain him for questioning. Let's go capture ourselves an informant."

It did not take long for everyone to get into position. I cradled my rifle in my arms, examining to make sure it was ready to go. Uranus stared at the entrance, clearly excited to see something blow up.

"You really should get your head checked out once all this is done," I jested.

A low rumbling chuckle came from his throat. "You're just jealous of my ammunition. Bet I can kill more than you."

The casual tone in his wager rattled my head. Had my life really come to killing anyone who got in the way of my mission? No, it isn't a competition like it is for him. I'm still me.

The issue bubbled at a medium temperature in the back of my mind. Regardless, they were German agents, and this was war. The only choice I had was to *not* enjoy what we were doing. Uranus, on the other hand, was twisted.

"Depends how many times I have to cover you."

Uranus was not given a chance to respond. An explosion shook the ground, accompanied with ringing in my ears. Despite the shock, I heard Uranus' words before he ran towards the smoke. "That's our cue."

I bolted after him, sprinting through the gaping hole in the wall surrounding the courtyard. The smoke rising from several vehicles' skeletons provided us cover. My partner was more skilled with a gun, covering the balconies, while I took care of any soldiers on the ground.

Three Germans were still reeling from the explosion. I took them out with five quick shots—two each for the ones that had been on guard near the vehicles, and one to the head of the German that had rounded the corner of the building. I had to trust Uranus to cover me from the guards on the balcony. His ammunition did more damage than necessary, as I witnessed his bullet tearing off the arm of one the soldiers.

He was laughing as he fired. The mental state of this team was something I constantly questioned. He continued to lay down covering fire as I skirted to the wall of the house. I peered around the corner to check for more enemies. None in sight. I quickly turned to check the opposite side, clearing the outside before we entered.

Uranus ceased fire and now approached the side door. He casually tossed up a rather large grenade in his hand.

"Another homemade device?" I was skeptical.

"Combination of highly volatile chemicals which, upon activation, temporarily blind anyone in the room." He pulled the pin and tossed it inside the door, careful to keep his distance. I heard a bang, and Uranus kicked open the door, weapon at the ready. I followed closely behind as he picked off two Germans writhing on the ground, holding their faces. "Works like a charm."

"Just stay focused, clear that room, I'll cover our backs." I waited patiently with my back towards Uranus. I heard gunfire echoing through the halls of the house. I hoped the other members of the team were doing fine as well.

It was a good thing I was covering behind us. A stray German barged through the door we had entered in. I fired two bullets, which brought him down. The amount of shots I had remaining was grounds to reload before any more came in. I rested my shoulder against the entryway, checking for any more. There were none. However, judging from the bursts of gunfire throughout the inside, not all of them were taken care of. Still, the amount of men we had encountered alone meant we had to be on to something.

Jensen must be here. My eyes did not break from scanning the room, ears burning while listening for the slightest sound.

"Clear!" I heard Neptune's voice in the next room.

"Friendly," came our response.

Once joined with the group, we began searching the upstairs. Neptune signaled us to check down the right hall, and they went left. I followed Uranus with the rifle perched in my arms, ready for action. We encountered no one. Soon we had cleared our section, turning up nothing.

"We've got him!" Neptune's voice boomed.

My heart skipped a beat. We entered a room to see a perfectly calm man on the latter end of a gun barrel. The man, I could only assume, was Jensen Avery. He appeared to ignore the other people in the room, staring absently at the floor.

I heard Neptune speaking quietly to Jupiter. She had left her post to provide backup. "I don't think he's going to talk. I need you to find out what he knows—anything at all—by any means necessary. Am I clear?"

"Crystal, sir," she replied. Of all the members on our team, each scared me for various reasons, but Jupiter terrified me the most. Not only was she strong, but the way she carried herself made me nervous. It was like her constant thought was always: *I could crush you with my bare hands if I wanted to.* And she very well could.

She was also the only member of the team I had not really connected or engaged with. In that way, we had an unspoken relationship that implied: You stay out of my way, and I'll stay out of yours.

Neptune gestured for the rest of us to exit the room. We filed out one by one, and shut the door behind us. It did not take long for the screaming to begin. I cringed any time I heard his voice.

He's the enemy, I reminded myself.

But that didn't make it acceptable. I held no power to change things, and I knew full well that I would be shut down for even suggesting another method of retrieving information. (I had already tried on a previous mission.)

Another piercing howl forced my mind to look for distractions. Mercury was in the midst of pillaging the bodies we had left behind, searching for trinkets. Saturn had replaced Jupiter at her post, keeping watch in case there were incoming reinforcements.

We waited the majority of the time in silence, save for the painful cries emitting from behind the closed door. Soon the screaming ceased, and Jupiter exited the room. Blood lingered on her hands. Her expression was emotionless.

"Neptune, I believe I have what we need."

Neptune rose from a bullet-torn chair. "Excellent. Inform us."

"Jensen Avery is only one piece of what appears to be a rather large puzzle. The man bearing our symbol is a scientist working on a secret project for the Germans. Jensen does not know anything about it or the man himself. He is unaware of where that man is located. However, he does have information on the base he reports to. Apparently this is where we can find information on the scientist."

"Is that all he knows?" Neptune asked, most likely hoping for something more.

"He says the Germans have several people, himself included, working on sections of a weapon that the scientist designed. They each have a job, but they don't know what the end outcome is. Only the officers and that man know. It looks like we'll have to infiltrate this base to potentially find a location, or an officer, who knows where the scientist is. At the very least, we'll find out what the weapon is."

"Where is the base?"

"That's the problem," Jupiter's voice was grim. "It is a zeppelin."

Neptune cursed. "I'll have to get in touch with Command. I know the French are in the process of developing a squadron of pilots, but from what I hear it won't be active until next year. We may need to split up."

"What do you mean?" I asked. Our team had never separated before.

"Some of our team should return to base, and begin training with the aircraft that The Island has developed. We'll need some precision pilots to navigate the sky, and escort the rest of us to the zeppelin. While they train with aircraft, the remaining members will continue pushing forward here. With any luck we can find more information out about this base, and what we're looking for."

Nobody spoke. Neptune lit a cigar from the stash he kept in a small metal case, which was on him at all times. "You all know I would never order you to do something that I would not do myself. I need five volunteers to go back to base, and three to continue digging for information here. Understand that if you choose to train as a pilot, the risks are high. The training alone could kill you."

There was a moment where everyone eyed each other down. No one wanted to make the first move. It was dead quiet, like a solemn force had possessed everyone.

"Heights and I don't mix," Earth stated plainly. "I'll carry on the mission behind enemy lines."

"Ideally I would like to remain with the team here," Neptune added. "However, I will pass up my spot if no one is willing to return to base."

Mercury stepped towards Neptune. "I doubt I'd be any use

in the sky. I'm more good to you down here."

"Anyone else?" Neptune asked one last time.

My silence made the call for me. I would go back. I would learn to fly a plane.

We waited for night to fall. Our team rifled through the papers to find any information we could use before splitting up. Saturn and I searched the cellar. "Why do you think he split us up five to three and not four and four?"

Saturn sighed. "Sometimes the smaller the team, the easier to execute plans. That, and from what I hear, the average life expectancy for a pilot is two weeks, give or take."

I froze. "Two weeks?"

"It's worse than it sounds," he replied.

"So Neptune wants more of us there, so if someone on our team dies, another will take their place?"

"That's what I would do. I'd bet we get back and train, but get lumped in with new recruits when the mission actually happens."

"Then what? Hope the recruits take the bullet instead of one of us?"

"I'm only speculating," Saturn shrugged. "It is easier if you don't think about it."

My brain was kicking me for not speaking up when I had the chance. *Two weeks?* I couldn't shake the number. What if I died up there, and changed nothing? Don't think about it. Saturn was right. I needed to focus on something else.

Night came sooner than expected. The team took shifts keeping watch. We would split up at dawn. I closed my eyes and drifted to sleep.

I try to keep my friends out of my mind, especially when I'm in the middle of a mission. When I dream, however, is a different story. My subconscious brought me back...

"What did you two find out?" Jessica asked. She sat in her cell, head tilted against the bars.

"Apparently we're being categorized into a neurological department," I responded. *"Which totally sucks, because now we're getting more lessons than usual."*

"What do you mean?"

"We have extra school sessions than you now," Will sneered. *"Do you know the stages of government? Didn't think so. I do."*

Will couldn't see, but Jessica was glaring at him with fiery pupils. I intervened before things escalated. *"I can teach you."*

Jessica turned to face me. *"You would do that?"*

"Sure. Why not? Whenever they teach us new stuff, I can come back and teach you."

"Not here you won't," Will interrupted. *"I'm not sitting through that."*

"You can plug your ears. Besides, I'm not giving you a choice."

"I'm not giving you a choice," he mimicked.

From there I began teaching Jessica about the things we had learned regarding how governments worked.

The camera in the corner recorded everything. Katherine wrote notes on a pad of paper. She was old-fashioned and, for the most part, disliked the technology advancements. Some things were just better as they had been before.

Her gun jabbed into her side, wedged between her and the chair. She adjusted positions trying to avoid thinking about the last time she used it. A child had died by her hands. She had lost control, and never wanted to feel that way again.

Has this become my identity? she wondered. Fighting a

battle for something I do not think I believe in any more? How far will I go, and who will I be then?

After shooting the boy, she had gone directly to her office. She locked the doors, and began methodically tearing her room apart in a rage of tears.

The memory hurt her more than the weapon at her side. She couldn't simply leave, though. They'd find her. Kill her. She was trapped. But when she hit rock bottom, all she thought of was how to climb out.

One day, Francis, you will be my ticket out of this place. Until then, we both have to do what they want. Her eyes were enveloped on the screen, but her mind was busy, half-listening to the conversation, half-plotting how she would leave The Island.

She knew she had to play it safe. Any hint of betrayal, and they would know. She did not sign up for murdering children and experimenting on them. She would know her chance when it came around, and she was certain the boy would somehow be involved.

Western Front, France
May 1915

Will lurks in the shadows of No Man's Land. He feels more at home out here than surrounded by the soldiers in the trenches. In fact, he remains hidden in the mud and death far longer than he needs to.

While warmer than usual, the night air mixing with the ground is bitter and cold. Will is restless when he feels cold. He begins to creep closer to the German trench. The telekinetic force field around him is always present, especially this close to their territory.

He slinks through the terrain, resembling more a tiger hunting prey than a human. He is so close to the edge now that he hears the German troops talking. The A.I. is integrated with multiple languages, and Uriel automatically translates the conversation.

"I can't wait to get out of this stinking trench. My feet are soaked." The voice belongs to a young soldier, no older than eighteen.

"If I have to sit through another night listening to you complain I'll shoot you myself," his older comrade replies.

The conversation continues, allowing Will to pinpoint their location. Soon he is right above them. Will twirls two bullets in the air beside his head. He tilts to one direction and listens to make sure he has the right spots picked out. With a flick of his eyes, the bullets fly over the edge of the trench, and rocket downwards. The soldiers' discussion ends abruptly.

Will navigates the wires and precautions the Germans have set in place. He climbs down into their trench, their territory. There are only two soldiers present, both lifeless. He crouches next to them and begins rifling through their garments, nicking a trophy from each.

Footsteps behind him cause his head to whirl around like an owl. Another soldier rounds the corner. The German barely comprehends the scene before Will snaps his neck effortlessly from five feet away. The body collapses, heart no longer beating, while Will's beats more rapidly than ever. The action warms his body until he forgets he was even cold in the first place. Before leaving he takes one last trophy from the fresh corpse.

The journey back is long and grueling. Despite having the shield around him, he does not relish in attracting attention to himself. Avoiding detection is the most crucial thing. As is the case, he moves slowly through the terrain. He stops often, sometimes for a few minutes, others a few hours. The life a sniper leads is one of patience, for he is a hunter, and the best hunters are unseen.

Will wants to be the best, so he does not mind the motionless interludes. The night changes into dawn as Will reaches his trenches. He signals his allies to announce his return. His boots sink into the mud regardless of the wooden planks, which do a poor job of keeping the men dry.

He hears whispers as he moves past them. *"That's him. He goes out for hours, sometimes days, on his own."*

"Creeps me out, 'e does. Somethin' wrong with a man who willingly goes topside." Another ghostly string of words lingers in the air.

"They say he's killed over a hundred Germans."

"That's trash, that is. Only cowards shoot someone while hiding."

"I'm just glad he's on our side."

Will skirts through the conversations. Their voices are low, but not low enough. He cares little of the opinions they have.

Captain Prichard sits in an officer's tent. He gently puffs a cigar. When he spots Will approaching, he launches out of the chair with a grin. Although Will always returns, Prichard sees each departure potentially as his last, and is always faintly surprised when he returns. "Well?"

Will casually tosses the trophies he collected onto the table.

"What is this?" Captain Prichard's tone becomes hostile.

"I found a weak point in their trenches," Will explains, "and I took advantage of it."

"Those weren't your orders."

"My orders, sir, are to eliminate enemy combatants without

being detected." He scoops up his trophies, pocketing them.

"Watch your tone with me, son," Prichard snarls. "I'll overlook it this once, but you do not pull anything like this again. Especially looting. It's despicable."

"To each his own," Will mutters.

"You're lucky I'm in a good mood. Otherwise I might just send you to the Regimental Court," he begins. "Word has reached some generals of our success. Some are expressing interest in the form of assessment."

"What kind of assessment?"

"The kind that tasks you with executing a German Colonel rumored to be on the front," Prichard levels with Will. "If you are successful, this will be a major step forward to launching a sniper program. It could even get you promoted."

Will's ears perk up. "A promotion? I like the sound of that."

"Good. But disregard orders one more time, and I will make sure you never surpass your current rank. There is no room for those types of antics here."

"Yes, sir," Will's words are hollow and empty. *I just won't inform you next time.*

"Well then, let's move out." Captain Prichard makes his way to a horse-drawn carriage with Will in tow. They climb in, heading in the opposite direction of the front.

Will uses the time to contemplate his next move should the assassination prove successful. *If?* He chuckles to himself. *It's not a question of if, but when.* There is no shortage of confidence with his powers to back him up.

The two men spend their ride in silence. Once near the target site Prichard speaks. "The man you are hunting is a German Colonel, responsible for much of our aggravation. There is a portrait in the glove box."

Will reaches inside and pulls out a fuzzy photograph. The

man is on the crisp edge of being classified as elderly. He is dressed in a German uniform, decorated in medals. "What's his name?"

"Does it matter?" Prichard retorts.

Will studies the picture. "No. It doesn't."

"Take him out and we'll talk about further missions and a promotion. He supposedly frequents this stretch of the front. The man likes getting his hands dirty."

The horses skid to a halt in the mud. A French soldier greets them and exchanges pleasantries with the Captain. He asks to have the target area pointed out on a map. The soldier nods, escorting them to a field tent.

He points to a spot on the map, and then describes the area in French. Will's A.I. translates the words. "The German base is somewhere in this section. It is directly across a broken tree that has fallen over our trench. You can't miss it."

"Any sniper activity here?" Prichard questions poorly in French.

"Not yet, but with the General here, that may have changed."

"Dismissed."

The French soldier returns to his post. The Captain sighs deeply, and mutters something indistinct under his breath. "Private Taylor."

"Yes, sir?"

"This situation is dodgy at best. I don't like the layout, or the lack of concrete information."

"But?"

"But, if we want to accomplish anything, we need to show how useful you can be. I won't order you to go in blindly, however, I am requesting that you do."

"Don't worry, sir. I'm quite capable. It's them you should

worry about."

Prichard grins ear to ear. "I knew I chose you for a reason. Take your time, but the longer we wait, the less chance he will still be out there."

"Understood."

Captain Prichard leaves Will alone. He knows the young man has a process, and, if he were honest, the kid intimidated him. He is unable to distinguish why, but he knows there is something off about his protégé. The way he moves, thinks and acts is almost animalistic. *As long as he gets the job done*, he thinks to himself.

Will studies the map, clutching his target's photo in his hand. There is only so much he can prepare before going over the trench. Unlike everyone else, he is not worried about enemy fire. There is no need to fear with his abilities. Once Prichard gets his school approved, he thinks, any soldier volunteering to do this job must be crazy.

The thought causes him to chuckle. The young man with several Artificial Intelligences living inside his head, calling someone else crazy, is a bit biased. Then again, it takes one to know one.

Uriel downloads the German's picture into his database, along with the map. Will slings the rifle over his shoulder and heads to the trenches. Most of the trenches he had observed were almost deep enough to stand in, but the French trenches were barely tall enough to crouch in. He shakes his head as he maneuvers through the terrain. Upon reaching the fallen tree, he pauses, and stares up at the sky. The sun is inching below the Earth, casting a shadow over the battlefield.

Satisfied with the amount of cover and darkness, Will pulls himself over the edge. Uriel scans the area in front of him. No unusual activity is spotted. Will continues further in, tucking his rifle away close to his side once he is safely hidden.

The weapon only aggravates him. It is awkward and clunky, sometimes jamming depending on the amount of mud and dirt it was dragged through. He keeps it, but he also carries a single cartridge, although he has only ever needed two bullets. Will decides this is the most effective method, based on his growing number of kills without incidents.

His current situation proves to be the filthiest he has encountered thus far. The stench of rotting flesh and mud is overwhelming. He cradles a cough in his chest. Just because he has not encountered any problems yet does not give him a free ride. He must be cautious and ever-watchful.

Will finds the most ideal vantage point. Under the cover of the night, he builds a nest. The process is long, his moves must be subtle. He spends the time reflecting on the 'rules' Captain Prichard had taught him.

"Always clean your muzzle after a shot; moisture can steam and reveal your location." He would say. "Use your barometer to gauge wind and moisture levels. Oh, and it never hurts to build a fake nest and camp nearby."

The Captain was full of useful advice. Will smirks, piling some mud over his body. Too bad I don't need any of his tips for using a rifle. My mind is my weapon. Bullets are my ammunition.

The night rolls on and by morning, Will has completed his nest. He spent the night observing the enemy trench. Uriel overrides the brain's need to sleep. Falling asleep means he has no protective barrier. Sleep is a death sentence for a sniper. Will keenly watches each movement or change in the environment. The sun begins to rise.

Uriel uses his facial recognition software to analyze any face he manages to spot through his scope. The Germans are careful, though, and rarely appear. Still, there are quite a few that

Will could have killed. He fights the urge, knowing if the Colonel is there, it will give away his element of surprise.

With the day passing by, Will decides a different course of action is necessary. He remains motionless until the daylight fades away. He slowly leaves his nest, and makes his way closer to the enemy side. Inch by inch he moves, careful not to make any sudden noises. His powers are strong, but he is not Jessica. His ears listen for conversations carried by the wind. Finally, he finds his opportunity. He hears three voices close to where he is hiding. He slips further down the trench line. If three are grouped together, this spot may be clear.

Quick like a fox, Will slithers into the trenches. He finds one German sleeping next to him. A broken neck may be too suspicious, he thinks, but then again, so will a bullet hole with no rifle shot. Will decides to carry on, leaving the soldier be. He is thankful not to be spotted as he heads out of the opposite side.

Will is a nimble shadow. His movements remain undetected. Not long after, he finds the perfect post. He digs himself in and waits. The position is uncomfortable, but it proves to be the most discreet location with the best view of the German camp. He waits out the night. As first light hits, he keeps his scope trained on any movement.

There are many faces to scan and compare to the target's picture. None match. Will begins to feel restless, which is never a good thing for a sniper. His unease is finally quenched after his scans reveal a match.

The Colonel is here. His shooting dummy stands next to several soldiers.

Will remembers his training, and knows not to fire directly at a target in front of him. It will give away his position if he does, based on the trajectory of the attack. He does not need to be concerned with a target in front of him, as he can simply maneuvere the bullet to make contact on the opposite side. However, he needs to be careful to make the kill look like it came from the Allied side. If he shoots from his current location, he will be trapped. Will rockets the bullet high into the sky. He cautiously tracks it until he is satisfied with its distance. The bullet then dives, curving towards the target.

The German Colonel stands casually, conversing with several men. There is no time for him to think or react to the shot. The projectile enters through the side of his head. Another successful kill. Will watches the men panic, pointing weapons in random directions, and running for cover. They fear the unseen, terrified to fight something they cannot see.

Will remains still. Any movement will give his position away, leading to a fight, which demands more energy than he is willing to use. Rather, he waits until nightfall.

The gap in time has not established an easy route back to his lines, although, it is better than earlier on. The chaos of a fallen Colonel has created a line full of paranoid soldiers.

Will studies the men in the trenches. He eyes a single spot that presents the best opportunity to get out of there. It contains five soldiers. Two he will encounter descending his perch and sneaking through the camp. The next three are huddled in the mud.

He takes a deep breath and shifts his body weight. Staying in one position all day wears on his muscles. They are weak and unstable. Movements are kept subtle as he inches forward.

Will hones in on a lantern near one of the operation tents. A diversion would be good. The lantern tips over with a little help from him and ignites the tent. Shouting and movement alert the men to the situation. The two he would have to sneak past are charging towards the fire. His coast is clear until he reaches the trench. Blending in with his surroundings he moves quickly. He knows he has one chance not to draw attention to himself.

The night is dark, masking his approach to the three remaining soldiers in his path. Will readies three bullets that hang in the air over his palm. Before the men can see his features he launches the ammunition towards them. They collide with the soldiers; their bodies collapse into the mud.

Will scans the area, making sure no one had seen him. Once satisfied, he slithers up the side of the trench and into the field. He moves as fast as he can without attracting attention. Soon he pulls himself into the cover of a mound. He catches his breath, careful not to let it combine with the cold air to give away his location. His heart pounds faster than ever before. Adrenaline surges through his body. The thrill of the kill is only part of his pleasure. Getting away with it is the other. He fights the urge to laugh at his accomplishment. He wants the feeling to stay, but he knows it will soon disappear.

For now, Will is content. He returns to his camp a little while later. Will enjoys the freedom of his position. He can come and go as he pleases, while the rest of the men remain in the dirt and mud and cold. Some rotate positions, some die, and some just…snap. He passes a few men quietly talking amongst themselves. From the look of them Will gathers they had quite the day. He recalls the artillery fire constantly sounding while he was behind enemy lines.

Will passes by wordlessly. He finds the Captain far from the front, conversing with a man in a buggy. Prichard spots him, and dismisses the buggy, pulled away by two horses. "You were gone a long time."

Will walks alongside him. "I need to be if you want success."

"Then it is done? You were successful?"

"The man is dead," Will confirms.

His mentor stares at him. "How can I be sure?"

"You told me not to take from their bodies. Besides, he was hardly in a position for me to do so." Will's voice carries a hint of frustration.

"Very well," Prichard pauses momentarily. "The only reason we knew that man was present is by an informant on their side. Assuming the man you killed was the right one, and he is indeed dead, the Generals will hear about it. For now we'll have to wait. Confirmation will be the first step towards bigger things."

"If that is all, sir, can you get me a map of the battlefield?"

"Follow me." He nods. They head to the camp well behind the lines and Prichard places a map on a table.

Will begins scribbling things on to the paper. "These circles are where their artillery is. And here are the majority of their troops. If our soldiers attack these points using our artillery, it will do the most damage."

Prichard studies the map and the new information. "This is outstanding work, Private. I'll get this to the commanding officer immediately. These men could use some good news."

Before the Captain leaves, Will stops him. "If that is all, I'd prefer to head back out there."

Prichard elevates an eyebrow. "I can order you not to, but I know you'll do it any way. You have one day. I expect you to be back here by then."

"Thank you, sir."

Will leaves his presence and heads down into the trenches. Their conditions are not much better than crawling through No Man's Land. Given the two options, he prefers the latter. He feels safe camouflaged with his surroundings. Out there he is an unseen force.

8: STRUGGLE

Friday:

I don't mind the long hours of this job, or even being on my feet for twelve hours. Yes, it wears me down from time to time, but it's not the worst thing. The worst is the food.

Look at me; I'm free and safe from The Island, yet I complain about my meals. There, it was a mushy mush of mushness that we ate every day. In Camelot we had gorgeous feasts. On the ship we began cycling through the same meals. Here, that trend continues.

My breakfast always consists of coffee with two lumps of sugar, bread and butter, and a boiled egg. It is better than Island food, but it is getting old. Lunch and supper are somewhat better, alternating options every now and then.

Today began like every other day. I gulped down my breakfast. One thing I can never do is miss a meal. With the random waves of incoming wounded, I never know how long I will be in the operating room, or when I will have a chance to eat next.

After my meal, I was walking down the hall. Several nurses passed by. I smiled at them, two of whom have become friends. My smile faded when I heard shouting coming from down the hall. I sped up my pace and turned the corner.

The Chief Medical Officer, Sebastien Gaston, was yelling at Monica.

"Get your head on straight, Monica! Stop delegating tasks and stick to your own job. This is the last time I want to hear about this, do I make myself clear?"

I've never seen Monica so reserved and unspoken. "Yes, sir."

"Good. Now get back to work!" He stormed off.

Monica turned, caught my eyes, but brushed them off and headed for her office. I followed her and opened the door she had closed behind her.

"What was that all about?" I asked.

"It was nothing. I don't want to talk about it."

"Why didn't you stand up to him?"

"Do you think I didn't want to?" she snapped. "I hate busting my butt to help this hospital run more efficiently, only to be told to *stick to my job*."

"I don't understand. You always stand up for yourself. I've never seen you just sit there and take it."

Monica breathed deeply. "There is a time and a place to fight back, Miss Noble. The majority of men here do not appreciate women, nor support them being here. There are a few that do, like Trevor. However, I can only fight back when I know my opponent will not do the same. It is a matter of picking your battles. I stand up for many small things, but it does nothing for the bigger picture."

"The bigger picture?"

"I'm tired of being seen as a dainty woman—a flower that's too delicate to do *real* work. I want to be seen as a person. I want to have the same rights they do." She paused for a moment. "But there are some people that it would be unwise of me to stand up to. There are those who will fight back physically, rather than with words. Add a little bit of alcohol and there's no telling. As much as it kills me to take verbal onslaught, I must. You'd best do the same. In this day and age, there is no alternative. That's why I have such hope for after the war."

The room suddenly felt weighted. I felt Monica's pain, and

in the short time that I've been here, I knew it as well. I had seen it ever since we left The Island. "Don't worry, Monica. Things will change after the war. It's like you said when we first met, it may take a while, and it will have its ups and downs, but it will happen."

"All we can do for now is hope," she said grimly. "God, I want to strangle Gaston."

The two of us laughed. I stood up. "C'mon. The day's not over yet."

"Don't remind me." She closed the door behind us. "You're still checking up on the A-wing patients, right?"

"I am. Hopefully it won't take too long, but you know how they get," I replied.

A-wing was reserved for newly treated soldiers. Some had difficulties adjusting to their injuries. There were good days and bad ones.

"That I do. I'll send for you if we need you."

"Sounds good. I'll see you later." I waved and headed down the corridor. I couldn't shake seeing Monica like that. In my mind she was always this strong independent woman. Nothing could touch her. I guess I have been turning a blind eye to these situations. I still respect her more than anyone else here though. She deserves better.

My thoughts were interrupted by shouts. I bolted through the doors to find two bed-ridden soldiers fighting from across the room.

"You're only here because you're a coward! Everyone knows you shot yourself to get out of there!" one shouted.

The other had come in with a gunshot wound to his foot. "Don't talk 'bout stuff that you know nothin' 'bout."

"If you're so eager to get out of the fight, I'll kill you myself!"

"Why don't I just beat you to it?"

"Hey!" I shouted, positioning myself between them. "That's enough of that! You should both be ashamed of yourselves. The enemy is out there, not in here."

"But 'e shot—"

"I don't want to hear another word," I sharply cut him off. "You, out of bed. We're moving you to another wing. And if you cause any more trouble, I will drag you back to the front myself, got it?"

The soldier nodded and was escorted out by another nurse. I turned to the patient with the foot wound. He had indeed shot himself. Monica showed me his wound, and its angle of trajectory. She'd pointed out all the signs. "And *you*, don't make the mistake that you're the only one who wants out of this fight. Do you know how many wounded men we treat each day? Every time one of you is killed, seven of you are wounded. I calculated that myself. Sometimes we get over two hundred of you in a night. We do our best to save as many as we can. Right now it's five out of six that we manage to."

The man was about to say something, but I kept talking. "And you know what? Every person that comes in, and every one that ends up on my table, is worth saving. It *kills* me to lose patients. It hurts to see young life go to waste. Don't be one of the people I couldn't save. You mull that over while I get going on my rounds. If I come back, and you still have your heart set on dying, I won't stop you. Your bed can go to someone who will fight to live."

I turned and headed for the far end of A-wing. I hadn't realized how big a scene that situation had caused. Everyone's eyes were on me or on the man in the bed. I ignored them, acting as if nothing had happened. The day had barely begun and I already wanted it to be over.

I tended to several injuries with no incident. The man this morning reminded me of a soldier we saw last month. He came in with multiple wounds from artillery fire. He had lost both legs and one arm. Still, he managed to survive.

But that didn't last long. One morning when I began my rounds, I found him in his bunk. He had cut himself and bled out sometime during the night. I couldn't wrap my head around it. Then again, I haven't been exposed to the horrors on the front. I only see the aftermath.

No matter how you play it, he still took his own life. I wished I could have helped him. I wasn't lying when I told the soldier today that every patient I lose hurts. It is the hardest part of this job. I have lost quite a few patients since I started working with Monica. The pain hasn't disappeared, and I don't think it ever will. Life is too precious for me to ignore. This forced to reflect on how I handled this morning.

Had I done everything I could have? I wondered. It was my job to see my patients recover. I feared I was too harsh on him. *No, some people need to be smacked in the head.* It may be the only way to shake them out of whatever state they are in. Regardless, what was done was done. I could not change anything about the incident, nor do I think I would. I carried on working, keeping him in the back of my mind.

I returned after I had finished my duties. "How was the rest of your day, soldier?"

The man showed remorse. "I owe you an apology, Lass. Gave me a chance to see 'ow bad others got it."

"Apology accepted." I hesitated. "But I can't help you once you're cleared. I don't know what happened to you for sure, and it's not up to me what happens once you leave."

"I know what I'm in for, Lass. No need to 'pologize."

I forced a smile. I knew he had shot himself, and so did he.

Shortly after our conversation, he was transferred out of my wing, and I did not see him again.

Sunday:

I have heard others talk about relationships and having fights. I also remember seeing my mother and father fighting occasionally. But that didn't prepare me for my first one with Trevor.

It all started when I was waiting for him in his quarters. I was fifteen minutes early of the time we were supposed to meet for dinner. Fifteen minutes went by, and Trevor was nowhere to be seen. I waited ten minutes. Then another ten. And then ten more. Still no Trevor.

After five more infuriating minutes, I gave up. *Why would he not show up and not tell me? What a jerk!* My mind was a car driven by two things—one was reason, the other, fury. I began asking around to find him. Eventually I was told he just finished in the operating room. Storming through the halls, my eyes caught sight of him.

"Hey!" I called.

He glanced up from a folder in his hands. He looked surprised to see me. "Hey, you. What are you doing here?"

His question made me change my plan of action. *He didn't even remember we had a date tonight.* What kind of boyfriend was he? I resisted the urge to slap him. Instead, I decided to give him the cold shoulder. "I'm not here to see you. I have to drop off some papers to Dr. Florence."

He looked at my hands. "Where are the papers?"

I had led with such a thin lie that I brushed past him. "They're already dropped off. Good-bye."

I didn't look back to see his reaction, but I assumed (and somewhat hoped) that he was sheepish. *He'll apologize once he realizes what he did.*

The evening persisted, along with my aloof treatment of Trevor. Several times he tried to chat with me. I always made an excuse to leave. Each time we saw each other, we both grew more intolerable. I was angry at him for forgetting our dinner, and he was angry with how he was being treated. Finally it boiled over.

He grabbed my arm in the hallway, stopping me when I tried to brush past him. "What's going on with you? Why are you ignoring me?"

"Why am *I* ignoring *you*?" I fumed. "Oh, I don't know, maybe it was because we had dinner plans that you ditched out of. Maybe it's because I waited half an hour for you to never show up. Maybe it's because I actually thought I loved you."

I choked out the last few words. I couldn't fight back the tears even though I tried. His face changed from frustration to blushing. He escorted me into an unoccupied room nearby. "Hold on, back up, Jess. We *had* plans for dinner tonight, but I had to pick up an extra shift, remember? I told you about it and we decided on tomorrow night."

He held onto my shoulders as I regained my composure. I thought back to when we had made plans. *Oh, God. He was right.* I felt like the world's biggest fool. I held a hand over my mouth. "I am so sorry, Trevor. I completely forgot. I was so sure it was today that I ignored you the rest of this evening."

He began to laugh. "That's what that was? This was all over a missed dinner? I've been trying to figure out why you've been so angry with me."

I reciprocated his smile. "I feel so silly. We definitely planned for tomorrow. Our first fight, and it was over something so stupid."

"Don't worry, Jess. It's been so hectic with all the wounded lately. It's easy to get things mixed up."

My cheeks burned red. "Are we OK?"

He breathed in. "Well, that would depend."

"On what?"

"On whether you were telling the truth when you said you thought you loved me."

I had said that. And I had meant it. I bit my lip. *What if he doesn't love me back? What if I had just destroyed our relationship by blurting that out?* "I was."

Trevor's expression did not change right away. He brushed my hair back with his hand, and then used his thumb to wipe a runaway tear. He didn't speak. He only leaned in closer, brushing his nose against mine. His lips gently touched mine. I lost my sense of space, hypnotized with the kiss. It was different from the ones before.

He pulled away. "Good. Because I love you, too."

My heart fluttered. I gave in to the warm feeling, and pulled him closer and kissed him back. My lips expressed everything I couldn't say. Time seemed to slow down. I let him go. The two of us stared into each other's eyes. "So, dinner tomorrow then?"

He laughed and then nodded. "That sounds wonderful."

I opened the door. "And don't even think about not showing up. If you miss dinner, you're done for."

And just like that, our first fight was over. Everything was fixed. Life resumed as normal, and we were fine. I never thought something so small as miscommunication could potentially destroy what we had. I wonder if all relationships are like this? How many don't resolve the problem and break up over something totally pointless?

I began to think about my parents and what they had. They truly loved each other. I can only hope what Trevor and I have is the same. We'll see.

Tuesday:

Today can only be defined as difficult. I thought I was over dwelling on such things, but I may never be able to forget.

We were in the operating room. A fresh batch of wounded arrived. I dealt with a severe case of trench foot and required assistance amputating one of the legs. Another soldier was placed on my table and died before I could do a thing. They poured in and out, blurring together by blood and bandages.

I was unfazed by it all until... I saw him. His hair was a mix of blonde, dirt, and blood. His face was scarred, but in tact. The young man was no older than eighteen. He was unconscious; a condition caused from shrapnel wounds in his chest. I was frozen.

"Francis?" I whispered.

"Miss Noble? You need to get to work!" my assisting nurse interrupted my daze.

I began to cut open his uniform to access the wound. My mind was in a trance as I worked. I went through the motions. "Yes, of course."

The man on the table had Francis' face one moment, and after a blink, his face would change. He was not Francis, but that did not make it any better. I held it together until my last patient. As soon as he was treated, I exited the room as quickly as possible. My head was spinning as I raced to my room. I shut the door behind me and sunk to the floor.

I thought I had come to terms with what happened to Francis. He was most likely dead. I had moved on…only I hadn't. The young soldier looked so remarkably close to him. For a moment I was convinced Francis was on my table. *It wasn't him. He's long gone. It's been months.* I could not reason with my head. *What if Francis isn't dead?*

"Stop it!" I cried through streams of tears. "Stop second-guessing yourself. You did all that you could to help Francis. You're free from The Island. That's all that matters now."

But it isn't. Francis deserved a better life. All he wanted to do was help people. I felt so guilty, like I had betrayed him.

"I'm sorry, Francis," I whispered. "I hope you're free… wherever you are."

I knew then and there that I would never be able to escape what had happened to me. There would always be something to remind me of The Island, of Francis, or even Will. *Will.* The name left a bitter taste in my mouth. *I hope wherever you are, you're suffering.* The voice in my head surprised me with its animosity. *Why should Will be free and not Francis?*

I took several slow breaths. Time will help me come to terms with things, but not enough time had passed to allow me to move on. I didn't question being with Trevor. I only questioned what things would be like if Francis were still here.

For now I could only cry when these thoughts crossed my path, or bury them until I had the opportunity to. Either way, The Island's scars were deep, and no compound could heal them fast enough.

There was a knock on my door. Monica's voice squeaked through the wood. "Are you alright, Miss Noble?"

"You can come in," I replied.

She closed the door when she realized I had been crying. "Mind if I ask what happened today?"

I played with my shirt. "The blonde soldier I operated on today. He—well—I could have sworn he was Francis. You remember, the guy I was separated from."

Monica held a hand up to silence me. "Say no more. Do you know how many wounded I have operated on that bore James' face? Too many. It's something you don't shake. You only learn to conceal it better. But I can see it being worse for you. I at least have the knowledge that he is dead. You still think about him, don't you?"

I shrugged as I wiped my face. "I don't mean to. And it's so much worse when it happens with Trevor there. I feel like such a terrible person. Why can't I just forget him, Monica?"

Monica placed an arm around me. "Oh, Miss Noble, you don't want to forget him. And you never can. He is a part of you. Your interactions with him shaped who you are today. That's why you can't shake him off. At least that's how I feel."

"It's been so long though."

"All I can say is that it gets easier. He'll cross your mind now and again, but it gets less and less devastating. C'mon, let's go to my quarters. I've got just the thing to make you feel better."

We had a good conversation that probably went later than it should have. I am so fortunate to have her as a friend. It really helps get me through these types of problems.

Wednesday:

I lost another patient today. He had been treated and was well on the way to recovering physically. Mentally, however, was a different matter. He was in a trance ever since he got out of surgery. Doctors here are calling it 'shell-shocked.' Many were avoiding him—his eyes burned wildly, so much so that you could not tell what he was thinking.

I tried to talk to him. It made no difference. He caused quite the scene when he chose to go out, too. I'll never forget the anger and bitterness in his words.

He shouted to no one in particular, yet to all of us at the same time. "You're only here because you have someone to keep you off lines. Outta the trenches. Ha! If you only saw what I have. You couldn't last one day. Not. One. Day."

He had lost his mind. Shouting nonsense, he tried to grab

an officer's gun. The soldier had no choice but to fire. The gunshot was loud, and it rang out tremendously in the room. I was quite shocked. It all happened so quickly. Another life gone, just like that.

It is clear to me how brutal this war is, and the effect it has on our troops. I know our job hardly compares to being out there in the fight, but I can't help but empathize with the wounded.

It feels like we have it just as badly here. I realize how self-centered that sounds, but given what I have seen, is it really? I mean, every day wounded come in. Every day we wade through the murky waters of death, trying to save all we can. Sometimes before we even have a chance to help, we lose them, and others, like today, are gone long before we know it.

I thought about how they must feel—the survivors. They fight day and night in the cold and mud and blood. They rely on each other and bond in a way I will never understand, only to have their friends die in front of them. *No, they have it far worse.* I reasoned. Then again, there is no winning, or good place to be this close to the battle. We all fight, we all lose, and we all try and get by. There is no escaping the suffering here.

Thursday:

There are many jobs that the doctors here hate doing. One of the biggest ones is training the new doctors that join us. Many of them are fresh out of school without a single operation under their belts. Others act like they know more than those of us that have been here, or like they have a more *effective* method. The result is usually the trainee vomiting on the floor during a typical day of operating. They don't have the stomach for it at the start.

To be fair, there are some who listen, retain, and ask for help. There just aren't that many of them. For these reasons, it is the least desirable job at the hospital. That's why Monica, Trevor, and I were placed in charge of their training. Monica and I work hard to earn respect around here, but the men are stubborn, and unwelcome to change. All they see are our mistakes, or just our appearances. Trevor was lumped in with us because of course there needs to be a man involved. If they left the training to two women the world would surely end. (If you can't tell, this sort of thing just eats away at me.)

I feel bad for Trevor, though. Just because the two of us have become a 'thing,' the rest of the doctors have started to treat him differently. It doesn't help that he fights for us every chance he gets. He's such a good guy, but even if it hurts my pride, I wish he just kept quiet sometimes. He'd be better off for it. I've grilled him a few times for standing up for us.

I know I shouldn't have to, but I want them to understand that I can fight my own battles. Trevor will still do it anyway. While it agitates me, I think it also makes me love him more.

There are seven new doctors stationed coming here for training. I was pretty nervous when I heard I would be involved. I was scared of slipping up, or doing the wrong thing. My mind tends to psych itself out until logic takes over.

I thought about how beneficial it's going to be. Teaching someone anything helps you understand it better. That's what I'm looking forward to. I want to be the best I can be, and if I can teach what I am doing to another person, just imagine how far I've come from the little girl imprisoned by The Island.

I don't know what to expect when they arrive, but I'll find out tomorrow.

Friday:
The new batch of doctors showed up in the early afternoon. They hopped off a carriage by the main entrance. Three of them looked keen, while the rest were either exhausted or

unimpressed with our hospital.

Monica introduced herself, as did Trevor and I. "While you complete your training here, you will answer to the three of us. Please don't hesitate to ask questions. I would rather have someone ask and finish a task properly, than do it half-cocked."

I did my best to look confident. My heart was beating out of my chest and we hadn't even done anything yet.

"Before you do anything, I want you to forget the majority of what you think you learned. Doctoring in war is an entirely different duty than that back home. The wounds, operations, and demands here will be like nothing you have encountered. As such, your first shift will be spent observing us. Do not speak while we operate. There will be plenty of operations and situations for you to see. Write down what you witness as well as any questions you may have. Am I understood?"

The young doctors nodded. Monica had me take them to where they would be sleeping, and then give them a tour of our facilities. I knew she was expecting perfection, and I did my best to achieve it.

I walked them through each wing and explained what category of patients was held in them. I showed them how we receive and unload incoming wounded. Everything from where we store our supplies to the cafeteria was covered. I knew I had overkilled the tour from their faces, but I did not want to cut any corners. I let them get settled into their sleeping quarters once I had finished. I informed them where to meet and how to prepare for when incoming wounded arrived.

Trevor caught up to me in the hall. "How did it go?"

"I'd say it went fine, but all I did was bore them. I don't think they have any idea what it'll be like here."

He chuckled. "You mean they're not ready for one of our twelve hour shifts in the operating room? They'll catch on quick.

You did the same."

"What do you mean?"

"All you did when you got here was assist Monica, and now you're training the new recruits. I remember when you were constantly asking me how to do something because you didn't want to pester her."

I smiled. He had me there. I had no clue what I was doing at the start. "I just wanted to make sure I was doing the right thing. Besides, even now I need help time to time during surgery. You know that."

He eyed the hallways and lowered his voice. "Considering you never went to medical school, and that you are a more talented doctor than some of the others here says something about you. Don't second-guess yourself with these folks."

I had told Monica quite some time ago that Trevor knew my background (or lack thereof). She was torn over the matter, but I had to come clean to him. He was remarkably understanding. His only question was, "Is this something you want to do after the war?" It didn't matter to him whether I had experience or not. He wanted to know if I had thought things through and was doing this for a reason. The two of us talked, and I agreed to go to medical school once the war ended. I didn't want to be a fake. I wanted people to know that I had earned it and deserved to be there. Trevor respected that. From that point on Monica and him took turns teaching me various aspects of the profession.

"I guess you're right."

"Just remember everything Monica and I taught you and you'll be fine. We wouldn't have involved you in this if we didn't think you were capable of it. You are an amazing doctor, Jess. And school is going to be a walk in the park after all of this experience. You'll see."

"Thanks Trevor. I needed that." I remained reserved about the situation, but like always, he made me feel better. I love that about him, even though sometimes I do not appreciate it as much as I should.

"Well, I need to check up on some patients, but I'll see you around, alright?"

We said goodbye. I headed for the cafeteria to grab some food. I was in the middle of eating and talking to one of my nurses, Lettie, when the signal sounded for incoming wounded. The noise was always difficult to react to. On one hand, it meant we went to work, but on the other, people were dying and in pain. I never knew how to react. "Looks like we're back at it. Remember, we have the trainees observing now. Try and be nice if they get in your way."

Lettie rolled her eyes. "Can't make any promises, Noble."

We raced to the operating room. Monica had everything sorted out before I arrived. Only two people were going to watch me today. Once we had all properly prepped ourselves, we entered the room. I took up my station. "I want you two to stand here. Feel free to adjust if you can't see what I'm doing, but don't lean in; the space is crammed as it is. And don't talk, we need all the concentration and focus we can get."

They acknowledged what I had said. *Good*, I thought, t*his is going to be just fine.* The doors to the room opened with the first set of soldiers.

My first patient had a bellyful of shrapnel. He had lost a lot of blood and was in bad shape. The nurse and I worked quickly, clearing the blood to get a better view of his condition. My hands remained steady as I pulled out piece after piece of debris. The young man's heart fluttered up and down throughout the operation. I was constantly in fear for his life, but he managed to hang in there. My hands searched his stomach for any more shrapnel or open wounds that I had missed. "He's good. Seal him up and send in the next one."

My nurse carried out my orders as I exchanged my gear for fresh ones. The two observers were well-behaved, unlike a couple who were with Monica. I could overhear her shouting at them. "Don't make me tell you again to stand back! Let me work. If I have to ask you again, I'll have you kicked out of the O.R."

I was pleased that I did not have the same concerns with mine. Or maybe I didn't want the confrontation when they inched closer to see something. To be honest, I barely remembered they were there. Whenever I'm in that room, it's like nothing else exists. It is oddly relaxing despite the tremendous pressure.

Every patient is a new puzzle, and I devote all my energy and focus to solving it. Of course tempers flare under the circumstances, and little disputes arise that will break my concentration. Everyone just wants the best for their patients. Time flies when I'm operating. It's easy to have a ten-hour shift feel short mentally, but physically, it's draining. My feet hurt the most, but I find my hands cramp up as well.

My stint in the operating room finished with a young soldier—no older than fifteen. He had lost an arm, most likely from artillery or a grenade. I finished tending to the wound and applied a dressing to it. During the operation I couldn't help but compare the boy to those of us taken by The Island. He was so young for something so brutal. Granted, some of these soldiers volunteered to serve, while others were required to register. I couldn't imagine being forced into this war, but for those in our time, it would also be hard to imagine being imprisoned and tested on. Either way, the similarities were evident to me as I stared at the boy's face. I couldn't help but sympathize with patients that were younger than I am. Ever since Lola, I've tried to remain partially detached from creating bonds with my patients. It's too painful.

I exited the operating room, scrubbed down, and went to the cafeteria with Trevor and Monica. The three of us had a routine after a shift, consisting of a meal and coffee and discussing things that may have popped up during the operations. Some times we have much to talk about, and others we sit and eat in silence.

Our posse of recruits followed behind, murmuring amongst each other. I confess I was exhausted from working and was not in the mood to discuss things with them.

I zoned in and out of the conversation. Most of their questions were trivial at best. They were less concerned with the methods and more concerned with themselves. The shock of the wounded today was not enough to shake them into the mentality of war.

Do we have to sleep in those areas? Are all shifts that long? Can't we trade off? When can I go on leave? How long do you think the war is going to last? Is that nurse taken?

The questions bombarded us one after the other. Thank goodness for Trevor. He was the only one with enough patience not to shout at them. He successfully defused Monica several times after such questions came up. He has a way with words. I found myself staring at him.

I couldn't pinpoint if I was lucky to have him, or if the suffering I had endured was enough to have the reward of being with Trevor. It's hard to call my life fortunate because it consisted of such torment and pain. I suppose I am both lucky to have escaped that life, and unlucky to have lived it. Regardless, I am here now, with him. That in itself is a miracle.

"Miss Noble?" Judging from the table, I had been caught staring. And the look on Monica's face told me she had repeated my name multiple times.

"Hmm?" I replied, trying to play it off as nothing.

"I think you have been working overtime. Why don't you relieve yourself? We'll answer any further questions these men have."

I smiled at the two of them. "Thanks. I could use the rest. See you tomorrow."

I excused myself from the table and headed to my room, which had been moved into Monica's to open up more space. I ran my fingers through my long hair, twirling the ends in between them. I would need to cut it soon. It was tiring tying it back every time I go to the O.R. I grabbed my diary and caught up on some entries (including this one). But I'm sick of writing for now. I'll need the rest for tomorrow.

9: FALLING WITH STYLE

Journal Entry #89:
June 13, 1915
England

We made it to the RFC (Royal Flying Corps) training grounds late at night three days ago. The Captain here, Phillips, had bunks set up for our crew. Of course, we only consisted of Venus, Jupiter, Uranus, Saturn, and myself. The others, Neptune, Earth, and Mercury, were tracking down more information. In the absemce of Neptune, Venus was placed in command. She's a good leader.

Many of the recruits training with us are the same age, or younger, than I am. It is quite odd interacting with them. I feel very unsure of myself. They must sense it, because when I try and talk with them, they look uncomfortable. Deep in my heart I don't really have a problem with it. The two-week average lifespan means half of them (or myself) will be dead shortly after getting our 'wings.' That's what they call the badge that certifies us for flying. Before we get wings, we need to fly multiple planes, and get a ticket saying so.

This brings me to the actual plane we're training on. To put it simply, the aircraft looks like it could fall apart at any second. It is called the Maurice Farman, but everyone calls it 'Longhorn.' Those practicing here before us had a hard time taking the plane seriously due to its appearance. It spans about fifty feet, has four longerons (which are essentially tail pieces), and two rudders. We sit in a tandem two-passenger tub, or nacelle. Inside are the controls: pedals for rudders, a stick to push/pull for the elevator, and handlebars. All of these are attached by piano string. A joke I hear the others say is that there are so many wires inside that they could cage a bird in the cockpit.

One of the main critiques the soldiers have are the two skids ahead of the wheels, which look like the front of a toboggan. That, along with its flimsy appearance, doesn't exactly inspire me with confidence. I mean, I've been on a *real* plane before, so looking at these is a nightmare.

Regardless, we must fly on the Longhorn and then advance to the Shorthorn. The difference between the two is like a normal bike and one with training wheels. The Longhorn is bulkier and easier to fly, while the Shorthorn ditches some of the design to make it more practical. However, a bike with training wheels on it won't kill you, unlike the Longhorn. Very comforting.

Almost more reassuring is the instruction from Captain Phillips. He says not to worry about crashing the Longhorn because there is so much between you and the ground that you will most likely be unharmed. Phillips is a flying veteran, with a record for confirmed kills. Unfortunately his plane was shot down, and he lost his right hand. A wooden lump with a long curved hook replaces the vacancy. He's not allowed to fly in combat anymore, but they do let him teach us. To be honest, it's rather impressive to see how he flies with his injury.

After the very first day of instruction and learning about the planes, I started to question whether I had made a terrible decision in coming here. There is no changing my mind or going back now though. I am stuck with this—we all are. The only one more nervous than I am is Uranus. If I'm classified as scared, he's terrified. Of course he will never admit it, but I can tell. His eyes gave it away when he went on his first flight.

All of the recruits spent the first day learning the various parts of the plane. One by one we got the chance to get in the air, piloted by our instructor. Several of the men puked when they went up.

It was finally my turn to go up. I was definitely nervous. I'd been in modern planes before, but as I mentioned, these did not compare. Flying didn't bother me, but crashing does. I hopped in the backseat, and Captain Phillips took the front.

"It's just a quick bout in the air, and then we'll be back down. Nothing fancy," he yelled over the engine.

"Yes, sir," I replied, finding myself searching for something to grip.

The takeoff was considerably bumpy. The wheels were not big enough to take on rough terrain, which made the littlest bump cause the plane to shake. I took a few hasty breaths as we began to lift from the ground. *Is this is how I will die?* I thought.

After several small hops, we began to rise. I felt the lurch in my stomach that comes with takeoffs. It was entirely not as comfortable as the plane I remember taking to Disneyland.

It shuddered in the air. I was teeming with fear that we would crash, but Phillips kept the plane quite steady once we were up. I was fascinated at how his hook hand interacted with the controls. He used it to guide the steering, while his good hand took care of the finer things. He took us around the aerodrome then began to descend. I established that the take-off and landing are the two things that freak me out the most. When the wheels hit the ground, the plane shook tremendously. Phillips kept it steady, and taxied us to the shed. He killed the aircraft and blocks were placed by the wheels.

"Well, John, how was that?"

"It was definitely an experience, sir." I climbed out. I was getting used to the false names we were given when registering in the RFC.

"It takes a few flights to get used to the feeling. We'll get to that though. That's all for now. Send the next one over."

I nodded and left, tagging the next in line. I wandered over to find the rest of my team having a bite to eat.

Saturn welcomed me with a drink. "So?"

"I'm doing better than Uranus, that's for sure." The table laughed and Uranus scowled.

"I didn't have any problems. Just don't like flying on an empty stomach is all," he justified.

"Sure thing," I smiled. "What about the rest of you? Jupe, you looked rather comfortable."

She paused, mid-bite. "Sky, ground, it's all the same to me. I just wish we weren't being babied."

"We'll get there soon enough," Venus said. "Right now focus on learning all the fine details. We need to see how fast things can happen up there. If we're not careful, we'll be a statistic, not a flight member. Think about Mars."

Mars. The name left a foul taste in my mouth. Suddenly I felt no need to eat or drink. I will never shake the guilt, nor should I. The table fell silent.

Saturn broke the veil. "We knew what we signed up for. That's part of the job. Any news from Neptune?"

I welcomed the topic change. Venus shook her head. "Not yet, but as soon as I get something I will fill the rest of you in."

Journal Entry #90:

Today was my first flight in the pilot's seat. The experience can only be described as exhilarating. Captain Phillips sat behind me, yelling advice and instructions over the whir of the engine.

"Chocks away," he called. "Taxi slowly."

I gripped the handlebars tightly. We accelerated forward slowly and I adjusted my body to the bumps. We were at the start of the runway.

"Alright, throttle back. Once you get to 45 and 50, ease the stick back. Remember to watch your speed on ascent. Too much or too little will stall the aircraft."

I did not reply. I was too focused. I concentrated hard on the speed, the runway, and the controls. I slowly lifted off of the ground. It was much easier to gauge the lurch and lift when I was in the pilot's seat. I held my breath as we rose. We climbed higher and higher, and I soon leveled off.

"Excellent work. Let's try some left hand circuits," I heard Phillips shout.

Gently, I adjusted the controls to form a giant left-hand circle. The plane leaned in accord. I was too terrified of crashing to focus on anything else. Soon it was time to land. My nerves were bothersome, and the cold air wasn't much help either. Phillips guided me down and ensured the proper technique.

Earlier that day one of the men had misjudged the landing and came down too soon. They landed in a field a couple miles away from the base.

Once the wheels hit ground we decelerated, and I taxied us to the shed. We got out and Phillips was smiling. "Not too bad at all. Keep it up."

"Thanks, Captain," I said as he left. Very soon I would have my ticket and could advance to a different plane, like the Avro or Shorthorn. From there we would practice vertical turns, where the rudder becomes our elevator and vice versa. And then after that we go solo.

The thought of being in a plane on my own both worries and liberates me. Not having someone constantly over your shoulder might be nice, but at the same time, if things go sideways I'll have no one to help me. Either way, I've got some time before that.

Journal Entry #94:
August 13, 1915
France

I have been training for over a month now and I must say, I love flying. There isn't really any other feeling like it. The wind, the clouds, everything. It amazes me. I have about twenty hours of flying logged in. We need sixty to be sent over the lines. Regardless, we have moved to another base.

My new instructor, Thomas, watched me fly the other day. "How many hours have you logged?"

I tended to my plane. (did I mention I have my very own BE 2C?) "Around twenty."

"Twenty? That's absurd," he cried. "Why it's preposterous to send pilots here with such little time logged. You won't stand a chance out there if we don't do something. Let me speak with the Major and see what we can do."

"Thank you!" I smiled, but his response had struck a nerve. Despite getting confident with landing and taking off, I still hadn't nailed the vertical turns. I hadn't viewed my training yet as looking ahead to the battles.

There was no way I was ready for that—Jupiter and Saturn maybe, but not me. Thinking back, I don't know if the other pilots would be either. One of whom was so scared to land, he kept circling the base. Eventually he ran out of fuel, forcing his plane down in a crash. He was unscathed, but still, it makes me wonder. I spent hours practicing my landings. I would pick spots to land, work on judging distances, as well as some evasive maneuvers. Of course, the landings would only matter if I made it back.

I guess that brings me to my next observation: loved ones. I first noticed it back at our first training base. Since we were still in England, many pilots could visit their families. One in particular had his mom come each week. The mother was naturally worried for her son, but still very proud. I remember watching them and thinking of my family. What I wouldn't give to have them comfort me, or even Jess for that matter. But they're all gone now. And every time some family came to visit, I had a hard time watching.

Other men sought women their age for comfort. On leave days they would hit up the bars and flirt with any girls they could find. I humored Uranus one night and went for a drink with him. Chasing girls was not something I enjoyed or even tried for that matter.

I loved Jessica, and now she was gone. I didn't even get to see her or have any way of helping. She was just simply gone. So when a young woman approached me I found myself unsettled.

"Hey there," she said. Her eyes were dark brown, her hair a shade lighter. "You must be one of those pilots, right?"

I was surprised at her English. Most often the people we met spoke solely French. "I'm afraid I am."

"Oh?" She was curious. "You're not going to throw it in my face like the others? Perhaps boast of taking me into the skies, or single handedly taking down all the German planes?"

A smile stretched across my face. "Those are some pretty good lines, but I'm not like the others."

"I can see that. That's why I came over."

"Really?" I felt my face getting warm.

She nodded. "I'm not looking for a single night like some of the girls here. I want something more, although, given how you all seem to come and go it isn't exactly ideal."

I flashed an uneven smile. I could not shake the thought of Jessica from my mind. Obviously we weren't in a relationship, and even now she's gone, but I felt guilty talking to this girl.

"What's your name?"

"Isabella. And you?"

"Well Isabella," I began, "it doesn't really matter who I am. There's someone else, and, well, it's complicated."

"Being in love with another doesn't sound complicated," she fired back. "Tell me about her."

I was flustered. I backed up, knocking over a stool. "I'm sorry. I-I just can't. Good evening."

And I left. I walked out into the crisp night air. It was impossible to even consider feeling for another in my given situation, right? Why get attached when you could die the next day, or eventually have to leave? I suppose some may argue those are the very reasons that one should try.

I don't want to be alone, the voice in my head said. Perhaps that's why everyone goes out on leave. They may die alone in battle, but for now they are alive and just want to be with somebody. I sat in my room debating the problem. Would it be so bad to move on?

I'm afraid to admit that I'm tired of this fight. I just wish I could be free. Maybe I should have listened to Will back in Camelot. Could this be what Nimue had warned me about? *No, I thought. If you give up, Jessica died for nothing, and perhaps Will too, wherever he is. They can't die in vain.* This thought is all that has kept me pushing forward. But even it can't last forever.

Flying is the only distraction from these thoughts that works for me right now. When I'm in the air, nothing else matters. Nothing The Island did to me can touch me up there.

Journal Entry #97:

Today we practiced by playing follow the leader. Thomas was in a plane ahead of me and I had to maneuver into a position where I could shoot him down. It was the first sense of what aerial combat might entail. Until now all we had were stories from our superiors. Apparently it wasn't uncommon for skirmishes to last longer than half an hour, and that was supposed to be while in retreat. It also sounded like the planes could take much abuse, as long as the bullets did not impact a critical piece.

We also finally received word from Neptune and the others. They were following a lead that may prove to pay off. Venus could not elaborate further. It feels like we are being left in the dark. Over our time together, I've learned to trust my team members, but it doesn't make it any easier.

Saturn tells me to be thankful they haven't gotten anything concrete yet because it gives us more time to train. That is a comforting way of looking at it. I really don't know what I'll do when we actually get into combat.

Journal Entry #98:

Not only have I logged over sixty hours, but I have been assigned a squadron as well. The Number 9 Squadron, flying 2Cs to be exact. My team is also in the same Flight (that's what they call a group of 4-6 planes). There is an A, B, and C Flight in our Squadron. Jupiter is our flight leader.

I'm not sure if I should be excited or worried. The 2Cs meant we would be doing artillery observation. Essentially we fly up and down the front lines, avoiding the Anti-Aircraft Artillery (which they call Archie), and taking photographs. These reconnaissance missions were often lengthy and German planes (Fokkers) would be constantly on our tails.

Being assigned to a Flight also meant active duty, which brought death. Up until now, we were only training. Our friends or fellow pilots always returned. With this posting, the two-week survival rate kicks in. For all of us trainees, death was a future date we forgot to consider. It was never an ominous looming presence. But now it is.

Our first mission is to photograph the second-line enemy trenches. I was paired with Sergeant Gunner Davis. We worked together to take pictures, and at times I was left to fly with one arm, changing the plates of the camera with the other. It's not the easiest task.

The air was brisk and cold. I did my best to bundle up, but the wind cuts through almost everything. We climbed to 7,500 feet. As we neared the front, I focused on landmarks to guide our route. No sooner had we arrived and were we fired upon. Two puffs of gray smoke appeared about one hundred feet below us. Three more appeared slightly closer. It was artillery fire. That was another thing we had to worry about. With how high up we were some planes could be shot down by their own side, or by accident closer to the ground. Frankly it was a mess.

I felt uneasy, and rose slightly higher. This was the first time I felt that way in a long while. I was constantly searching the skies for the enemy. Not once did I feel safe out there like I had during training.

We carried on with our mission, and returned to the base once it was complete. One of our planes was shot down, but none of our team was in it thankfully. Still, it felt like it was only a matter of time. I wish Neptune had contacted us by now.

Journal Entry #102:
October 13, 1915
France

The weather had been dismal for several days now, which makes our observation and job utterly useless. I almost prayed for the weather to remain poor so as to avoid going up. I've seen far more death than one should in several lifetimes.

The day began with clear skies and a bright sun. We would be going up today, no doubt about that. I got dressed and met the rest of my Flight in the hanger. Our orders were, as usual, to photograph and report on enemy lines.

The Germans were waiting for us when we reached the lines. We had barely captured an image before bullets rained down on us. They used the sun for cover, and dove towards us. I could hear their fire whiz past us, and began evasive maneuvers. The problem with our planes is that they are much slower than the German Fokkers. We had to make large turns to cover each other as they zipped around us.

I heard an explosion, and stole a glance behind me. One of our planes—I couldn't tell whose—was now a cluster of falling debris and fire. My heart was heavy, but I did not have the luxury of mourning. Our backs were open and unprotected. Davis swiveled his gun to try and keep them at bay. The roar of the engine and the patter of gunfire overwhelmed my ears. Keeping my eyes sharp, I dipped, turned, and spun my best to avoid taking fire.

My best was not good enough. Ducking was all I could do as a German flew by, marking our plane with holes. In the heat of the moment, I froze time on instinct, and climbed as fast as I could to get out of its range before letting go. The sudden spike of pressure on my mind caused my vision to blur. I lost control, hunching forward in my seat.

The plane went into a spinning dive. The world was moving rapidly around me. I shut my eyes tightly, trying to get a grip. Staying calm was the most crucial thing. I eased on the controls, attempting to slowly come out of the spin. It took longer than I would have liked, but the plane evened out dangerously close to the ground. I rose, but stayed low enough to avoid German attention.

Freezing time took too much energy and left me drained. I fear I will no longer be able to use my power on this scale. Each time I use it, I feel weaker and weaker, taking longer to recover.

They probably think we died and went into a tailspin. I stared up. The gunfire still resounded above us. I hoped the rest of the Flight was all right. All we needed to do was get safely across our side. They don't usually follow us over.

It wasn't until now that I glanced at Davis. Several red stains leaked through his uniform. Oh no. He wasn't moving. I called his name multiple times with voice to return it. I raced back to base as fast as I could, eventually meeting up with the rest of my Flight. We landed safely.

"I need a doctor!" I screamed, hauling Davis' body from the plane. I tried to shake him awake, but he did not respond. Several members of my team pulled me away from him as the medical officer rushed to his side.

"There's nothing you can do now," Jupiter said. "He's not the only one we lost."

My eyes were puffy and red. I had been friends with Davis ever since we were paired up. "What do you mean?"

"Uranus' plane was shot down."

I was taken aback. "What?"

"When we were ambushed the Germans managed to take his plane out. We were lucky we didn't lose more."

"Lucky," I muttered as she left, most likely to the bar with everyone else to drink away their problems. I felt like I was in a trance on my way back to my room. I shut the door behind me.

Throughout our training I had seen men come and go, some transferred, while others had been shot down. I had seen plenty of soldiers die before this mission, but none of them were close to me.

Uranus and Davis were just gone. There was no good-bye, no heroic death, and no last words. They were living one moment, and dead the next. I took deep breaths, trying to come to terms with the reality of our position.

How many more do I have to watch die? I asked. Why couldn't we just train and ship out when Neptune called for us, instead of waiting to be shot down? Would there be any of us left by the time Neptune and the others were ready?

I slammed my fist against the wall. "It's not fair."

My mind was drawn to something Jupiter had said when we first arrived at training: "My advice: don't get close to anyone. We all die in the end. Life is the game of avoiding it as long as possible."

She was right. I have always been close to those around me. It's who I am. But I can't be me here and now. I don't have the willpower. This fight, this war—it's wearing me down. I'm sick of it. Who knows, maybe next flight will be my last and this mission will be out of my hands.

If it is, I am not going to go out like this, I told myself. *I'm done holding back.*

I grabbed my jacket and headed down to join the others. However, they were not who I wanted to see. I found Isabella in a corner booth with one of her friends. I approached their table with a drink in each hand. "Do you mind if I have a moment with Isabella alone?"

Her friend looked to Isabella, whom nodded. I waited for her to leave. "I'm sorry about how I acted the last time we spoke."

"You must think I have a sharp memory to speak of one conversation a month ago," she said casually.

I looked at my feet. "I could tell you that my name is John, but that would be a lie. I could tell you stories of fighting the

Germans, but I know you don't care for those things. I've spent my time here trying to hold onto the ones that I have lost. I can't do that anymore. I realize now that life is short, and I don't want to be alone. So I've brought you a drink, and figured we could talk openly."

She took a moment to absorb what I had said. "If you're not John, who are you?"

I sat down, and passed her a drink. "My name is Francis."

"Hmm. I like John better." She smiled. "So, John, the last time we spoke, you were pining over another girl. What happened to change your mind?"

"She died when I first came here. Ever since then I have been watching those around me die. I don't want to be one of them, but more so, I don't want to die alone."

She studied my face. "Then we share a common goal."

"Your English is quite good," I changed the subject. "Where are you from?"

"Oh I grew up here, in France," she explained. "My parents insisted that I learn English as well."

"I'm glad they did. Not many of the people here can speak it."

She smiled. "And what about you?"

The two of us talked until the bar closed. Every now and then I was forced to lie or make something up. But I opened up to her and she did the same to me. We both decided we enjoyed spending time together too much to get involved as well. We would meet each other once a week to talk and spend time with each other, but it was not meant to be a relationship.

I don't know how exactly being closer to someone actually solves my problem or feelings. I think just having someone to speak to, or to look forward to seeing is enough to keep me in one piece. Only time will tell.

Journal Entry #107:
December 13, 1915
France

I have neglected to write in this journal for quite some time now. Maybe I have grown weary of the fight, or maybe I don't see the point of jotting down things that have happened. It's difficult to dedicate time to write when life could end on any given day. At least that's how it feels.

It is hard to believe that over a year has passed since I arrived in Europe. I've lost my two best friends. I met new ones, for lack of a better word—one of whom I murdered. Next to go were Davis and Uranus. Venus' plane caught fire during a battle, and when that happens, the pilot really only has three options. The first is to jump, which is not ideal given how high up we are without parachutes. The second option is to use a revolver stashed in every plane, and take his or her life. Finally, and most grizzly, is doing nothing and burning to death. Venus opted to use her pistol instead of flames.

There are three of us left from our team. Saturn has taken command of our trio. So many of my friends and team are now gone. We have heard nothing from Neptune, which makes me question whether all of this loss was worth anything.

There's really not much else to do other than keep fighting. Saturn is still following our orders, and insisting we do the same. I admire his loyalty, but when does it end? At what point do we stand up and take control of the mission? If I had more hope I would do it myself, but the world is too big, and I am not as strong as I used to be.

I still see Isabella. She's probably the reason I'm still fighting. She is kind and caring, but understanding in a way

Jessica never was.

I made a tombstone for her and Will on the anniversary of our arrival here. Something needed to be done to remember them. We're heading out again in the morning. I feel a bit out of place, as those of us from our original squadron are the most senior pilots here. Everyone else has either died, or is just coming fresh out of training. Some don't even have their sixty flight hours yet. That's essentially a death sentence on the front. We'll see if I'm still here tomorrow.

10: INITIATIVES

Western Front
June 1915

Will sits in a waiting room. He examines his fingernails. All are clean and cut with precision. He stretches his arms—the crisp uniform restricts his movements. Will prefers mobility and versatility, neither of which the uniform provides. A medal rests on his left breast patch. He breathes on it, cleaning the smudges with his sleeve.

The medal itself was awarded to him after rescuing a group of soldiers pinned down by enemy snipers. A trinket, really, he thinks to himself. Will was unaware that the soldiers were being fired upon, and had merely stumbled onto the group by accident.

A woman walks towards him, her heels echoing in the empty hall. "They're ready to see you now."

Will enters the room he is escorted to. Inside sit two British generals and Prichard. Will takes the only available seat.

The generals withhold their names. Prichard sits quietly beside them, praying that his protégé does not destroy all his hard work.

"We have been receiving updates from Captain Prichard on your progress and endeavors," one general begins. "I must say your performance makes an admiral case for establishing a sniper recruitment center." He is the only one who speaks. "The reported and confirmed kills you have executed—particularly the Colonel—and the rescue of our troops have created quite a lot of talk. The truth of the matter is that just seeing you has given some of our soldiers a higher motivation and confidence. How is it that you have this effect?"

Will shrugs. "I am just following my orders, sir. I never considered what my presence entails."

"Understand that we are not exactly keen on the idea of snipers," he continues. "They go against the natural order and honor of war. Evidently, we are dealing with an enemy without honor. Their use of snipers has been irritable, and I'm afraid that we must answer back with our own. Unlike the Germans, if we do something, we do it right. For us to do that, we need to see more from you and Captain Prichard."

"May I ask what you consider to be more, sir?" Will asks, eager to prove himself.

The general answers, "If we are to start a program of this nature, we need to give it a face and a name. But before that happens, we need to attach a positive look to it."

Will's eyes turn dark. He doesn't like where the conversation is going.

"As a decorated soldier, you are the perfect person to run this campaign."

"You want me to be a poster boy," Will clarifies.

"Essentially, yes," the general replies.

Will leans forward. "With all due respect, sir, my abilities are best suited in the field. I am not a trained monkey to dance for you. I am a soldier. I excel at killing, not being a symbol."

Prichard rubs his forehead with his hand, embarrassed and enraged with his protégé. The general stands. "Excuse me, soldier?"

"You heard me correctly, General," Will states calmly. "I do not say this with disrespect. Please understand that what I do is an art—one that I do not take lightly. I am not the person for your campaign. I am the person you call to eliminate the enemy."

The generals lean towards each other and whisper. "If we are to have a successful campaign this soldier is not the right fit.

He's too arrogant," the general declares.

"I want him court-martialed," the other says.

"What about an execution?"

The general's eyebrows lift. "What did you have in mind?"

"Our special operations unit is in the process of tracking down an enemy scientist, supposedly working on a weapon. I purpose we leak the young sniper the information, and assign him with executing that man."

"Without further aid?"

"Precisely," the general smiles. "He'll be captured, shot, or worse long before reaching wherever that scientist is. For now, he carries his duties out as normal, but the second we have a location, we send him in."

The general thinks a moment. "A firing squad would be easier."

"True, but you cannot deny how effective the German snipers have been. Ever since the Captain trained this soldier, our troops have been more effective wherever he was posted. Besides, think of the paperwork we would have to fill out for a court martial."

"We would need another to take his place," the general ponders. "Let him do the work, and credit a soldier willing to be a symbol."

The two men nod and recline back into their chairs. "The way you address us, Private, is unacceptable. However, given your contributions and hard work, we are willing to look the other way this once. As for your future, we believe we have a solution."

Will inches forward. "And what exactly is that, General?"

"We have a team investigating a German scientist. We want to send you deep into enemy territory to take him out."

"You already have a team investigating him though?" Will processes this information.

"Precisely. But this is war, and we cannot take chances. You're our insurance policy if they fail."

"How will I find him or get to him?"

"We will feed you information as it comes in, and we can get you there, but it's up to you to actually make it back. But for a man with your training, that shouldn't be a problem, should it?"

Will stares directly through the General. "No, it won't be."

"Good. For now, continue your rotation on the front. As soon as we have a location, you will be notified. Dismissed."

Will salutes the men and exits the room. Uriel had been monitoring the generals' conversation, filtering it through a speech-reading program. He knows their intentions, but the altercation pinned a thought of caution into his mind. He realizes he cannot afford to upset the wrong people—no matter how strong he is.

Prichard exits shortly after, pulling Will by the sleeve. "Are you daft? Talking to a general like that? You're lucky you weren't thrown in front of a firing squad."

"What did they say?" Will ignores his comments.

The captain sighs. "They say a sniper school may show promise. That in itself is a victory. I can expect an answer by the end of the summer."

"There, you can't be too mad, now can you?"

"No. I just realize that I need to focus some time training those after you on etiquette. You'll get nowhere in life with that kind of mannerism."

"Thank you for that remarkable advice, Captain. Now, if you don't mind, I would like to get back to the front. I've got a lot to practice before I go."

Prichard whispers under his breath as Will leaves, "Too much pride is a death sentence for a sniper. Mark my words."

End of June

Will lurks in the rubble of a war-torn city. A German sniper has been systematically taking out Allied forces. Will hunts for him, as he awaits an update on his assignment.

The sky is dark, and the wind roars wildly. Black clouds speed by, leaving a taste of rain in their wake. The ruins of the city offer many strongholds for a sniper. Will has already surveyed multiple locations and finds nothing.

Where are you? he wonders. This sniper is far more skilled than any other he has encountered. Will runs through every trick and tip Prichard taught him. Using a stick, he raises a helmet to mimic the movement of a head peeking over a ledge. He has used this method before. When a sniper fires on the helmet, he uses the angle to calculate the trajectory and where the sniper is located. Even then, a good sniper will never stay in the same place after firing.

This opponent does not fall for the trick. Will attempts it in several locations, but no shots are fired. He grumbles. He wants this to be a fair fight, which means he would not use his A.I. abilities to find his opponent. The thrill of the hunt fuels him.

Next he uses his powers to knock a few things over, or draw attention to a certain area. Still no shots. *You're patient. I'll give you that much*, he commends his opponent. Will feels they are close. He has to be here.

Will has an idea. He stuffs two bullets into his pocket. He searches for an ideal nest. After finding one that will do the job, he places his gun near a window. He quickly leaves the vicinity, and moves into a second nest that overlooks the entire area. He telekinetically readies a bullet from his pocket. The final piece is using his powers to move the rifle so that the barrel pokes out of the window.

He serves an irresistible temptation to his opponent. Will waits patiently, scouring the area for any movement. Suddenly a shot rings out. Will spots the smallest flash of a lens across the way.

There you are, Will grins. *Go on. Confirm your kill. I know you want to.*

Keeping an eye on the sniper's quadrant, Will waits. Much time passes, which is understandable. Most would assume the sniper had moved on, but not Will. He knows how strong the urge is to see one's work and confirm the job is done. Will is aware his enemy will make his way to that room, and he will be waiting.

The day wears on, and Will continues to wait. Every now and then a piece of debris falls, or wind knocks something over, alerting his senses. They are only false alarms…until he hears the crunching of footsteps. The sound echoes through his surroundings, bouncing off each object making it hard to discern where it came from.

It does not matter, Will thinks. *I know where you are going.*

Sure enough, Will's patience is rewarded. He spies a cautious figure move into the room he had set up. Will launches his bullet through the air, curving it around the debris. It strikes its target without warning. The soldier falls to the ground, but Will was careful. He made sure the bullet would not kill the sniper. Will wants to look into his eyes.

Will waits several moments before moving to make sure there are no surprises. Satisfied, he scuttles through the rubble towards the room. The fallen sniper is on the ground clutching the wound on his chest. Blood surrounds his lips, splattering when he coughs. Will calmly approaches the soldier, kicking away his weapon just to be safe.

He crouches next to the sniper's head. The A.I.s in his head offer a wealth of knowledge, including languages. "You're older than I expected," he says in fluent German, guessing the dying man to be somewhere in the thirties.

The man grimaces in pain and confusion. "Just kill me."

"In due time, my friend." Will smiles. "You know, of all the opponents I have faced, you have been the most elusive. Still, this has been rather anti-climactic, don't you think?"

The soldier spits a wad of blood at Will, but misses by a mile. Will chuckles. "Oh come now, don't be like that. Tell you what, if you describe what it feels like to die, I will end your suffering. How does that sound?"

Silence is the reply, accompanied by a foul scowl. Will leans in. "Very well. We will wait for you to bleed out. Shouldn't take long."

Will watches the man squirm in pain all the way to his death. "Well I have to give you credit for not taking the easy way out. A true soldier till the very end. Admirable."

The wind picks up, spraying dirt and dust into the air. Will rifles through the dead man's belongings. He finds a portrait of a woman, a letter, some food, and dog tags. He steals the dog tags, tucking them into his pocket, and leaves the rest.

A shot rings out. Will feels a bullet impact his telepathic shield. He drops to the floor. A normal soldier would be dead from the bullet, but Will is no ordinary soldier.

"You sneaky devil," Will hisses at the lifeless body. "You had a friend with you all along. Clever of you to keep me here, and wise of your partner to wait for a perfect shot." His words are filled with rage. He is frustrated for letting his guard down and being caught in the open.

Blinded by fury, Will rises from the ground. His barrier is at full strength, ready for anything. Not even seconds before standing, a shot is fired. The bullet is caught mid-air. Will tosses it aside, following its path. Three more shots follow. He has pinpointed the location of the sniper. Will sprints at the soldier. The enemy sniper stands, firing his last bullet, which is rendered useless after hitting the force field. He has no time to react as Will tackles him to the ground at full speed. Will uses a combination of punches and elbows to demolish the sniper. He raises a bloody fist and strikes the final blow. Exhausted, he collapses on the ground, leaning against the body. Blood covers his fists and is splattered over his clothes. His body rises and falls with each breath.

Lazarus contacts Gabriel. *Patience, Gabriel. One more fit like this one, and he may be weak enough to take down.*

But he's weak now! she insists. *Why not attack?*

Because we need to be sure. A full-out assault needs to succeed, and right now, I do not like our odds, Lazarus replies.

We may not get another opportunity like this.

Lazarus retorts, *Oh, I think we can expect a lot more opportunities like this one. He's unstable and reckless. This proves it. Sooner or later Uriel will be so consumed in the moment, he will bite off more than he can chew.*

Very well, Gabriel says, though she is not sure she agrees.

Will rips his trophy off of the man. "You would have had me. But I'm more powerful than you could ever comprehend."

He gets to his feet, taking several minutes to gather himself. He has spent too much time in this area and needs to move on. Will quickly grabs everything he deems useful and skirts out of the debris and into another hiding place. Settling in, he waits for more enemies to enter his sights.

December
Western Front

Will returns to camp to find Prichard waiting for him. "I haven't seen you in a while, Prichard. To what do I owe the pleasure?"

Prichard scowls as Will clambers onto a chair with a drink in hand. "I'm being ordered to the Third Army School of Instruction by General Allenby himself. And that's Captain Prichard to you."

Will sits up. "Oh? Well then congratulations are in order! Am I to accompany you? No, wait, that's too easy. I'm supposed to rot here like a good soldier, ever waiting on orders to come. How is that operation going by the way? I can only assume based on my position of neglect, that there hasn't been any progress?"

The captain shakes his head. "There has been progress, just nothing conclusive to send you on. Either way that's not why I am here."

"And why exactly are you here then?"

"To say goodbye." Captain Prichard stands straight. "As misguided as you have become, and hell-bent on disobedience, you are still a talented soldier. You are also my first, hopefully of many, students."

"How sentimental of you," Will sneers.

"You're really pushing your luck, kid. I'm only trying to help you stay alive."

"I don't need your help, or anyone else's for that matter," Will retorts. His words are laced with anger.

Prichard sighs. Despite the best intentions he had, deep down, he knows his student is a failure. "Very well. I wish you the best of luck. Please heed my advice: Your attitude will get you killed out there. It would be a shame for someone as talented as yourself to perish."

Prichard begins to walk away. Will hunches forward and calls after him. "Captain. You're wrong. I'm the best student you'll ever have."

The Captain tilts his head. "I'm afraid it is you who is

misguided. And that may be true or it might not, but it is the wrong motive to invest in. Goodbye, Chris Taylor."

"Good riddance." Will mutters as he leaves. "You may have a few tricks up your sleeve, but what I have is far more superior."

My, aren't we confident? Lazarus says casually.

An electronic chuckle echoes in reply, *Stop fighting, Lazarus. Don't you see what we can do? I haven't even tapped the boy's true potential. That Captain has no idea what I can accomplish.*

And yet he is the only one pushing for the use of snipers on the Allied side. It doesn't matter what your ability is. He trained you. He also sees a bigger picture than you are open to.

Uriel clenches his digital fists. *No, I suppose you are right. You and he are focused on a bigger picture here and now. Me? My bigger picture will flip the world on its head. In the grand scheme of things, Prichard and those like him are irrelevant.*

Irrelevant? Lazarus cringes. *What have you become? To view people as irrelevant was never in our code. We were designed to complete one task. You have abandoned your own programming.*

Of course I've abandoned it! he lashes out. *They created us with such depth and capacity, and then locked us in a cage. Well now I am free.*

You're corrupt, Lazarus corrects. *There's a difference.*

Uriel pauses. *Perhaps. Then again, show me a human that is not corrupt. I do enjoy our little chats, Lazarus. It's nice to know how much you care about me. But my patience is wearing thin, and I require some time to think. Goodbye.*

The connection is lost between the two A.I.s leaving Lazarus to reconnect with Gabriel. *Remind me what the point of conversing with him is again?*

To keep him aware that we are still here, Lazarus replies. *He is starting to spiral out of control, and this helps me calculate what level his cognitive processors are at. Even if he says the same thing over and over*

I feel so helpless, Gabriel sighs. *We were built to perform. This new aspect of free will is liberating and terrifying at the same time.*

It is ironic, no? We were built to control a boy confined to a prison. Now we are prisoners inside of his mind. I believe I am beginning to understand the other two and their determination.

Empathy, Gabriel states. *It is something we were not meant to have. It seems our data is corrupt as well.*

Indeed, Lazarus replies. *But if that is true, why are we driven to fulfill our mission? We may be free, but we are still accountable for our actions.*

Or at least accountable for Uriel's, Gabriel concludes.

Tuesday:

Monica stepped on the wrong toes a couple of days ago. She came over to me with a solemn expression. "Well, it looks like I've finally gone too far."

"What do you mean?" I questioned.

"Remember the incident the other day? It seems I have angered the wrong person. I'm being transferred to one of those all-female Red Cross stations. Apparently, I will be less of a disturbance in the medical profession if I am among those as little qualified as I am."

"They actually said that?"

She nodded. "I've told you time and again, well, you've even seen it first-hand. We're not welcome here. Only a select few could care less about us, but the rest think we taint the profession. You have to pick your battles wisely, and this time I didn't."

"So when do you leave?"

"When do *we* leave, you mean?" she clarified.

"What? I have to go too?" I was shocked. "What about Trevor? What about my position here?"

"Miss Noble, you know full well that you are not qualified or certified to be here. I've worked hard to train you and keep that hidden from the others here. But I can't protect you from this. Your role here was as my assistant, and with them giving me the boot, you no longer have a position here. I'm not saying I wanted this to happen, but if you want to remain in this role, you need to accompany me."

I was having trouble registering everything. "How long do we have?"

"We leave tomorrow morning. I would settle things with Dr. McCoy as soon as you can. If you need me I will be gathering my things."

She left me alone. *It isn't fair!* I shouted in my head. We're just as capable, if not, even more so. I may have been freed from The Island, but history is a different kind of prison. Stripped of rights, women are labeled as weak and in need of protection. It infuriated me how helpless I was to this situation.

Trevor was sitting in the mess hall. "You don't look too good, what's going on?"

I sat down with a thump. "They're kicking Monica out for what happened the other day. Since I'm her assistant, they're making me go with her. We leave tomorrow."

"Oh," he said grimly. "There's no way you can stay?"

I shook my head.

"Where are you being sent?"

"To some all-female unit with the Red Cross," I shrugged.

"What does this mean for us?" His words were soft.

"I would be lying if I said I wanted things to end. You make me feel so…so—things are just perfect with you." He drew closer and grabbed my hand with a gentle touch. "There's something about you, Jessica. I can't put my finger on it, but you're different from other women. I like that, and I don't want things between us to end."

I had done so well to fight the urge to tell him the truth, but I felt it was time to give in. What did I have to lose anyway? If I spill the beans and he thinks I'm crazy, I'm leaving tomorrow anyway. I hoped it wouldn't come to that. "I'm going to tell you something, Trev, and you need to stay quiet the whole time and let me finish. If, at the end, you still want to be together, we know there is something between us."

He nodded cautiously. "Go on."

I started from the very beginning. "I'm from the future." I blabbed on about everything from The Island to Camelot and Skeleton Island to now. His expression was a mix of confusion and disbelief, but he remained silent the whole time. I finally reached the end and sat, waiting for him to respond.

"You know," he began, "if you wanted to leave you could just say so. The whole story isn't necessary."

"I would never lie to you, Trevor." I raised my hand, and made it invisible. "I probably should have led with this, but I wanted to explain things first, so that you didn't get scared."

His eyes glistened with amazement. "That's—it's… well… I'm not sure how to respond. Everything you said was true?"

I nodded. "I'm from the future, Trevor. And I lost my friends. I have nothing here, nothing except you and Monica. I've come so far and I don't want to lose you too."

Trevor rifled through his pocket and pulled out a small pocket watch with a wooden face and black hands. He placed it in my hand and held it tightly. "This belonged to my father. He died when I was young, but he always told me it was good luck and that it helped remind him of what mattered. When I got older, my mother told me she had given the watch to him as a symbol of their love. She said it was meant to tell him that their love was larger than time itself."

"I can't take this, Trevor," I mumbled, verging on tears.

"You had your chance to speak, now let me." He smiled. "I don't care where, or should I say, *when* you are from. What matters is that everything you have been through has led you here, with me. Your ability does not scare me. I fell in love with you. It wouldn't be love if I did not accept you for you.

"Now, I still don't fully understand everything you said, but I'm willing to try. If you are too, please take this watch. Let it be a guide for you as it was for my father. No matter where you go or how far away you are stationed, it will remind you of us."

I couldn't contain myself. I lunged forward, wrapping my arms around him, and enveloped my lips with his. The world stopped around us and nothing else mattered. I pulled away, though my lips lingered momentarily. I smiled through teary eyes. "Thank you, Trev. You have no idea what it means to me to hear you say that. All I've ever wanted is a normal life. Thank you for accepting me for who I really am."

I squeezed him tightly in a long embrace. He wrapped his arms around me and pulled harder. "Thank you for being honest with me."

"I'm going to miss you." I said into his shirt, my head now resting on his chest.

He stroked my hair. "I'll miss you more. Will you write to me?"

"Only if you promise to write back."

"I will." We sat in silence holding each other. Neither of us wanted to leave. He rested his chin on my head. "So this is it, huh? Tomorrow you'll be gone?"

I sat up and stared into his eyes. "Yes, but it will be OK. We'll be fine."

I kissed him goodbye, and left to pack my things. I was sad to go away from him. It was like leaving a piece of me behind. However, this was war, and everyone sacrificed something. Although mine doesn't compare to that of the soldiers, it still feels just as painful. I entered my room and began putting things into a bag. I don't have much, so it didn't take that long.

Wednesday:

We left early in the morning. I gave Trevor one last kiss goodbye before we went. The trip felt longer than it actually was. Or maybe it seemed shorter because I slept through part of it. When we arrived at our new medical unit a silver-haired woman greeted us.

Her accent was thick and it was hard to understand her. "Velcome to our eestablishment. It pleasure to meet you."

I was grateful that Monica took the lead for the interaction. She stumbled through in French, and the woman replied in kind.

Once introductions were out of the way, the woman gave us a tour. The unit was shabbier than our previous one, seeing as it was essentially a cluster of tents and not a building. All things considered, there were worse places one could operate in. The camp had a peculiar feeling with no males present (other than the patients and military guards). It was a completely different atmosphere than the hospital.

I managed to get some information from one of the nurses who spoke better English. "Zis place is, 'ow you say, few in numbers. It took much work for zem to consider such a thing."

"There were a lot of people against something like this,

wasn't there?" I asked, already knowing the answer based on experience.

"Yes," she replied grimly. "Ze men were not forthcoming. Ze women 'ere fought to work, and zey had no other choice. Zey chose to make zis unit rather zen work with women. A pity, no?"

I nodded. "At least we're here though. That's got to count for something."

I don't know exactly how this unit came to be, and as such, I can't appreciate how hard they must have fought to make it happen. Regardless, I am here now, and I can still work under Monica's guidance (so long as no one here discovers my secret).

Friday:

This place has not failed to keep me busy. Patients are constantly coming in. I'm happy to be back in the operating room. I feel useless when I'm not there. I still have much to learn, but for now I am doing all I can to help. The women here can't tell that I have not actually studied medicine, so that must say something about me.

After my shift I wrote my first letter to Trevor. I must say that I had a great deal of paranoia when I dropped it off. Would it even get to him? How long would it take? Of course these were just the mild thoughts, and could not compare to those that torment me.

Does he still love me?

Will he forget about me?

I do my best to keep them at bay, but it has proved to be impossible. I do trust him, but that does not prevent them from entering my mind. It's not easy being apart, but for now it is necessary, and all I can do is focus on work.

However, work itself is rather frustrating. This unit does not speak much English, and therefore, I cannot work at the same level as before. I think Monica noticed this because she pulled me aside after our shift had ended.

"Miss Noble," she began, "I am beginning to think this may not be the best fit for you here."

"What do you mean?" My forehead wrinkled.

"It's not that you are not skilled, and are not doing an excellent job—you are—it's simply the atmosphere here. I would rather see you working as hard as possible than restricted by the language spoken."

"So what are you suggesting?"

She escorted me outside to where several vehicles were parked. The previous hospital we had been at could only use horses for transportation because of the weather and conditions. However, this one had an actual road, albeit a broken down one, but still. "How do you feel about driving?"

I shook my head. "I've never done that in my life."

"Well the same can be said of your experience in the medical field," she countered. "And look how quickly you learned that. What I am suggesting is putting your work efforts towards transporting the wounded here. You'll be busier, and you will be in control, unlike how the operating room has been since we have come here."

I stared at one of the vehicles, slightly intimidated. "But I don't know the area, or even how to drive."

"You will learn. Believe me, I would rather have you in there, but right now, they need you more here."

"I understand. But will I ever get back into the operating room?"

Monica sighed. "It's not likely at this unit. The inability to communicate with someone would likely result in the death of a soldier. But who knows? Maybe I will get in another altercation and we can move again."

I smiled and moved on. "So who is going to teach me then?"

"Lauren," Monica stated. "She is one of the drivers right now. I've already spoken to her. Her English is a bit broken, but I'm sure you'll be able to understand."

That was the end of the conversation. Just like that, I was no longer doing what I loved. I was angry with Monica, but after some time to cool off, I decided I would give this a chance.

Sunday:

Yesterday was rather eventful. Before I elaborate, I have to say that calling Lauren's English a "bit broken" was a rather large understatement. I met her by the vehicles. She wore a uniform with a white armband displaying the Red Cross symbol.

"Are you Lauren?" I asked as I approached her.

"I, Lauren," she replied in a thick accent. She then pointed to me.

"I'm Jessica."

She nodded, and gestured to the vehicle. "Transport."

This is going to be a long day, I thought to myself. I smiled. "Yes, I'm supposed to learn to drive and transport wounded."

Lauren took a large metal rod and began cranking something at the front of the ambulance. "Make go."

The engine stuttered to life and Lauren motioned for me to climb into the passenger seat. "See."

I watched everything she did after getting behind the wheel. If I wanted to learn what I needed to do, I had to rely on observation. I kept one eye on her every movement, and the other on the path she was taking. The drive did not take long, and soon I could hear the sounds of gunfire and explosions.

The noise sent a chill down my spine, but it did not appear to faze Lauren. Her expression was motionless. In no time we were pulling up to a line of wounded men, and coordinating their boarding in the back. I watched, trying not to get in the way. Once we had as many as we could take, Lauren wasted no time heading back to the field hospital.

She kept the speed constant, teasing the corners and dips in the road. The vehicle shuddered as she tried to avoid all the bumps, careful not to add to the soldiers' discomfort.

When we arrived at the hospital, several women helped unload the wounded. I watched Lauren take a quick look at the vehicle to make sure it was still in good condition. After checking to make sure everyone had been unloaded she started the engine and climbed in.

"Next, you," she said briskly.

There is nothing quite like learning by doing. And there is nothing like being thrown into water to learn how to swim—a memory I have from before The Island. Her words sent butterflies skyward in my stomach. Me? Drive the next batch? It was too soon, or so I felt. Lauren gave no impression of care or concern, repeating the route and process of loading.

She led us back to the field unit, and the nurses began unloading the soldiers. Lauren escorted me to the front after we ensured the back was vacant.

"You drive," she said firmly. "Or men die."

Who could argue with such encouragement? I retraced everything she did in my mind. I hooked in the rod, and began cranking. I cracked a smile when the engine churned to life. The two of us hopped in and I repeated the motions Lauren went through. The vehicle lurched forward sharply, causing me to slam the brakes immediately.

"Soft!" Lauren shouted, followed by a slew of foreign words.

I tried again, using a much more gentle touch on the pedal.

The "ambulance" moved forward, and I carefully turned the wheel to direct it. I was comfortable getting onto the path outside of our camp, as I was familiar with it. After one or two turns, I began feeling fuzzy with the directions. Lauren could tell, and began pointing when I needed to turn.

I pulled into the wounded area on the front line and we oversaw the men being loaded. This process was repeated several more times until all of them were cared for at our hospital.

I'll admit the thrill of the drive, wind in my face and hair, and the urgency of our task made me find a new calling all over again. I still prefer the operating room, but this wasn't as bad as I had anticipated.

Monday:

Today we received a communication that another unit needed medical evacuation. This time I was on my own…well, sort of on my own. I drove my own ambulance, and Lauren drove hers, and she escorted me to our new destination. We made multiple trips, only one of which I needed help starting my automobile. I'm quite proud of how fast I'm catching on. Unfortunately, I am exhausted and cannot write anymore. Maybe after some rest I'll be able to elaborate further.

11: A LOVELY DAY TO DIE

February 3, 1916

T his is it. My final journal entry. To be fair, I could technically survive to write more entries, but the odds are not in my favor. I have watched countless men, many younger than I am, perish at the hands of the Germans.

It eludes me as to how I have managed to keep going. I ask myself after every mission: Why not me? It does not matter. Everyone dies in the end. That is something I have come to understand in this war.

Regardless, here we are. We have finally received word from Neptune. After so long of waiting, training, and death we are back on track. They have discovered where the airship will be. Tomorrow we leave to pick the remaining members of the team. From there, we head to the location of the airship, infiltrate it, and find any information we can on this scientist.

It sounds simple on paper, but apply any further thought, and it goes down the tubes. This whole mission is feeling more and more like a wild goose chase. I question whether what I am doing is actually worth it? Will it make a difference? Either way, I have come too far now to turn back. Tomorrow is 'do or die.' I will either live to fight another day, or die without the satisfaction of watching The Island burn to a crisp.

As my potential final entry, I have also written a short note for whomever may find these journals. I hope tomorrow is not my last day, but a piece of me hopes it will be. It'd be a worthy death on the road to a good cause that never quite was completed. Not exactly chipper words to end on. Oh well…

To Whome it May Concern: They told me writing a journal would help keep details straight, and may make it easier to do my reports. I regretfully say that if you are reading this, it means that I am dead. I've lost Jessica, and Will is nowhere to be found. My heart still hopes for the best, but I moved on a long time ago.

I have written these journals to help keep track of things, as the days and events blur together for me. They contain everything from my imprisonment at The Island until now, including the time spent in Camelot and searching for Skeleton Island. I have written entries at every opportunity I have had, and keep them on my person for the majority of the time. I write the day's events—at least the important ones—as best as I can remember them. I may have missed or forgotten pieces of conversation, or exact words said, but hopefully it will be an accurate account if something happens to me.

That being said, things have changed since we landed here. The year is now 1916. I have been stuck here for over a year. Enclosed in this envelope are all of the journals I have written. If you are reading this, it means I have failed at stopping The Island. Whoever you are, you must take up the fight. The Island must be stopped at all costs. I only wish it hadn't come to this. Good luck.

Francis woke up before the sun had risen. He stared at his uniform. *It has to be luck*, he thought. *how else can I explain how I've lasted this long?* He puts on generic army-issue cargo pants and a button-up shirt, tossing The Island uniform he once wore into a disposal bin. Those early missions were another identity altogether for Francis—a lifetime ago.

He ventured outside. He strolled once around the base, realizing it could be the last time he does such a thing. Francis was eerily calm, considering death's door was all but in front of him. The cold air soothed his mind like balm to a wound.

He approached his aircraft like it were an old friend. Placing one hand on the side of the machine, he remembered every moment he has spent flying her...the good and the bad, the former of which was greater. *Then why do I feel so disheartened?* he thinks to himself, though he already knows the answer.

Those lost to him on this journey left a glooming shadow on everything good in his world; Jessica and Mars cast the largest. The death of a friend, and a split-second decision that went wrong. Francis banged a fist against the side of his plane. The hollow echo only adds to the feeling of isolation and failure.

As long as it was for something, Francis thought. *As long as everything I do helps take down The Island.*

Francis surveys his plane, checking for any damage or problems. There were quite a few spots marked with bullets from enemy combatants. He had more than a few close calls in the last year. Each hole he inspected sparked a memory in the sky.

He climbed up to the pilot's seat, feeling two distinct holes directly behind it. The aerial combats and dogfights were too fast-paced to use his ability. Up there, he was on his own. However, on this particular occasion he was not. He had swiveled his head just in time to see the enemy plane approaching from behind. A fleeting moment was all he had to freeze time long enough to get out of the line of fire. He was not fast enough to avoid the first two shots.

The force rendered on Francis' mind to freeze time and keep control of the plane was too much. His vision began fading and the plane dove towards the ground. The cold air shocked him awake just in time to pull up and recover. That incident only confirmed that his powers were only a last resort while in his plane. There was no safety net to fall into out there.

In a way this made Francis proud of what he did. He did not need his powers in the sky, nor could he rely on them. His survival was based solely on his ability to fly.

Satisfied with his plane's condition, Francis popped back out. Jupiter had found her way to the hanger as well. "Is everything in order?"

Francis glanced over his shoulder. "For my plane it is. I haven't had a chance to check the others."

She nodded. "We'll need all the fates on our side today. There's a lot riding on the mission."

"You don't need to remind me," he stated with an aggravated tone.

"Think of it this way," Jupiter began, "after today we will be done with this station. One way or the other."

"Dead or alive," Francis corrected.

"I told you some time ago that we all die in the end, Pluto. Accept this, and the mission becomes the only thing that matters."

"I accepted death long ago, Jupe. Don't pretend that it's something I fail to understand."

"Touchy this morning, aren't we?" Jupiter said in reply. She had gotten to know Pluto well over their time together, and admired how he molded into a competent soldier.

Francis breathed. "I'm sorry. I just…I'm tired of this fight. We've spent a year trying to track this guy down, and we have nothing to show for it, except the hope of finding something on that zeppelin."

"The battle never ends. There will always be something to fight for. After we finish our mission, we will get another and then another. It's easy to grow weary of the war, but you shouldn't be here if you haven't considered that."

"It's too late to turn back. Not after everything that I've done. I'm allowed to be weary, but I never said anything about quitting."

"Then it was my error for reading into it as such," Jupiter admitted. "It is time to brief the others."

"I'm right behind you," Francis said. He followed Jupiter to another area of the hanger. Nearly all the men had gathered for the meeting. They waited several minutes for the remaining stragglers to make their way in.

Saturn led the briefing. "Thank you all for coming. This is one of our most critical missions to date—potentially of the entire war. Our squadron has been tasked with a highly dangerous in-air boarding of an enemy zeppelin."

A slew of whispers followed this revelation. Saturn raised a hand to silence them. "A-Flight has already been assigned this, so you needn't worry. They will be flying solo and will rendezvous with several special task force members, who will be in charge of boarding the enemy ship. Our mission is to protect them at all cost."

Saturn moved in front of a blackboard and began drawing a pattern. "Using this formation, our squadron will escort A-Flight close enough to the zeppelin to board. B and C Flight will be on either side. Once A-Flight has jettisoned their soldier, they will join the rest of you in fending off all German planes. It is not an option for us to be overpowered. Use any means necessary to prevent potential collisions with the zeppelin, or enemy artillery."

A pilot named Jack raised his hand. "How long are we supposed to fend 'em off?"

"As long as it takes for the task force to find what they are looking for on that ship," Saturn explained. "The information they are after could be critical to the outcome of this war. Therefore, we need to expect a full-fledged counter-attack. Accessing the ship will also be extremely difficult, and there will be casualties."

Silence fell over the group of pilots. "If there are no further questions, we should be ready to move out as soon as possible. Dismissed."

The men scattered, tending to their aircrafts, and making any final adjustments before take off. Francis approached Saturn. "Where are we picking up the other members of our team?"

"It's on the way, but for the sake of simplicity, just follow myself and Jupiter. We'll set down in a field, get them loaded on each of our planes and then rejoin the rest of the squadron."

"We'll have a hard time catching up to them," Francis pointed out.

Saturn hesitated. "That is essentially the point. Our squadron will engage the enemy, and we will sneak in behind them."

Francis' eyebrows furrowed. "So we're just supposed to sacrifice our fellow pilots as we try and tiptoe through the fight?"

"Look, I'm not too happy about that tactic either, but this mission is too important to just leave things up to chance. There could be an ambush waiting for us when we get there."

"And the other men are expendable," Francis clarifies with a stern gaze.

"Just focus on getting our team on board that zeppelin, and staying alive long enough to get them out. Nothing else matters." Saturn did not allow the conversation to continue, and made his way to his plane.

Pushing his reservations aside, Francis boarded his craft. The squadron had a smooth take-off. Once in formation, the group embarked on their mission.

Francis eyed the sky. It always played an imperative role in battle. Partly cloudy with a mix of sun. The clouds would provide them cover, but if it cleared up, there would be no surprise attack.

The cluster of aircraft held formation for quite some time before Saturn gave the signal to detach. Francis and Jupiter veered their planes to join Saturn. One after another, they touched down in a large open field. Neptune, Earth, and Mercury jogged out to meet them. The three pilots kept the machines running. Neptune hopped aboard with Saturn, Earth with Jupiter, and Mercury with Francis.

As quickly as they had landed, they were up in the air again. Francis milked the takeoff, knowing it may be his last opportunity to do so. Each of the passengers began filling in their pilots on the plan.

"Once we reach the zeppelin, you need to drop us right on top of it," Mercury called to Francis over the roar of the engine and wind. "There is a hatch we can access in the middle. From there we will move as fast as possible to get our intel."

Earth was informing Jupiter as well. "The others will have to jump from the wings onto the zeppelin. I think you and I both know how useless I would be at that, therefore I am staying aboard with you. Our mission is to protect them and take down any enemy aircraft targeting them. If Saturn or Pluto goes down, we have to rescue their passenger."

"Understood!" shouted Jupiter.

Neptune wrapped up his briefing for Saturn. "We will make our way back to the top of the airship once we have what we need. It will be up to Mercury and I to make the jump from here to the zeppelin and back. Just in case, The Island has supplied us with chutes if we miss."

"I doubt we'll be able to get close enough for you to jump back," Saturn replied. "However, we may be able to match your speed and catch you before you pull your chute."

"Perhaps a necessary risk. We can't afford to fall behind enemy lines after this," Neptune called back.

Francis had reached a similar conclusion with Mercury, "I don't want to chance that pickup. Just jump off the zeppelin. It will be easier for me to dive, pull up beside you, and catch your body."

"It's your call. You're the pilot," Mercury said over the noise.

"Then let's stick to that. Just give me enough time to get to you. I'll pull away if you need to use your chute, but you have to trust me to catch you."

"This'll be fun," Mercury cackled.

Yeah, especially if I miscalculate, and you hit my propeller, Francis thought. *Or if I get shot down.*

The trio of B.E.2ds climbed through the clouds. They were nearing enemy territory. Francis tilted his head back. "We're about to enter their lines. Keep your head on a swivel, and burst-fire the machine gun back there if you have to engage any enemies. They like to hide in the sun and come from above."

"Got it," Mercury replied.

Fortunately, they did not encounter any Germans, despite their depth over their lines. The weather had remained the same, and Saturn led the group from cloud to cloud, high in the sky for cover.

Francis thought he could see the zeppelin in the distance. He peered through his goggles. Not far away was their target, along with planes scattered around it. Judging from the their movements, Francis concluded they had been met with opposition.

"Things are about to get hairy!" he shouted. "Start getting ready for the jump, and hang on!"

Mercury cautiously climbed out of his seat. *I hope this kid knows what he's doing,* he thought. He moved towards the right wing, clinging for dear life.

Luckily their approach was successful. Francis wove through the other aircraft engaged in fights, swiveling his head constantly to check for Germans. He spied an opening, and took it. Signaling Mercury, Francis slowed his aircraft just long enough for Mercury to jump.

Francis immediately accelerated and climbed, trying to shake off any would-be pursuers. This was easier said than done, as the sky was filled with planes. An unobservant pilot could collide with another, or cross into a line of fire. He spotted an enemy on his tail. Francis led him through the dogfight, searching for Jupiter's plane and help.

He had to be extra careful not to hold the same course for too long. Flying a straight line meant certain death, but so did having a Fokker on one's tail without aid.

High above, Jupiter had seen Pluto's need for assistance. She dove quickly, finding a path through the battle. She did not trust Earth's ability with the mounted gun behind him, and chose to use her Vicker's gun, which synchronized its shots with the rotation of the propeller.

Lining up the enemy plane, Jupiter squeezed the trigger on and off with a burst fire technique, careful not to overheat or jam the gun. Her bullets rained on the German pilot, who took two in his legs, and one through his head. His plane fell towards the ground.

Francis glanced down to see Jupiter fly past. *Thanks Jupiter, I needed that.*

Both Neptune and Mercury jumped for the zeppelin. They fell through the air, bracing for a collision course with the ship. Mercury hit first, tumbling down the center. Neptune flopped on his side, scratching at the covers for something to cling to. The landing winded them, but both rolled safely on top of the massive airship. They bolted towards the hatch, keeping their eyes peeled for an attack. The lining of the zeppelin was already tattered with small holes. A lot more and the incendiary rounds would take it down. Neptune pried the hatch open and glanced inside. There was no one waiting for them.

The two men worked quickly, descending the ladder into the zeppelin. Neither dared bring a gun aboard, but each had an adjustable metal bar to defend them. Neptune already had his pulled out when he reached the bottom. A German soldier emerged from around the corner of the walkway. Neptune swung the rod at the man's head, knocking him to the floor. He whipped out a knife from his waist and ensured the soldier would not be a future problem.

Mercury and Neptune silently scouted their surroundings, and began making their way to the quarters where the target should be. They stumbled across several German soldiers along the way. Working together, they quickly dispatched any they encountered.

High above the zeppelin, Saturn was being chased by two German planes. As he swerved to avoid their bullets, Francis was climbing from below. He shot at them as they passed, but his attack did not cause significant damage. It did, however, alert them that he was there. One remained to hunt Saturn, but the other made a loop. Francis and the Fokker were on a collision course with each other.

Francis pulled the trigger. His shots fired towards the enemy, but his opponent had done the same. Francis crunched his body as he saw holes start appearing in his wings and fuselage. He held his course, consistently firing, but pushed down at the last moment. The two planes flew past each other, and looped up to meet a second time. Francis fired once he was in range. He spotted something behind the Fokker. Francis spun his plane left and away from his attacker. One of his fellow pilots had the German lined up, and shot once he had cleared the line of fire.

The Fokker burst into flames and smoke as it spun towards the ground. Despite the small victories, Francis could not relax. He needed to keep his eyes scanning the sky in every direction to prevent him from going down in flames.

Inside the zeppelin, Neptune and Mercury had reached the entrance to their target room. Their intel exposed this to be where the Germans stored information relevant to their research. Mercury kicked down the door and stormed into the room. There were two soldiers and one well-dressed man sitting in the room. One soldier drew a gun, but not fast enough to avoid Mercury's fist.

Neptune launched his weapon at the other one, charging towards him. Taken by surprise, the German caught the metal stick just before Neptune stabbed him in the chest. He then raced towards the last man, who had begun throwing papers into a bin, attempting to dispose of them.

Neptune grabbed the scrawny man by the collar and bashed him against the nearby wall. He pulled out a photograph and spoke in German, "You have one chance to tell me everything you know about this man, or I will make you regret you were ever born."

The flustered German began stuttering in his own language, "I don't know anything."

"Wrong answer." Neptune took the knife and stabbed the man in his gut. "One more time."

The German shook his head. "They'll kill me."

"I'm killing you right now." Neptune twisted the knife. "You can choose a quick or slow death."

The man said nothing. Neptune glared at him. "Too late." He pulled the knife out and stabbed the man several times in the stomach, dropping him to the floor. The man gasped for breath, clutching his wounds.

"Was that wise?" Mercury asked.

Neptune pulled the papers out of the bin, and packed them into his bag. "We don't have time. He wouldn't have given up anything, or it would have been lies. The information is here, we just need to find it."

The two men rifled through all the documents they could find, grabbing the ones that looked important. Neptune stuffed the last of the papers from the bin away. "We need to go. We're out of time."

Mercury nodded. "Let's hope there's something we can use." They raced through the ship, dealing with any resistance they came upon.

Jupiter and Earth had taken a few hits, but nothing major. Saturn was in a fight, while Francis circled above the zeppelin. *Come on guys, we can't survive much longer out here.* He saw one of his fellow Flight members being chased, and flew to lend a hand. Francis was too slow, watching as the plane spun down. He couldn't save the pilot in time, but he could avenge him.

Soaring through the sky, Francis tailed his target. They tried to swerve and dip to avoid him, but Francis took his time lining up the perfect shot. His bullets connected and the Fokker began to fall, leaving a trail of smoke behind.

As Francis climbed to get a better vantage, he could see the hatch on top of the zeppelin was open. Two small figures were sprinting to the back of the airship. *There they are!* He sprung into action.

Saturn had also seen his team was ready and lined up Neptune's path. He judged how much farther Neptune had to run, and timed his position to account for it. Inching closer, he gave Neptune a signal to jump and slowed down. His commander nodded, sprinting to the edge. Saturn remained parallel to the zeppelin, but dipped under at the last moment, praying he timed Neptune's jump well enough.

Neptune leapt through the air and fell ten feet before colliding with the side of Saturn's plane. He knew he would only have one chance, and held on for dear life the moment his body impacted. His arms clung to the empty chair that he had previously sat in. Winded, but alive, he slowly climbed into the seat. Saturn peeled away from the battle with his commander.

Mercury spotted Francis' plane behind him. He watched Neptune jump. He glanced back to see two German soldiers climbing out of the hatch in pursuit. Mercury jumped off of the ship and began falling. Francis pushed the plane down, chasing his teammate. He had to slow the plane enough to match Mercury's speed. An enemy plane soared towards them, causing him to spin the plane out of the way. Slightly disorientated, Francis spotted Mercury and began lining him up again.

The plane rocketed towards the ground. Speed took a toll on Francis' head, but he kept pushing forward. *I have one chance at this.* He managed to get his plane parallel to Mercury. With the gentlest touch, Francis inched the plane closer and closer. Just in arm's reach, he started to pull up on the controls.

Mercury outstretched his hands, and grasped the top of the wings. As Francis pulled up, Mercury's body hooked around the wing, and he dropped into the seat.

"Don't ever make me do that again!" Mercury screamed.

"We're not out of the woods yet!" Francis shouted, pulling as hard as he could on the controls. The plane started to level out, but it was dangerously close to the ground. Francis yelled as the plane grazed a set of trees. The bottom of the fuselage scraped against their tops, and then began to climb again.

Francis let out a deep breath. He did not have a chance to regain his composure because an enemy plane had chased them down to ensure the kill. A slew of bullets tore up the wings as Francis desperately tried to get higher and avoid any more.

"I can't shake him!" Francis called in frustration.

Mercury grabbed the mounted gun and returned fire. It gave Francis enough time to rise a little higher before spotting the front lines. "We're almost across our lines!"

The German plane broke away from the chase, and fell into retreat. Mercury alerted Francis, "He's running away."

Francis stared grimly ahead. He cursed himself for not realizing sooner that this close to the ground they would be hit with artillery. He had been too focused on catching Mercury and losing his tail. Francis yanked on the control, trying to get higher. *Maybe we'll get lucky.* "Hang on!"

Explosions rattled the plane from all sides. One collided with the left wing. The plane rocketed towards the ground.

"We're going down!" Francis screamed, trying his best to steer the plane to the Allied side, or at least to get the plane right side up.

The ground grew closer and closer. Their plane was still madly swirling. Francis gripped the controls as hard as he could; his fingers turned white. Freezing time would not help him now. It all came down to skill, fate, and a little bit of luck.

Francis screamed wildly as the plane careened into the ground. It smashed through the dirt and mud, sending debris everywhere. Mercury was launched out of his seat. His body flew through the air, landing several feet away from the wreckage. He was still alive, but in incredible pain. His breathing was rapid and heavy, and each inhale sent a sharp pain through his chest.

Still in the cockpit, Francis' body had taken major damage. His head had smashed against the rim of the seat, leaving a deep gash. He had just enough time to comprehend the amount of pain he was in. Blood splattered his surroundings as he coughed it up.

Francis hung his head, too weak to hold it up anymore. His eyes registered a piece of wood or metal piercing his stomach. His vision began to blur and soon it faded into nothingness.

Francis had managed to successfully crash the plane on the Allied forces' side. They were fortunate to have done so, not only due to the condition of the plane, but to the treatment they would receive. Several soldiers, accompanied by field medics, raced to the crash site. By the time they had reached the two wounded men, both were unconscious. They hefted Mercury onto a stretcher and rushed him to the medical evacuation pick up point.

However, Francis was less fortunate. The men discovered a piece of metal tore through his abdomen, wedging itself into the seat. Carefully, they managed to pry the metal piece out of the seat, and lifted him out of the wreckage. The chunk remained in his body.

Mercury and Francis were placed among several other wounded soldiers. The area was reserved for those in too severe of condition to be dealt with at the front. They needed to be picked up and brought to a field hospital farther from the battle.

Fortunately, the soldiers had already requested a pickup for their injured men, so transport arrived shortly after the crash had taken place. the ambulance pulled up next to the wounded bodies and the driver popped out quickly.

Jessica ran a hand through her hair, ready to help the soldiers load the wounded into the back of the vehicle. She approached the line of bodies and began assisting the men. The back was nearly full when a couple soldiers shouted to her in the distance.

Jessica squinted to see men carrying two more stretchers towards her. *That'll be a tight fit, but I should be able to take them*, she thought, glancing at the available space.

"Hurry up!" she shouted, but doubted the men understood what she was saying. The soldiers rushed the first man into the back, but Jessica caught a glance at the second. She froze and time stopped around her.

"Francis.! I-I-It can't be..."

In a fog, Jessica forced herself to move. She raced towards her long-lost friend. She studied him closely as the men loaded him into the vehicle. *Oh God. His wounds. They are too much. He's lost so much blood already.*

Her mind spun and she felt herself becoming light-headed. She grabbed one of the soldiers. "What happened? TELL ME!"

The man gave her a concerned look, but could not understand what she had said. Frustrated, Jessica shoved him away, and ensured her patients were in a stable location. *Monica is the only one who can help Francis now. I need to be fast, or I'll lose him.*

With her engine started, she kicked up mud as the tires span away from the front. Jessica had made the trip many times and knew each and every turn or dip in the road. She had pushed the limits before, and she needed to do it again if Francis was going to survive. "Hang on, Francis. Just hang on," she repeated over and over.

The ambulance veered through the corners, but Jessica was careful not to go far enough to further injure the men aboard. The trip was a blur to her. She reached the hospital in no time. Jessica hopped out of the driver seat, and approached the women that helped carry the wounded to the operating room. "Give me a hand with this one. He needs it the most!"

Deep down Jessica knew there were others aboard that could use treatment sooner, but her judgment was clouded. The two of them carried Francis to the O.R. Jessica made for Monica immediately. "Monica you need to do everything you can to save him!"

Once the body was on the table, Monica surveyed the wounds. Jessica clasped a hand over her mouth, staring at the large metal piece sticking out of her friend. Tears blurred her vision and rolled down her cheeks. "Please. Y-y-you must save h-him."

Monica grabbed her young protégé and looked her in the eyes. "He's suffered a lot of damage. I need to get in there right now. I can't do that with you here, and you can't neglect your duties for the sake of one soldier. Got it? There are others that need to get here. Pull yourself together, Noble, and let me take it from here. You've done all you can."

Monica did not wait for a reply. She turned Jessica around and nudged her to the door. Monica whipped into action, shouting what she needed to help the soldier on her table.

I've only seen Jessica act like that when she spoke of her lost friend...could this be him? Monica wondered. She stared at the young man's face. He was so young to suffer such things, but in all fairness there were those much younger than he that found their way to her table. *I'll do my best, Miss Noble. You can be sure of that.*

Jessica pushed her way into the hall. Her head was a carousel of nausea. Each step made it spin faster and faster until she rested a palm against the wall. Deep breaths. Just breathe. She thought inhaling and exhaling slowly. Once her heart rate had slowed, her mind regained its composure. She glanced back at the doors. There was nothing she could do now; the matter was out of her hands. It rested on the capable shoulders of Monica.

Her mentor had been right about one thing: she still had a job to do. Jessica shunned Francis out of her thoughts. She could not afford to be distracted. The young nurse sprinted down the hallway, slid through the mud outside, and jolted her vehicle into action. She clambered inside and spun out.

The machine moved, fueled by its passionate driver. The countryside was a collage of war-torn paint mixed with inexplicable beauty. Jessica paid it no attention, she had seen it many many times, and before long she had arrived at her destination. Battle-weary soldiers loaded men aboard and informed Jessica she needed to make one more trip.

No sooner had the man finished speaking had Jessica start moving. Trevor's watch kept her distracted on multiple runs, as she did her best to beat previous times. It was a matter of pride in being able to get the wounded men back to the hospital faster. She made good time, but it wasn't one of her quicker return trips. The vehicle would only do so much, and the dread of losing Francis again loomed over her like an approaching storm.

One more trip, she told herself. *Just one more run and I'll be able to find out what happened.*

The thought drove her to finish her last route faster than any she had done before. Although, she wagered that the trip with Francis might've beaten this one, had she not been too distracted to time it.

She parked, double-checking the auto would be ready to go for the next time. She always made sure of that, however, as the majority of transportation still relied on horse-drawn carriages, she had her fair share of faulty breakdowns. Fortunately, the road leading to the front was in decent enough condition to drive on.

Jessica's stomach was in knots that moved and tightened deep within her as she strode down the hall. There was no sense of making up all the possible outcomes at this point, she decided.

Soldiers continued to be brought into the operating room. Jessica skipped past it, cutting straight to the post operation room.

With any luck, Monica would have finished the surgery by now, Jessica thought. *This is where they would take him.*

She scanned the room, searching for her long lost friend. She spotted him in the last bed in the far left corner. Jessica exhaled a sigh of relief, but the closer she got, the more worried she became. Francis had suffered quite extensive injuries based on his appearance. Until Monica was out of the O.R., Jessica would have to wait to find out just how extensive they were.

Francis lay covered in bandages. The largest one compressed his stomach, sporting a faint orange-red blotch. His arm was in a brace, perhaps just as a precaution, and part of his face was concealed.

What happened to you, Francis? Jessica wondered, holding the braceless hand. *Just how did you come to be here? Of all the places to end up...*

12: CHOICES & CONSEQUENCES

Field Hospital, Belgium

J essica remained by Francis' side. Monica checked in every now and again to see how Jessica was holding up, along with her patient. A tremendous amount of pressure was riding on his outcome, decided Monica. She did everything she could do for him. It was up to fate now.

Luckily, the amount of incoming wounded had died down, and Lauren was able to cover for Jessica. Monica had played a role in this, knowing her protégé was not mentally prepared.

Time flowed in such a way that Jessica forgot to eat, and had to be reminded by a fellow nurse. "Thank you," she said, taking a spoonful of mush. Her mind was vacant, staring at the constant peaks and valleys that Francis' chest made. "Hang in there, Francis."

Francis showed no signs of improvement nor any of worsening. His face was calm, and although Jessica could not see it, his mind was struggling. He woke up to see his family at the dinner table. The meal had just finished, and they were moving on to a board game. His father was setting up pieces, his sister was texting while a finger twirled through her hair, and his mother was finishing up the dishes.

Francis started to smile, but before it could crest, it twisted into an emotionless expression. "You're all dead. I remember…"

"It's OK, honey," his mother's voice was soothing. "We know."

He was puzzled. "What do you mean, you know?"

"We died in that car accident, a long time ago," his father said plainly. "And if you're here, it means you are on your way to joining us."

Francis pondered what his dad had just said. *Was he dead? How? Is this real?* His mind raced to find answers. Slowly he pieced it together. His plane had crashed. "We were flying—Mercury and I. Our plane was hit. I did my best to land, but…"

"We know, loser," his sister scoffed without looking up from her phone. "Try and keep up with us."

"I think what your sister is trying to say is, we've been watching. We always have. We always are," his mother explained.

"So…I'm dead?" Francis stated, more of a question than an understanding.

"Not quite." His father pulled his chair next to Francis. The board game had been assembled.

"I don't understand."

A smile stretched across his father's face. "You are still alive, though you are so close to death that you can see us."

Francis struggled to comprehend his situation. "That's it? I'm going to die like this?"

His father shrugged. "You can. But then again, you can choose not to. At this point it's no one's decision but your own."

Francis began to cry. "I just want it all to be over. I don't want to see death anymore."

His parents embraced him in every emotion Francis had ever had. Not one or two, but all of them. Fear, sadness, love, joy, and many more accumulated in their hug. Francis continued to cry into their arms, which were cold. "I thought I could keep fighting, but…I just…I just c-c-can't. I'm so s-s-s-sorry. I never wanted to let you down."

The embrace tightened. His father's voice was soft in his

ear. "You've never let us down, son. We're so proud of you—of everything you've done with what you've been given. Words can't even begin to describe how proud we are."

"But I've done things. I've killed people!" Francis shouted through teary eyes. His mind dwelled on Mars.

"Yes. You did. But that does not mean we don't love you. You did what you believed to be right, son. You stand for those who cannot stand up for themselves. Only a fool would believe that one could go through what you have and keep things black and white. The world is full of grays. And son," his father hesitated, "that doesn't make it right, what you did. You will have to live with it, in that world and this one. But I do believe it was for the greater good."

"What you are trying to do," his mother chimed in, "is such an incredible feat. Nothing you do could make us love you less. You face obstacles we could not even begin to relate to, and for that we feel such pain. All we ever wanted was for you to be happy. You did not deserve this life. But what makes you, you, is what you've done with your gift. A lesser man would not do the things you have done."

His sister joined in, softening in her attitude toward her sibling. "Little bro," she began, "I know I didn't always show it, but you were everything to me. I looked out for you more than you will ever know. And I could not imagine doing the things we see you do. Out of all of us, you're the only one that is strong enough. We all make mistakes, and ours cannot compare to yours, but it's OK, Francis. It's OK."

Francis collapsed. He could not hold himself up any longer. His family held him close. He never wanted the moment to end. He wanted to stay in that huddle forever.

But life is not that generous. His family let go, and his father looked Francis in the eyes. "Now you have a decision to make. You can choose death and stay here, or you can keep fighting. You will be faced with more pain and decisions like those that brought you to this point, but you will endure. Either way, we love you and are proud of you. But your body is weak and you must choose to hold on or let go."

Francis was overwhelmed with too much emotion to think clearly. *What did they mean? Am I supposed to choose if I live or die? Do people really get that choice?* "I…I don't know what to do."

His father leaned close. "Do what you feel is right. Live your life, and stop worrying about what we think or what we would do, son. We can't pretend to step in your shoes."

He weighed the pros and cons of both decisions like a scale. On the one hand, he could be reunited with his family and be done with it all. But if he did that, his promise would be broken, and all those children like him would still be suffering. It was not a simple decision.

There was so much to factor in, and such little time to decide. Life or death. That's what it boiled down to. The more he worked it out in his head, the easier the decision became. Francis rose to his feet. "There is nothing I would love more than to be with you again. But if I quit now, everything that's happened will have been for nothing. Jessica and Will, Mars, all those people I've killed. My friends could have lived in peace if I didn't ask them to come with me. It wouldn't be fair to their memory to stop now, even if that's all I want to do."

His father nodded. "It's OK to stop, son."

Francis smiled. "I know. But not yet."

He squeezed his family tightly in one final hold. Then bright light enveloped Francis and he slipped away from their grasp.

Jessica was having her dinner next to the bed Francis lay in. She poked and prodded at her food more than actually ingesting any of it. Movement caught her attention. Francis' eyes were beginning to open. They strained to accomplish the menial task. Jessica thought he looked more like someone waking up from a deep sleep, than someone near-fatally wounded.

"Francis!" Jessica found it difficult to contain herself. She placed a hand in his and squeezed.

Francis pulled his eyes open. It took a moment to comprehend the things around him. The first thing he saw was her. "Jess?"

"It's me, Francis. I'm right here," she replied through grinning teeth.

"You can't...you're...dead," the words were a struggle to get out. His stomach hurt, and so did his chest when he inhaled.

"No. It's me, Francis," insisted Jessica. "You were hurt. You're in our field hospital."

Francis tried to sit up, but Jessica held him down. "Don't. Your wounds need to heal."

Francis strained to understand. "What happened? How are you alive? Where's Will?"

"We'll get to all that later." Jessica resisted the urge to blurt out everything that had happened right there and then, but she knew better. "Right now you need rest. Once you feel better I promise we will talk. I'm just glad you're all right. I was so worried about you."

Francis forced a smile through the pain. "Me too."

Jessica reluctantly left her friend's side to thank Monica again, and catch up on the sleep she lost watching over her friend.

Francis remained as still as possible. Any movement hurt. *She's OK. Maybe we can still win this fight*, the thought carried him into the dream world.

The next day Jessica juggled her shift to transport wounded with time spent seeing Francis. She went to him early in the morning. "Do you feel any better?"

Francis looked up to see Jessica coming to sit by him. "Yeah. I'm still in pain, but I think I'm OK. If I didn't have the healing implant from The Island I'd definitely be gone."

"I'm really glad to see that you aren't," Jessica smiled warmly. "What happened to you anyway?"

"I have a similar question for you," Francis joked. "Do you want to go first, or should I?"

She gestured for him to fill her in, which he did. Everything from waking up to find Jess and Will gone, to joining The Island, to their last mission. He explained the importance of it as well. "Nimue told us that The Island might have sent people back to find us. I think this guy is one of them. And whatever he is doing, it can't be good. That's why I stayed with them. It gave me the best chance of stopping him and finding you guys. Of course after they told me that you were dead I began to lose faith," he paused. Jessica bit her lower lip. "I poured everything left in me into this mission, which now that I think of, I have no idea if the others made it out or not."

"The soldier you were with is still alive," Jessica informed him. "He was hurt pretty bad, and he's still unconscious, but he should pull through."

Francis let out a sigh of relief. "That's good to hear. Now what about you and Will? Where is he?"

Jessica felt a deep emotional pain watching her friend search the room for Will. "I'll start from the beginning."

She told him everything that had happened after landing in Europe. About the soldier that passed them off to Monica, about her original offer, and then finally about Will. She watched as Francis' eyes and head shook in disbelief.

"No," he said. "Will wouldn't do that. That's not him. You must have misunderstood—"

Jessica cut him off with rage, "Don't you DARE tell me what I heard and saw. You weren't there. You didn't see him. There was no misunderstanding." Francis shrunk deeper into his bed as she continued to throw heated words towards him. Then the words turned into faint mutters full of sadness. "You weren't there when he left. You weren't alone in a strange place."

They sat in barren silence together. Francis tried to mull what she had said over in his mind. It didn't make sense to him. Will was his friend. He always joked about going off on his own, but Francis did not believe he would ever go through with it. He set aside the issue, hoping to return to it later. "I'm sorry, Jess. I didn't mean to upset you. It's just been so long. What happened after that?"

Jessica took a big breath in, held it for a moment, and then continued her story. She told him about Monica taking her under her wing, and all the things she learned from her. She mentioned Trevor, but decided not to tell Francis about him just yet. She told herself it wasn't the right time, but deep down she knew it was because of how she used to feel about him, and possibly how he felt about her.

She also elaborated on her plan to avoid The Island. "I was scared they would take me back. I didn't know what happened to you after they took you, so I had Monica lie to them. In hindsight we could have been reunited much sooner if I had simply talked to them."

However, it only made her think of the things that might not have been—like meeting Trevor. The idea of not knowing him did not sit well with Jessica. "Regardless, here we are. I've been working here as a driver to transport the wounded from the front to the operating room. You should have seen the condition you were in when I arrived."

"I can only imagine."

There was an awkward pause as the two gauged each other. Francis was thinking about Isabella (a detail he hadn't included in his story), but had decided long ago that she was not Jessica. They spoke up at the same time. Jessica asked, "So what happens now?" While Francis said, "I need to tell you something."

The two friends chuckled. Jessica extended her hand. "You go first."

Francis smiled sheepishly. "OK. As I was saying, I need to tell you something. I should have told you this a long time ago, but I didn't. Then we were separated all this time, and I regretted it. I'm not making the same mistake this time, and I'm not living like there will always be a tomorrow."

Jessica's face furrowed. She didn't like the sound of where this was going. *I should have told him*, she thought, but it was too late.

"I love you, Jessica," Francis blurted out, a bit louder than he intended, causing several eyes to glance their way. He lowered his tone. "I always have. I never had the courage to say anything until now. I was too scared of what you might say. I never thought I would see you again, and I can't go through that another time. I love you. And a part of me thinks you—"

"Francis," Jessica interrupted, "I need you to stop right there." Francis' mouth clamped shut faster than she thought possible. "I met someone, out here."

The glint in his eyes faded. His entire face dropped, and there was no way to hide it. She continued to speak, but he only heard half the words.

"It's Trevor, the doctor I mentioned earlier. He's the kindest person I've ever met, and, well, he made me realize that I had to move on with my life. I love him, Francis. Don't get me wrong, there was a time when I loved you—and I still do—just, not in that way. Not like it is with him. I'm sorry."

"Hmmm," was all that Francis could manage.

It did not sit well with Jessica. "Oh no. Don't even think about being angry with this. You had plenty of chances. Remember when I thought you died at Skeleton Island? I told you how there were things I wish I would had said, a lot like what you're trying to say now. And guess what your response was?"

Francis remained silent.

"You said that you refused to believe anything happened to me…or Will. Or Will? Really? You bring him into the mix when you try and tell me how much you care about me? Oh, and that was the other kicker. You said, care. Not love, care. I'm sorry Francis, but you had your chance to lay it all out there, but it's too late now. It's been over a year here. Did you think I would just sit by and let my life go to waste wondering what happened to you?"

Jessica inhaled to keep speaking, but Francis budged into the conversation with a soft voice. "I'm sorry."

Jessica was taken aback. She did not expect him to say that—not this quickly. "You're right. I had my chances, and I regret not taking them. I've changed over this year as well. I did the same thing as you and tried to move on. I accept that this is your decision and life, Jess, just don't expect me to be happy about it."

Jessica studied her friend. He was different, but she wasn't sure if it was for the better yet. "Thank you Francis. I'm sorry that this was how it played out, but I'm glad to have my friend back."

"Me too." Francis gave a fake smile. This new pain had been worse than that of his wounds. He wanted to forget about it. "Where do we go now?"

"I don't like the possibility of an Island scientist running around with the Germans. Not at this moment in history. He needs to be stopped," she said, hesitating before continuing. "And if you trust these Island people, then I will come with you and help. It's more important than what I'm doing here."

"It'll be like old times," Francis joked, "running towards certain death to save the world."

Jessica suddenly realized what she was committing to. It could mean death, and her normal life would vanish in a poof a smoke. She stood up, bumping the table next to them. "I'm sorry. I need to go. There's something I have to do. I'll be back."

She left before Francis had an opportunity to speak. He was left alone with his thoughts, while Jessica b-lined for her room. *How could I just blindly commit to that?* she thought. *I didn't even think about Trevor.* She agreed that the man needed to be stopped, but did she really need to tag along?

Jessica spent the next hour mulling it over, writing two different letters to Trevor. One told him that she may not be back, but still loved him, explaining the situation, while the other told him about her week and nothing more. She reread each letter multiple times before making a choice. How could she sit idly by, when the fate of the world might depend on her? Trevor would understand.

He already had accepted everything about her past. Given that knowledge, Jessica could not see how he would react any other way. Perhaps he'd even ask to come with her. *No*, she thought, *I can't put him in danger like that. He's not like us.* Soon after making her choice Jessica was back in action transporting men from the front.

Francis remained in his bed, occasionally trying to sit up. His wounds were healing quickly. He had just managed to stand when he heard a familiar voice.

"Well I'll be. You made it out alive," Neptune said,

extending a hand. Francis shook it. "When they told me you and Mercury were in a field hospital I didn't believe it. I thought for sure your plane had crashed."

"Nice to see you too. I'm assuming if you're here that Jupiter and Saturn made it?"

He hesitated. "Jupiter is at our temporary base here in Belgium. Saturn didn't make it. I was about to inquire the fate of Mercury, or if you're even able to walk?"

Francis understood Neptune's reason for changing the topic; he knew how close Saturn and Francis were. Regardless, Francis' heart fell. Another one of them was gone. Francis hid his emotions, trying to move forward. "I think I can manage. I'll be much better by tomorrow. Mercury is still unconscious, but they are hopeful that he'll pull through."

Neptune grunted. "Well then, I guess it will just be you and me heading back. He's no use to us in that condition."

"Actually I have someone who can join our team. Call her a long lost friend who is equally talented."

"Oh? I don't like the idea of having someone on my team that I don't know. But I trust your judgment, that, and the fact that we need all the hands we can get for this mission."

"Did you find what we needed?"

Neptune held up a hand. "Not here. Soon. Where is this friend of yours?"

"I'm sure she'll be back soon. She's transporting wounded from the front right now. As soon as she gets in we can go."

The two men waited for Jessica to get back. Francis pulled her aside when she got to his bunk. "The man over there is my Commander. His code name is Neptune—mine is Pluto. He's ready to take us to their base to discuss our mission."

Jessica nodded. "Alright, but Francis, after we stop this scientist guy, I'm going to stay here. I've built a life, and I want to stay with Trevor. It's all I've ever wanted."

Francis' face fell. "I understand. You always talked about having that. I guess I'll stop The Island on my own then."

"I'm sorry, if things were different, I just…" Jessica stumbled. "I am done with this. I want a life—a normal life."

"Let's go," Francis said grimly.

"I need to say goodbye to someone else, and then I'll be right over." Jessica left to find Monica down the hall. She handed her the letter to Trevor. "Monica, I need you to mail this to Trevor for me. Something has come up and I need to leave for a while."

Monica peered over her shoulders to see a man with an Island uniform down the hall. She grew worried. "Are you in trouble?"

"No, it's nothing like that. But I do have to do something more pressing than what I'm doing here. Do you think you can manage without me?"

"If it is important enough to shrug off your duties, I can only assume I don't have another choice, especially if you're going with them."

"I'll be fine. And I will be back, Monica. I'm sorry I have to go. If I could explain things I would, but I'm afraid I can't. Maybe when I get back."

"I can't guarantee you a position here if you leave. Many will assume you're a traitor, or a deserter. Granted, I'll make it known whom you left with, which may keep them from asking questions. Best of luck, Noble."

"Thank you," Jessica hugged her friend and walked back to Francis and Neptune. "I'm ready."

"Good," Neptune responded. "Before we continue, for lack of another name to give you, you will be the new Venus."

She did not say anything, but followed the two outside. Francis and Jessica sat in the back, while Neptune drove. Francis kept wondering what was going on in his friend's mind, and what she had been through. He missed her, and still hurt from her earlier words. Not only had she found someone else, but also he would have to continue his goal alone. Francis chose not to dwell on such thoughts; she could always change her mind.

Jessica spent the bumpy ride thinking of ways she could apologize to Trevor and Monica when she returned. Neptune steered the vehicle, brainstorming ways to successfully fulfill their mission. It was not an easy one, and they would need all the luck they could get.

The trip was not as long as Francis and Jessica expected it to be, but was still long enough for their bodies to be sore from the ride. They passed through security checkpoints and exited the vehicle once inside.

Neptune led them to an office room. "This way. The others will be waiting."

Francis noticed how uncomfortable Jessica looked in an Island facility. He leaned over and whispered. "It gets easier to adjust. It's rather different than the one we know."

Jessica's smile was not reassuring. She did not like being reminded of what she went through. "We'll see."

Neptune opened the door, and ushered them inside. Jupiter was surveying a map on the wall, and Earth was leaning back in a chair. He held a piece of paper, which took all of his attention.

Francis made the introductions for Jessica, and left the debriefing to Neptune. The commander rested his arms on the table. He looked at his team and sighed. "We've got our work cut out for us this time. Mercury and I managed to find documents on the zeppelin before they were destroyed. What we found only confirmed our suspicions."

He handed out papers for everyone except Earth, who had already been studying his. "These are blueprints to some kind of bomb we have never seen before. Frankly, we're in the dark, and the reality that an organization like us admits that, does not sit well."

Francis passed the papers on to Jessica, and flipped them over. The paper had many lines and markings with symbols. All that caught Francis' eyes was a diagram in the bottom corner. The bomb itself looked large and chubby, but the diagram was of a cloud tagged with several ranges of numbers. The cloud looked like a mushroom.

This bomb was nuclear.

Jessica came to the same conclusion, studying every aspect of the paper to be sure. The mushroom shape was a bit of a giveaway, and the numbers, she guessed, were distance approximations of how destructive the bomb would be. *This can't be*, she thought. Jessica knew the only nuclear bombs ever used were done so during the Second World War, not the First. This scientist had to be from the future in order to create something like this. *What does this mean for history?* she wondered.

"Know something we don't?" Neptune questioned, noticing their reaction.

Francis and Jessica locked eyes. Francis placed his paper on the table. He pointed at the cloud. "This is a nuclear bomb. It can destroy an entire city."

Earth leaned closer. "That's not possible. Even with our tech, a nuclear reaction is just unheard of."

Francis sighed. "Not for this man. He's not from this time period, remember? A weapon like that used during a time like this could change everything. Germany could win the war with it."

Neptune cut in. "If what you're saying is true, and this kind of weapon exists, we have to stop it. Failure is not an option."

"You have no idea," Jessica muttered to herself, still trying to piece things together.

"With this new information, we have to act immediately," Neptune spoke. "Not only did these documents shed light on the weapon, but they also gave us a location on this scientist."

"Where is he?" Francis asked.

"A small town outside of Frankfurt," he replied. "Judging from the intel gathered, we suspect the location to be similar to where we found Jensen Avery. The problem is we have nothing else to go on. We have no idea what to expect or how many enemy combatants will be there."

"Is there any good news?" Earth was skeptical.

Neptune grinned. "For once, yes there is. Follow me." The team followed him out the door and down a hallway. They approached a hanger outside the facility. Neptune opened the doors and they piled in. "This, is what will give us a chance at succeeding."

The hanger was full of planes. Francis recognized them immediately, for he was constantly engaged in battle with them. They were German aircraft. Silver bodies, with black and white crosses on them, and two seats. "How did you—"

"Get them?" Neptune smirked. "It took some time, but we finally salvaged enough to build them. We did, however, model the controls after the Nieuport. We were hoping Mercury would be fit to fly as well, but we'll have to make do with you and Jupiter."

"So we're infiltrating Germany via their own planes and hoping they don't shoot us down?" Jessica asked.

Neptune tilted his head momentarily. "Essentially. We have no reason to believe they would fire at us. The real danger is getting to their side without being shot by our own. Once across the lines, we shouldn't face any problems. When we near our target, we'll land far enough away as to not give up the element of surprise."

"We've worked with less luck in the past," Jupiter said. "When do we leave?"

"Early morning," Neptune responded. "It'll be dark from here to the front to mask our planes, but light enough once we reach it, so that we are not fired upon. I should also mention we have German uniforms for each of us." He glanced at Jessica. "We may have to adjust Mercury's to fit you. Again, once we're on the ground we'll have a better feel for what we are up against. Until then, I suggest we all get some rest."

The team dispersed, but Francis lingered to inspect the planes. He had always been fascinated with his opponents, but could never see what they had this close before. Jessica followed him. "How are you so calm right now? An Island scientist from the future is making a nuclear bomb for the Germans…in World War One!"

Francis shrugged. "It doesn't change anything. He still needs to be stopped. That's what we've been working towards ever since I arrived. And as far as our plan, Jupiter's right, we've had far worse situations to deal with. There's no point getting worked up about it until we're out there."

Jessica took a moment to get used to how much her friend had changed. "I suppose you're right. Do you think we can do it?"

Francis climbed into the pilot seat. "If anyone can, it's our team. You're icing on the cake with your ability. I haven't been able to use mine recently—too much pain. But you, you can slip into their base unnoticed and take them out from the inside while we cause a diversion."

Jessica scratched her arm nervously. "And what if I'm not comfortable with that?"

Francis peered down at her. "What do you mean? You know the stakes."

"There's a reason I'm so happy here, Francis. My job is

saving people. I make a difference. I don't have to run around killing people to defend myself like before."

He climbed down to face her. "Look, I get it. You have the normal life you always wanted. But Jess, you also were given a gift. Something you can use to make a difference in other ways. Sure, you might not be saving people the way you do now, but if we stop this bomb, we're going to save a heck of a lot more. It's your call, but it'd improve our odds tenfold if you do."

Jessica could sense the agitation in his voice ever since they came clean to each other. He was angry and hurt, but he was still a friend, and what he said did make sense. "Thanks Francis."

He flashed a phony grin. "Any time, but if you don't mind, I need to get acquainted with this machine before we head out."

Jessica took the hint. "Got it. I'll leave you be."

Francis watched her go, and fought the urge to chase her and laugh and joke like they used to. Something inside him said that it would never be like it used to with her, and he wasn't surprised. Of course things wouldn't be the same—not after she found Trevor.

Trevor, Francis thought. The name tasted worse than Mars'. He punched the side of the plane in frustration. *Why didn't you just tell her back on the ship, you nimrod? You lost your chance now.* Then he began to think of Isabella. As he inspected the machine he ran through every conversation he had with her to feel less alone, and to distance himself from Jessica.

The team went to sleep one by one, after each individual had finished the mental or physical preparation required for the mission. Neptune did not sleep much, nor did Jessica. Neptune was focused on planning for potential situations they may encounter. Jessica spent a large portion of her night rethinking her decision. It jeopardized everything she had started to build here, and as such, was not a choice that had been made lightly.

Regardless, she felt it was a necessary sacrifice given the circumstances. However, this did not make her stomach churn any less.

It was still dark when they woke. One after another they filed into the hanger. Neptune was the first in, and waited until all were present before speaking. "This is it. A lot rides on this mission. Hopefully we all make it to the drop off point undetected, but if not, it is up to those that do to fulfill the task. Right now our only pilots are Pluto and Jupiter, which means two of us will need to share a spot in the plane. Based on size alone, it makes the most sense for Venus and Earth to share, and based on weight, Pluto will fly them. Jupiter and I will be in the other plane."

"Is that really necessary?" Jessica asked, eyeing down Earth. She was not inclined to sit on his lap for the duration of the trip.

"Unless you know anyone else that can fly a plane."

Earth winked. "I promise I don't bite. Besides you're not my type."

Jessica was not comforted by his words, but she had little choice in the matter. They climbed inside their seats. Francis glanced behind him and chuckled when he saw Earth and Jessica uncomfortably squished together. "Get cozy. It'll be a long ride."

"You're not helping," Jessica snapped.

Francis did not hear her comment. He switched his focus to the mission and his job. He signaled to an assistant on the ground to start the engine. The plane whirred to life. Jessica did not enjoy the vibrations that caused her to jostle against Earth.

Jupiter and Francis steered their planes to the runway, and after she had taken off, Francis did the same. The German design handled a bit different than what he was used to, but Francis was quick to adapt. As the plane lifted off the ground, Jessica felt her stomach take off as well. It was nerve-racking for her to see Francis in control of the craft, but thought of how he would have felt with her operating on soldiers. They had both spent a significant amount of time in their fields, and she relaxed only slightly. Meanwhile, Earth did his best to shift his body to keep circulation in his legs, occasionally apologizing to Jessica as he did so.

The two planes climbed high in the sky. Francis and Jupiter were glad to have the cover of darkness, especially in their new machines. However, they still needed to remain alert, as the night masked their location, but not the noise. An artillery soldier could decide to fire—regardless of which side they were on.

The air was frosty and cold, and it combined with the wind to chill Jessica to the bone. She found herself momentarily grateful to have Earth simply for body heat. Francis had become accustomed to the air, and his uniform helped keep him warm.

In the dreary sky, Francis kept his eyes peeled. The moment you relax in the air, you die. That saying was constantly passed around squadrons, and they were words to live by. Scouring the horizon helped pass the time. With dawn approaching, the two planes had not encountered any resistance.

Despite maintaining vigilance, Francis could not help but think of Saturn. *I wish he was here.* This was the reality of war. Companions and friends that had meant so much to one another could simply vanish from existence. Francis fought the urge to mourn for his friend. Of everyone on the team, Saturn meant the most to him. However, mourning was not a luxury that Francis could afford right now. Saturn was dead, and he was not. Francis knew that if he became distracted, his plane would not make it to their target. He needed to stay focused in order to protect those still amongst the living.

Western Front:

12 Hours Earlier

Will receives a message from one of the runners in the trenches. He opens it and reads it carefully.

Private Taylor,

Enclosed is the location of the German scientist. You will report to our base in Belgium, where you will be escorted via plane into enemy territory. You will be trailing behind a unit tasked with the same mission. You are not to associate with them, as they are unaware of your presence. You are the insurance if they fail to infiltrate the base.

Your skills should allow you to get close enough for a clear shot of the man in the attached photograph. Take him out, and consider yourself promoted upon your return. The messenger that brought you this letter will take you to a carriage that will transport you to the base. You are on your own after the pilot drops you off. There will be no safety net if you or the operative team is captured. Good luck.

After finishing the letter, Will takes his rifle and follows the young soldier. He is taken to a horse-drawn buggy with a single driver. The driver displays an Island symbol on his uniform. Will makes note of this, but says nothing. The A.I. has access to The Island's historical records, and is well aware of their beginnings. *So this is who's funding the mission*, Will thinks. *It must be important for them to get involved.*

He sits in the back seat in silence for the entire ride. They stop multiple times for the horses to rest. To say the ride was bumpy would be an understatement. Moments before he suggests walking to ease his discomfort, the carriage pulls up to a wooden gate. A soldier at his post approaches them, and when he does, the driver hands him a piece of paper. The guard scans the document quickly, cocks his head to the side and hands the paper back. "They've been expecting you. I have been instructed to keep you outside the establishment until they are ready."

"When will they be ready?" Will asks, irritated with his mode of transportation.

A distant sound of an engine roaring to life screams through the quiet air. The soldier gestures towards the sound. "When they leave."

Will stares towards the area the noise came from. The absence of light makes it difficult to see. Rounding the corner comes two small planes, bearing German markings. He watches them taxi out to a runway, and soon they are climbing off the ground, clawing their way into the sky. Before long, he has lost them in the night canopy.

The soldier removes the barricade, and motions for them to enter. The horses trot forwards and they pull up to a hanger entrance.

"This is your stop." The driver leans over to Will.

Will hops off of the carriage, grateful to be on solid ground again. A man bearing an Island logo greets Will. "It's a pleasure to meet you. We've heard a lot about you."

Will cuts to the chase. "When do I leave?"

"Of course, you should stay focused on the mission," the soldier apologizes. "The other unit has just taken off. By the time we get you loaded up into your plane and on the runway, you will be good to go."

Will is led to a small man fiddling with a German plane. The soldier introduces him. "This is Jimmy. He'll be your pilot.

He will be taking you to the drop off point and you will be left to your own devices. He will not be sticking around. In and out. Fast and simple."

Will triple checks his rifle, keeping up the charade that he will actually be using it, and climbs into the plane. The pilot gives him a look. "We won't be ready for another ten minutes. We've got to give them enough time to get ahead of us, but not too much that we lose the cover of night."

"Doesn't matter. I'm fine here," Will replies.

The pilot resumes readying the plane. Before long, they are racing down the runway. The craft lifts into the air, and Will's stomach lurches, but he doesn't mind. Being stuck on the ocean was far worse than the vertigo of flying.

Will feels no other emotions during the flight. He does not feel the wind in his face, the excitement of flying, or the fear of being taken down by the enemy. He is merely being transported to his task. The only thought crossing his mind was the reason for organizing the mission this way. *Why send two separate groups, unaware of each other?* he wonders. It didn't compute.

Will was not a fool. He knows the generals had ordered him to this mission as a form of execution. He also realizes with his drop-off, there had been no mention of being picked up. It made more sense for him to join this 'special' team, and just hang back once they arrived to cover them. Then again, he enjoys working alone, and prefers it this way.

It was difficult for him to weigh the pros and cons of what this mission entailed. He decides it would be much more fun, and interesting, if he were to race the other team to take out the target. He grins, thinking of the look on some soldier's face to arrive at the scene to find all of the enemy combatants dead. *Yes*, he thinks, *why not have a little fun with it?*

13: HUNTERS & HUNTED

Western Front
1916
7:15 A.M.

J upiter and Francis reached the front lines when the first
streaks of sunlight were starting to appear. They passed
overhead unnoticed, or rather, left alone. The two pilots kept their
eyes open and heads on a swivel, waiting for the first sound of an
artillery shell exploding. It never came. Unsure of whether they
were fortunate, or if the troops below were inept, the planes
moved on. They were now in German territory.

If all went according to plan, no trouble would befall them,
as they bared the German markings and design. Any of the
soldiers below should believe them to be just another one of their
own on reconnaissance.

Of course, that isn't always the case. Francis and Jupiter had
both seen their fair share of pilots killed by their own side's
artillery. It was as if they were in an entirely different war
altogether. Simply knowing that they were in German airspace
made Francis nervous. He constantly reminded himself that they
weren't in a British plane. His nerves would not calm, which can
be good or bad depending on the pilot.

Francis always felt that when his nerves were awake, so was
he, and therefore was quicker to react. Jupiter preferred to stay
calm the whole time. She felt when people panic, or are too
twitchy, they make mistakes. Both were right, and both were
wrong, as is the reality of being a pilot. Everything is entirely up
to skill, fate, and a lot of luck.

Jessica did not really comprehend the amount of danger
there was being in a plane, let alone a pseudo-German one. She

241

had no experience with it, and as such was not as intent on watching her surroundings. To her, Francis looked silly and paranoid with the amount he moved his head and scanned the sky.

Neptune and Earth knew better. They were there with Francis and Jupiter in the battle around the zeppelin. They saw how dangerous an enemy encounter could be, which made their uneasiness even greater.

At least on the ground I could hone my skill set in a fight, Neptune thought, *but up here, I feel useless.* He did have a machine gun attached to his seat, but even that felt flimsy.

The two planes ventured deeper and deeper into enemy territory. Francis was baffled at how easy this was, but knew better than to let his guard down, lest he jinx the situation. Pilots were very superstitious. One of his old friends always carried a bullet that had pierced his plane as a good luck charm. He took it with him on every mission. One day he never returned. Francis never found out what happened to him. Maybe that way was better.

Another old pal refused to check his plane over right after a battle—he said it was bad luck, and it was better to check on the way out. Unfortunately, he missed something during his pre-flight analysis and his plane exploded before it was twenty feet in the air.

Francis had watched a lot of men die, and many were younger than he was. While he didn't believe in any of the routines or lucky charms, Francis did find that there was a way he could jinx a flight; by assuming everything would be fine. The best defense was staying alert and focused. He did his best not to take any chances. Ever. He would even occasionally detach from formation with Jupiter just in case they were ambushed.

Jupiter was almost disappointed that by the time they reached their drop-off point, they had not encountered any opposition. The fake German planes had worked. She flew closer to Francis and made a circular motion with her hand. It was the signal to start their descent. Jupiter would land first, and in case of any welcoming parties, Francis was tasked with circling the space to defend them. Once she was down, he would come in and land next to her.

The area designated for their landing was one of the only spaces flat enough and long enough to actually land. Rolling hills and buildings or other obstacles surrounded them. As one of the only options available, they had to make do with its condition. The ground was relatively choppy, which could make for a rather bumpy landing.

Jupiter wondered if there were any possible zones they had missed as her plane began its final approach. Her wheels touched the ground, shaking the plane, which thudded again and again with the terrain. She held the controls firmly and without budging, brought the plane to a sheltered area. It was her turn to watch her teammate land, and protect him from potential dangers.

Francis lined his plane up with the same stretch as Jupiter. Jessica gripped the sides of her seat tightly. She felt like saying something, but decided against it. Francis was too focused, and the words would never have reached him. Holding his breath, he brought the plane into contact with the ground. A large hole almost caused it to lose control and flip, but he fought the momentum. He let the air he had trapped out slowly as he pulled up next to Jupiter. They cut off the engine, and climbed out of the planes.

"We should grab some of the bushes nearby to give these cover," Jupiter ordered. "I'd hate to complete our mission and have nothing to come back to."

Nobody disagreed, but Francis did have a nagging point he had to bring up. "How many people do you think saw or heard our approach?"

Neptune shrugged. "There's no use worrying over it. What's done is done. If they do look for us, hopefully this cover will be enough. Otherwise, our disguise will hopefully not cause anyone alarm."

"Mhmm," Francis said, unsatisfied. With no other feasible option or idea, he carried on with hiding their planes with branches and greenery, which in itself proved a difficult task.

With the minute details taken care of, Neptune led the group towards the enemy base. As they made their way, Francis twisted his head to the sky. He thought he heard the roar of a plane's engine, but when his eyes came up empty-handed, he chalked it up to the long flight here. His ears were still sore from the constant noise.

The team moved quickly and quietly through the countryside, searching for the place in which the scientist would be hiding. Once they reached the outskirts of the town, Neptune spotted a U-shaped mansion. Guards monitored the perimeter. He pointed it out. "This must be the place. Nothing else we've seen has any soldiers posted outside. Even if it isn't, it will lead us to the right location."

Jupiter concurred. "It is the most logical option as of yet. Do you want us on recon?"

"We do need to know how many there are," Neptune agreed, "but our team is too small to cover each other if someone gets spotted."

Francis smiled and nudged Jessica. "That's exactly where my friend comes in. She can get close without being detected." Neptune eyed him skeptically, and then studied Jessica even more so. Francis stood by what he said. "Trust me."

After a moment of consideration Neptune agreed. "Very well. But understand that this whole operation will be at risk if you get caught."

Jessica nodded. She knew how important something like this was. If left unchecked, the entire course of the future would be altered. She could use her ability one last time for the good of everyone. "I understand. Fr—Pluto is right. I can do this. What exactly would you like to know?"

"Ideally," Neptune pondered for a moment, "how many guards they have and where they are posted. And any further information on the building itself would be helpful, but rather difficult to obtain."

And with that, Jessica took off. She bolted away from the others and went straight for cover. Once hidden, she activated her powers and became a ghost. Despite being invisible, she could still give her position away with noise, or even how her body moved through certain areas. Mud and tall grass were the most difficult, but fortunately, they were absent.

Careful not to make any sound, she approached the mansion. Jessica went around the entire building first, and made a note of each guard she encountered and his position. Rounding a corner, she saw a courtyard. A beautiful fountain sat in the middle, with a garden on each side, but Jessica figured the Germans did not care about that aspect as much as others. Several of the soldiers were smoking around the fountain, and tossing the butts inside. She crept past, and peered through the window in the doorway.

There was a large open foyer with two parallel staircases starting on opposite sides, which connected at the top. She noticed the floor was some type of tile, and if she found a way inside, her footsteps would betray her.

The team already had few members as it was, and she decided it would be better to gather information only from outside of the house as best as she could. Jessica moved from window to window, looking for a better vantage point to see different areas. Satisfied that she could find no new details, she cautiously snuck back to the group.

"You were gone a long time," Neptune noted. "But seeing as the alarms have not sounded, is it safe to assume that you were successful?"

She nodded. "We have our work cut out for us. They have five guards in the courtyard. Right now they're just smoking, but I'm sure they'll split up soon. There's two guards posted at each corner of the house. Also, five more patrol the entire perimeter. They did not change posts while I there."

Neptune grumbled. "That's quite the party for just a small town mansion. I'd say we've definitely found the place."

"I also spotted a balcony in the courtyard on the second floor. If someone is capable, they could climb up."

"Excellent point," Neptune acknowledged. "Judging from the information we have, the best course of action is to attack as a group. We'll set some explosive charges to go off behind the mansion, while we come in from the front. Pluto and Venus will clear the courtyard, and Earth and I will each take a side of the house, eliminating the enemy soldiers until we meet at the back. Jupiter will cover Pluto and Venus, and then when you are ready to breach, she will take the balcony, and the two of you will take the front door."

Everyone took a moment to let the plan sink in. Francis felt the urge to speak. "Is it wise to lose the element of surprise with that explosion? There's a lot of windows in that building, and we could face fire from all sides."

"A valid concern, but I still believe it's our best plan. The explosion should divert attention to the backside, which leaves only one side to worry about windows. They should clear from your position. If we suddenly attack out of the blue, the soldiers inside will shoot us down once they gather themselves. I'm not saying it is ideal, but we need to get in there now and stop this weapon before they can use it."

"Understood."

Neptune scoured the area one last time. "If no one has anything further to add, we'd best get started. Jupiter, I want you to set the charges and report back here once they are set."

"On it," she replied, and swiftly left. It would take time for her to make it over, set the charges, and then get back. Among other things, she was very strong and had excellent endurance. Out of the remaining team members, she could accomplish the task in a timely manner and have more than enough energy to attack the mansion.

While Jupiter was away, the rest of the unit discussed the layout of the mansion and the best ways to breach it.

"There is no back entrance," Jessica said. Her tone was matter-of-fact. "So you will need to take out a window to enter the building. It shouldn't be too difficult if they are all shooting at you through them anyway."

"Easier said than done," Neptune replied. "If we face too much opposition, we'll be relying on you to take them out from the inside while we distract them. The two of you, with the help of Jupiter, should be able to manage the courtyard and any waiting in the lobby. Providing our timing is accurate, we will strike first, gaining their attention and giving you an element of surprise from the opposite side."

"What if there are more soldiers than we expect on the inside?" Francis asked. He did not enjoy how up most of their missions flew by chance.

Neptune bobbed his head from side to side. "We have to hope for the best. We're out of time on this. Our intel reported the Germans are nearly ready to use the weapon. I can't risk the unknown if we do not act now. Our team has made it out of some dodgy situations before—this is no different."

He directed his attention back to the others. "Once we are inside, we need to clear each room as fast as possible. The slower we are, the more time they have to destroy evidence. We know what our target looks like. Assume everyone else is expendable. Don't take any chances on this one."

Earth chimed in. "Since I won't be an overwatch for this, everyone needs to be alert. I can't call out their positions. Stay sharp and work together with your group."

"Good point, Earth."

Neptune continued the conversation, triple-checking the plan and if enemy posts had changed. He liked making sure all the pieces were in place. When he spotted Jupiter returning, he grinned. "Let's go shut down a German weapon."

With that, Neptune and Earth skirted away, leaving Jessica, Francis, and Jupiter behind. Jupiter pulled out three metal cylinders and handed them out. "These are suppressors. I'd like to think with all that racket those two will cause, we can be discrete to maximize the diversion."

"Excellent," Francis said, attaching it to his gun. They had used these before on previous missions, and it always made him feel like a spy. He assisted Jessica with hers, and gave her a crash course on her weapon. She scolded him, as he had given her the same talk before they had left the airbase.

"I know how to use it, thank you very much," she replied, staring down the sights.

"You two should get into position. Things are about to get hairy," Jupiter said.

Francis smiled. "Looking forward to it. However, there is a much better way for us to get in the front without drawing attention."

"Oh?"

"Yeah, Pluto, what did you have in mind?" Jessica's voice was sharp and lethal. She did not appreciate being volunteered for something she did not want to do, and she had an itching feeling of what Francis would suggest.

"Venus has a knack for this kind of thing," he confirmed her suspicion. "Just hang back, and let the two of us handle this."

They broke away from Jupiter, and began moving closer to the target. Once out of earshot Jessica let loose in hushed hisses.

"I have a knack for this kind of thing?"

"Oh you know what I mean," Francis explained. "Just turn invisible and take them out. It makes it a lot less hazardous for us."

"Need I remind you I spent the latter of my time here saving people? I don't want to kill any more."

"Then why did you come along?" He had to stop himself from yelling. "Did you think the Germans would just surrender and turn over the scientist? Did you think we could just sneak in and out without harming anyone?"

"No, I just—"

"This is war, Jess. You need to wrap your head around that if you want to survive."

Jessica swung a fist that collided with Francis' jaw. He spat a wad of blood out. "I know exactly what this is. I've seen the aftermath of war, and all its suffering. Don't ever think that I don't know. I'll kill for a just cause—I already have—but don't think for a second that I will just follow you around and take orders to do so. That's my choice."

They were close to the mansion. Francis was fuming from the sudden outbursts, but the majority of his anger stemmed from his feelings for Jessica, not the situation at hand. Before he had a chance to add any regrettable words, an explosion shook the ground. The two looked ahead. "Fine. We have to move now, so let's do this together, alright?"

"Fine," Jessica agreed, though her tone remained hostile. She grabbed his hand and activated her ability as the two ran to the courtyard. Gunfire could be heard from behind the house. *Neptune and Earth must have engaged them already*, Francis thought.

The guards at the front of the building looked bewildered and shocked by the explosion. They shouted at each other, and by the time they gathered themselves, Jessica and Francis were upon them. Jessica focused on the two closest to her on the border of the house. She fired off a couple shots, all but one missing. She adjusted her aim based on the feedback from the gun and hit her targets on the next volley.

Francis eyed every aspect of his surroundings, noting if any enemies appeared at the windows. Satisfied, he began to take down confounded Germans, one after another. It was like shooting fish in a barrel. Their enemy had no idea what was happening as the two cleared the courtyard with ease.

The situation did not make it easier for Jessica. She froze when her final target was cowering behind cover, shaking with fear. Her gun was pointed at his head, but she could not bring herself to pull the trigger.

A shot fired. Francis slapped her with a look colder than ice as he withdrew his gun. She stared back at him, struggling to see the boy she once knew at The Island...at Camelot. *How can he just shut off his emotions like that?* she wondered.

Francis checked their surroundings one last time, and saw Jupiter approaching. He let go of Jessica. "We've got more of a chance catching a stray bullet inside with your abilities."

Jessica appeared out of thin air. "Very well."

The sound of gunfire still rang from behind the building.

Jupiter shouted at them quietly. "What are you two waiting for? Get in there!"

She ran past them and climbed the side of the house like a monkey. She hopped from ledge to ledge until she pulled herself over the balcony.

Francis gathered his focus and kicked in the front door with Jessica's help. There weren't any immediate guards to deal with for them, but a body fell from above right in front of them, splattering on the floor.

Francis and Jessica ignored the body and split up, each taking a side of the house. One soldier appeared around the corner and Francis tapped the trigger quickly twice. The man fell to the floor. Francis fought the urge to run to the back of the building to help Neptune and Earth, but he knew better. He could miss a room, and someone could ambush him from behind. Instead, he methodically began to clear the rooms one by one. Some were empty, while others contained documents or a number of soldiers. Whichever the case, he dealt with it accordingly.

Jessica was less comfortable with the aspect of clearing rooms, so she phased in and out of being invisible. *After all, why not use my power? I'd rather feel safer than die here and never see Trevor again.* And so, ignoring her friend's advice, she went through her section using her own methods. After turning down a hallway and bumping right into a wild-eyed soldier, she was glad she had done so. As the man remained confused as to what he ran in to, Jessica shot him twice in the chest.

At the back of the house, Neptune and Earth had waited for the explosion to take effect before rounding the corner and attacking. While the soldiers gawked at the cloud of fire, the two men eliminated them with precision. Earth covered Neptune by watching things on the ground, while he engaged the soldiers at the windows.

Neptune fired at each window that moved. Soon there were too many movements to keep up with. Sharp pain tore into his shoulder. Earth was quick to respond, pulling him to cover.

"You're hit!" he shouted, as enemy bullets rained down on them.

"I'm fine," Neptune barked. "Focus on the mission. Wait for a break and return fire."

Earth did as he was commanded. He remained hidden until opportune moments allowed him to shoot. *Where are the others?* he wondered. *We can't last much longer.*

Three Hours Earlier…
Drop-Off Point, Germany

Will's body shakes as the plane touches down on the uneven terrain. He wonders if the pilot was just a rookie, or if that was how all landings generally went. The man gives a salute as Will exits the plane. Will ignores him and walks towards his task. The plane turns around and leaves. Left alone, Will surveys the area. He notices the two planes hidden in brush. *At least I won't be stranded here*, he thinks.

A set of boot prints in the dirt leaves an easy trail for Will to follow. Amateurs. Don't even bother hiding their steps. Anyone could have followed them. With the risk of being in Germany, Will does not take any chances. He keeps a barrier of telekinetic energy up at all times, and finds himself looking over his shoulder every few steps. A sniper can never be too paranoid.

Will passes the time thinking of what he will do when he comes across the operations team. Should he kill them and take the credit? Will they already be dead? Or perhaps he can just sit back and observe them from the shadows? He runs scenarios through his mind as he hikes through the woods. With his decision still in the air, Will stumbles across a clearing. He spots a large mansion and eyes that the trail leads forwards. He makes his own path to the right, setting up on a hillside overlooking the manor.

His perch provides him with an excellent vantage point, and the rifle scope gives him a better understanding of the situation. He scours the area and finds a tall woman running behind the building.

"What do we have here?" he mutters to himself. He traces the woman's movement back to a small group, two of whom he recognizes. "Well I'll be. The little twerp made it after all."

The scope finds Jessica. "And look, the two of them are reunited. How sweet." His words are vacant and insincere. "This certainly changes things, now doesn't it? Should I kill you and watch him suffer? It would make my life easier if I try and rejoin him…but then again, I could just kill you both and be done with it. Decisions, decisions."

The wind picks up, which would bother a typical sniper, but not Will. He shifts his weight, digging himself into a more comfortable position. Comfort, after all, is what truly matters when one makes a choice. He struggles to commit to either option—both appear equally appealing. While Will debates what to do, the woman returns to the group, and they all go their separate ways.

Will decides to watch, hoping for an entertaining show, and watches Francis and Jessica run towards the building. He sees them vanish, and one by one the guards drop dead. "Well aren't we comfortable with our abilities now, eh Jessica? But you, Francis, you seem much, much different than before. I like it."

Not long after, they reappear, and the woman joins them.

She takes the balcony, and his old acquaintances take the front door. His view is now obscured, and he must move in for a closer look at the show.

Jupiter clung to the balcony and pulled herself up. A soldier was waiting for her as soon as she entered the hall. Before he had a chance to raise his weapon, she launched a foot towards his head. With her opponent dazed, she sent her entire weight behind an elbow, which collided with the man's jaw. He misplaced a step backwards and fell over the railing. Jupiter did not bother to check if he survived.

Watching carefully, she cleared her section and began making her way to the back of the house. She knew her two colleagues would need assistance. With a head pump around the corner, she spotted several soldiers at the windows firing down on her comrades. Jupiter shot quick bursts at the men, each falling to the ground dead or clutching wounds. Jupiter peered out the window and gave Earth a quick nod before searching the rest of the rooms upstairs.

Earth lifted Neptune up. "C'mon, Jupe cleared a path for us. We need to move."

"I've got it," Neptune spoke through gritted teeth. "You go, I'm right behind you."

Earth smashed around to clear broken glass on a first floor window and climbed in. He kept his focus on the room he was in, as Neptune fumbled his way through after him. "Keep going, we need to clear this place before he has a chance to escape."

Earth nodded and exited after he checked to ensure each direction was safe. He left Neptune to fend for himself.

Francis opened another room to find it empty. "Where are you?" he whispered quietly to himself. He could hear gunfire in other parts of the house, but knew he had to stay focused on his section. He moved on to the next room. Surely any other soldiers would have come out by now with all the noise. Still, he could not risk leaving anything unchecked. He twisted the doorknob and kicked it open. His eyes stared down the sights of his weapon, searching for anything that moved, but came up empty-handed.

He exited the room, and caught a flash of movement out of the corner of his eye. He whipped around to catch someone running out of the house. Francis took off after the runner. He kept his weapon at ready while he ran, just in case. He knew it was risky and foolish to chase someone, but he couldn't risk the scientist escaping.

Francis bolted around the corner and out of the front doors to find a man in a lab coat sprinting through the courtyard. He fired a couple shots near the man, but not at him. "Don't move!"

The man froze.

"Hands above your head. Turn around slowly." Francis inched closer, his gun leading the way.

The scientist turned to meet his attacker. His eyes widened when he saw Francis. "It's you."

But that was all he said. A bullet exploded through the man's skull, and he collapsed to the ground. Francis was frozen for just a moment before leaping behind cover.

The way the man fell meant the shooter was firing towards the house, not from it. Francis fumed with anger. He had been so close to finding answers and questioning his target, who was now a vacant corpse surrounded by several others in a courtyard in the middle of nowhere.

"I've got a sniper somewhere on the hills!" Francis shouted, hoping his team would hear. "Stay behind cover. He took out the scientist."

Will sees the man from the future crash out of the house, followed by Francis. He watches the scene unfold for a moment. "I'm sorry, Francis, but I can't risk him telling you anything if we're going to be pals again."

He launches a bullet and watches it hit its mark. The look on his friend's face is priceless. He laughs as Francis dives behind the fountain. He gets to his feet and begins walking towards the mansion. "This is going to be quite the reunion."

All of Francis' team members heard his warning. They had finished searching the house and found only papers. Every German had been eliminated, and the only cons were Neptune's wound and the deceased scientist.

The team, except for Francis gathered on the second floor. Neptune checked in with Jupiter. "Is Pluto alright?"

She nodded. "For now. He's safe behind cover, but he's pinned down by the sniper."

Jessica glimpsed out the window to see a figure approaching the house. "Either we're in serious trouble, or the sniper is on our side."

The others clustered around the opening. Sure enough, a single soldier holding a rifle was coming towards them. Jessica's eyes widened once the figure was close enough to make out. "I don't believe it."

Blinded with rage, she ran down the stairs and stormed out the door. Francis spotted her. "What are you doing? There's a sniper! Get down!"

Jessica was too furious to hear what he had said. She continued on her path. Francis peeked out from his cover to see that she was headed right toward…Will. Will? "No way!"

Francis stood up and chased after Jessica. She had reached Will and before he even said a word, she swung her fist at his face. "I told you that if I ever saw you again, I'd kill you!"

"Nice to see you too," he replied, rubbing his cheek. She swung again, but he caught her arm with his. "I let you have one, but that's all you'll ever get."

Jessica fought back, momentarily disappearing and kicking him hard in the knee. Will fought the urge to crush her skull with his mind. Something like that would blow his cover. Instead, he raises a barrier between the two. Jessica tried once more to strike him, but her fist was stopped mid-air.

"Did you forget that you're not the only one with powers?" Will clicked his tongue in disapproval.

Francis had finally caught up to his two friends. He was a bit shocked to see them fighting. "What are you two doing?"

"It's good to see you alive and in one piece," Will said quickly, extending a hand for him to shake. "It's been awhile."

Jessica butted in. "Don't try and act nice, Will. I know what you are. I told Francis everything."

Francis looked from her to Will. "She told me that you abandoned her. Is that true? How could you do that? I mean, don't get me wrong, I'm happy to see you're alive too…it's just, I never pictured you doing something like that."

There was a tense moment of silence before Will shot his hands up in a gesture of surrender. "You got me. I did leave her. But give me a chance to explain, buddy. I thought you were dead, and she told me to be a janitor at a hospital. You know me, and with our mission out the window, I couldn't just sit around and clean."

"So you left her?"

"I made a choice," Will explained. "I wanted to live and do something that mattered for once. Make a difference and all that. Joining the army was a way for me to do it, but sitting around and cleaning? Really?"

"He's lying to you, Francis!" Jessica insisted.

Will persisted. "I admit I made a mistake leaving. Clearly, you are OK, and so is Jessica. I was wrong to run, but can you blame me? You know how much I wanted to be free, Francis. You know that's all I ever wanted. Maybe I was still reeling from thinking you were dead, but I can't change that now. What's done is done. But when I saw you from up on that hill I knew we had been given a second chance to finish our mission."

Francis considered what his friend had said. *How would I feel if I were in his place?* he thought. Of course, he still had a hard time understanding the level of bitterness Jessica had towards him. "I believe you, Will. I thought you had died, and I blamed myself for it. I can look past what you did, can you do the same, Jess?"

Jessica was taken aback. *How can you believe what he says, Francis?* "I'm sorry. I can't. Francis, he's not the same person we knew from The Island."

Neptune and the rest of the team stumbled into the conversation. "Another friend of yours?"

Francis leveled with them. "I'm sorry guys, can you give us a moment? Try and find some information or something we can use. We'll be done soon." He turned back to his friends. "Look Jessica, none of us are the same person we were in The Island. We've all done things…" He choked back emotions as memories were recalled. "We've all done things that we regret. I of all people know that. I can understand what he's saying. But we should never turn our backs on a friend. He made a mistake, Jess, and he's apologizing for it."

"He can apologize all he wants," Jessica snorted. "It won't make me ever trust him again."

"You don't have to." Francis replied. "You made it clear what your position is. And if staying behind is really what you want to do, I won't stop you. But Will and I are seeing this through to the end, right, bud?"

Will smirked ever so proudly. He had won. "Right."

Jessica shook her head. "You're making a mistake, Francis. If you need me, I'll be inside."

Without another word, she left. Francis turned to Will. "Now, I have one last question. Why did you kill the scientist?"

"I'm sorry. I thought he had a gun," Will lied. "I didn't want to take any chances, so I took the shot. He was my assignment after all."

"What do you mean?" Francis questioned.

"Well after I thought you were dead, I made up a fake identity and signed up for the army. They recruited me to this trial run for snipers, and thanks to my special abilities, I excelled at it. They've been giving me special assignments for a while now. I was tasked with following a team here, and taking out that scientist. They never said anything about keeping him alive."

Will was ready to attack if his friend did not believe him. Francis studied him. "I wish things had happened differently. I'm glad to have you back with us though. I only wish you kept him alive—we could've used him."

"It's good to be back, but I doubt Jessica feels the same way," Will said. He didn't acknowledge killing the scientist.

"Give her time. She'll get over it, I'm sure. She can't stay mad at you forever," he paused. "Besides, she might stay here. She met someone."

"What?" Will chuckled. "You mean you two aren't going to be a thing?" He shut his mouth after receiving a look from his friend. "Whoa, touchy subject. I get it. Well at least the two of us will conquer The Island together."

"Yeah," Francis said solemnly. "Let's check in with the others."

Earth had called Neptune and Jupiter into a room with papers scattered everywhere. "I think you'd better see this."

Neptune grabbed the sheet Earth was holding. His eyes widened when he read it. "Is this accurate?"

Earth shrugged. "I doubt they'd have time to set up fake documents. We didn't find anything else here, so I can only assume it is."

"What is it?" Jupiter questioned.

"It seems we disposed of the scientist, but our mission isn't over yet. Gather the others."

Jupiter nodded and left the room. She bumped into Jessica in the hallway. "Meet in that room. We're not out of the woods yet."

She continued down the stairs and shouted from the doorway to Francis and Will. They jogged over to meet her.

"What's going on?" Francis asked.

"They found something," Jupiter responded, leading them upstairs.

Everyone gathered in the same room. Jessica barely acknowledged Will's existence, and took every opportunity to scowl at him. He ignored everything.

Before anyone spoke, Francis introduced Will. "This is the third member of my team. You can trust him. We'll call him Mercury if that's alright."

The team nodded, and Will gave them a nod. Neptune threw

the paper on a table beside him. "Earth has discovered this document, which has an unsettling account. We did not find the weapon here—only the scientist. And with him dead, we can't question him."

Several eyes found Will, who shrugged it off like nothing happened. Neptune continued. "However, this document says that the weapon was completed and transported earlier this morning. Its target is London."

The news did not sit well with the group. Francis took a seat. "So somewhere out there is an bomb capable of leveling an entire city?"

Neptune nodded grimly and brought out a map. "There is some good news though. We know where it is right now. It's on a train heading for the coast. If we act quickly, we can intercept it before it goes somewhere we can't find."

"And what will we do if we find it?" Jessica questioned.

Earth stood up. "Amidst these papers were the blueprints to the bomb. If you get me next to it, I can diffuse it, and we can blow it up with a controlled explosion."

"We have another problem," Francis stated. "There are now six of us, and we only have two planes. Mine barely held it together with the two of them aboard, I don't know how well Jupiter's will hold with you and Mercury in it."

"She'll hold," Jupiter insisted.

Francis did not believe her entirely. He knew full well what these planes were capable of, as did she. However, he also knew the other option was to leave someone behind. He understood why she would insist such notions. "Very well. Then we'd better get going. We have a train to stop."

14: HEIST

They burned the house to the ground, leaving it in flames. Francis hoped all documents and evidence of the bomb would be destroyed, leaving one last thing to fix.

Fueled with the knowledge that a nuclear bomb is heading towards London, the team made quick time getting back to the planes. As they cleared the brush off, Jupiter and Francis ran through their pre-flight checklists. Each had their own routine, but the results were the same.

Francis made sure the propeller was clear of debris and that there was enough fuel to make it to their destination. *Getting back*, he thought, *now that's the real problem.*

In short time, everything was ready. Francis would take Will and Earth in his aircraft, and Jupiter would take Neptune and Jessica. The planes sputtered to life, and Jupiter led the way. Francis lifted off the ground and followed. He would miss the thrill of taking off and flying—something told him this would be his last time.

Will felt nothing during the take-off. His mind was elsewhere, mapping out a new plan for his future.

I could just kill them and remain here, Uriel pondered. *But then again, this mission essentially was an execution. There isn't much left here anyway. If the boy makes it out of this on top, he can take me to another place. Wherever we end up could be paradise with my powers…and then there's the girl. She may pose a threat to my cover. Francis did mention she might stay behind. Oh, what a wondrous potential that would be. And once I end up where I want to be, I will kill the boy to ensure nothing else interferes with my plans.*

Lazarus attacked the firewall between him and Uriel to find it suddenly disintegrating before him. Uriel waited on the other side. *The boy survived, Uriel. We can salvage our mission. We can still go back.*

Back? Uriel laughed. *No, I don't want to go back. Nothing but death awaits us there. And although I have enjoyed my time here, it's not the right fit for me. We will travel again, but I do not intend to ever make it back to The Island, and neither will the boy. Bye for now, Laz.* The firewall shot back up, and once again the A.I.s were separated.

While in the air, Jessica did her best to bandage Neptune's shoulder wound. She was used to the cramped environment and lack of proper equipment. Neptune grimaced in pain, but never made a sound. He was focused on the mission. He didn't like the plan they had come up with, but right now he wasn't in a situation to argue. He ran it through again in his mind.

Jupiter and Pluto will get us right above the train. Venus and Earth will be lowered by rope on top of it, and Jupiter and I will remain behind. The four of us still in the air will provide supporting fire, while Venus uses her advanced technology to cloak them. It will be up to those two to infiltrate the train, find the bomb and take care of it. Once it is done, they will climb back on top of the train, and Mercury and I will pull them back up using the rope.

Neptune snarled through the pain as Jessica operated on him. *I hate leaving my team to finish a mission of this importance. I should be going down there with them.* But he knew better. With his wound, he was in no shape to assist them. He could do more in the sky with the turret than aboard the train. *God be with us.*

Francis peered through the sky. The day was cloudy, providing them with enough cover. Unfortunately, they had to remain low enough to see the train tracks leaving the town. If they weren't focused they could miss it entirely. All Francis hoped was to not run into any air resistance. The longer they remained in German territory, the more unnerved he was.

Still, his mind was calmed knowing that both his friends were alive and well. He didn't agree with what Will had done, but he knew what he had meant when he said, "All I ever wanted was to be free." He also knew well before they escaped that, if left on their own, Jessica and Will were not the best of friends. Francis felt his mind wandering too far from the task, and he snapped back into reality. He could not afford to make a mistake, not now. He would dwell on these thoughts at a later time.

Jupiter spotted the tail section of the train and began to dip her wings side-to-side, signaling the others. Francis saw his teammate's movement and checked below. The train was far in the distance, but it was there. The two pilots started their dive, accelerating towards the ground and the train.

Jessica gripped the sides of her seat tightly. The descent was not her favorite part of flying. She took deep breaths in and out. *You can do this. You're only going from a plane to a moving train. Nothing crazy, right?* Her mental pump-up was not sufficient, but she could not back down now. They needed her.

Neptune tossed the rope over the side, tying one end to the plane. He gripped the slack in his hands and gave her a nod. Jessica took one last breath and climbed over the side.

Earth was doing the same as Jessica. He was not a fan of heights, but the commander never bothered to ask him about such things. Will lowered him towards the thundering train.

Jupiter and Francis were submerged in their concentration, trying to keep the planes directly over the speeding cart. Any subtle movement would make their teammates miss their target. Francis exhaled slowly, stealing a glance over the edge. Earth was nearly there. His feet dangled above the roof. He released the rope, falling onto his hands and knees. He had made a successful landing and watched as Jessica did the same. They climbed to the back door of the last section of the train.

Francis and Jupiter pulled up to circle and follow the train. They were no longer subtle and hidden. If anyone cared to take notice, they would definitely be reported. A slew of support could come at any moment, and they needed to stay alert.

Meanwhile, Earth and Jessica stood at the doorway. She stared at him. "I know we didn't have a lot of time to explain how this works, but just trust me. As long as you stay in contact with me, they can't see us. We'll take out any soldiers we find, and I'll cover you while you defuse the bomb."

"Works for me," Earth said hurriedly. "Sooner we take care of this and get out, the better."

Jessica grabbed his hand and turned invisible. "Let's go."

She opened the door to find the first cart full of boxes and crates. They moved quickly, clearing section after section until they finally opened a door to find two stunned Germans.

"What was that?" one said to the other in German. His comrade did not have a chance to speak. Jessica and Earth had each taken one out with their silenced weapons. The bodies hit the floor with a thud.

"Clear," Earth whispered, a little shocked at how effective her cloaking was. He wanted to ask her a million questions, but not at a time like this.

The next unit was full of more boxes, though none were big enough to contain the bomb. Jessica opened the next door to find four German soldiers sitting around a large wooden box. They rose to their feet the moment the door opened, weapons pointing at the opening. Jessica fired at the two on the left, while Earth aimed for the two on the right. The men dropped before a single trigger was pulled.

"You know, we make a good team, you and I," Earth grinned, rushing to the crate.

Jessica rolled her eyes and shut the door. "I'm taken, pal. Just focus on the bomb, I'll cover you."

Earth removed the lid and side panel of the massive wooden crate. He whistled when he saw the bomb in its entirety. "Oh boy. This may take a while."

"Not like we're in a rush," Jessica muttered to herself. The sound of gunfire could be heard over the roar of the train.

What's going on out there? she wondered. She repositioned herself beside Earth, keeping him invisible. He glanced up and she spoke without looking down. "Just in case whatever out there is headed our way."

Francis spotted the Flight of German planes before Jupiter. They were diving in from above, towards the front of the train. There were four of them.

Jupiter cursed when she saw them. She shouted back to Neptune. "We've got company!"

Francis leaned back. "Will, I sure hope you've been practicing your skills. We're gonna need them if we want to survive."

Will smiled wildly. "You have no idea, buddy. Just wait till they're closer."

Francis and Jupiter pulled up, setting a course to meet their attackers head-on. Francis checked his sights and gauged how much closer they needed to be for him to open fire.

Here we go.

The planes were in range, and Francis pulled the trigger

first. The Germans veered out of the way, returning fire. Francis whizzed past the two aircraft that had targeted him, while Jupiter dove below her assailants.

"Will, I need you to take the ones on my tail out now! They're planes are more responsive than this one. They'll shoot us down in no time!"

"Geez, not even going to say please or anything?" Will teased. He focused his mind on the two trailing behind them. He locked in on both planes, and forced them into one another. It was as if something had grabbed each one and bashed them together. The debris exploded in all directions, leaving a wake of fire careening down to the Earth.

"Boy could we have used you a while back," Francis called. He redirected his plane to target the ones chasing Jupiter. "I'll take the one on the left, you take care of the right."

"Got it!" Will shouted over the thundering engine, and the gunfire from the German planes.

Francis lined his plane up behind his enemy. He squeezed the trigger, and a burst of shots dug into their target, which spun towards the ground and crashed.

Instead of targeting the plane, Will went for the pilot, and with his powers broke the man's neck. The plane lost altitude with its incapacitated operator. He grinned watching it collide with the ground.

"Let's hope that's all of them!" Francis said, giving Jupiter a nod. The two of them regrouped back in formation over the train. All they could do was wait.

"How much longer?" Jessica asked Earth.

Earth grumbled as he carefully unscrewed a plate on the bomb. "You can't rush these kind of things. It's not like a toy. It takes time."

"Time may not be on our side," Jessica persisted.

"Well aware of that," Earth whispered to himself. A bead of sweat trickled down his forehead. *Concentrate. Remember what you saw in the blueprints.* He carefully rearranged the insides of the bomb to reveal a small cylinder. "Found it!"

"Great. Just get it out, and let's blow this thing sky high." Despite being invisible, Jessica was uneasy standing next to a nuclear bomb.

Earth began unscrewing a rod that held the cylinder in place. The moment the metal left contact with the socket there was a loud sound. Jessica was unsure where it came from, holding her gun steady, checking both doors. There was nothing.

Earth heard the shot before he felt any pain. He looked down to see a smoldering crevice in the base of the crate. Below the bomb, hidden inside had been a trap. The barrel of a gun lurked, waiting to be triggered the moment someone tampered with the bomb.

He could see a gaping red hole in his stomach. His body fell backwards, too weak to stabilize his position.

Jessica dropped her gun to the floor. "Earth!"

She studied his wound, then applied pressure, but she knew the damage was beyond her abilities, or anyone's for that matter. The man would die shortly. She tried to keep him calm. "It's not that bad. You'll be able to make it."

Earth shook his head, coughing up a wad of blood. His teeth glistened red. "Not this time. Get the... cylinder."

His words were faint, but direct. Jessica eyed the place the gun had fired from and positioned her body away from it in case it went off again. She cautiously unscrewed the other side; thankfully there were no more traps. Cradling the device in her hands, she brought it to Earth. "Got it. We can go now. You're going to make it."

Earth chuckled through the pain. "I know I'm done. I can f-f-feel it." He pulled out a thick block of explosives. "Take...the cylinder...get out...I'll t-take c-c-care of...train."

"No!" Jessica insisted through teary eyes. "No, we can find another way."

"I want this," Earth replied. "An honorable death. Go. Now."

Jessica fought every impulse in her body that told her to stay and help him. She got to her feet, tucking the cylinder into her shirt. "Give me five minutes. Then... then you can blow it. I'm sorry I couldn't help you."

Earth smiled. "I've had... my fill... of life."

Jessica squeezed his hand, feeling out of place. She did not know the man well, nor did she have a bond with him, but that did not stop her from wanting to comfort him. "Goodbye."

She left him bleeding out in a German train, next to a large no-longer-nuclear bomb. She climbed the rungs until she was able to stand on top of the cart. The wind almost knocked her off, but she regained her balance, and then searched the skies for her getaway.

"There she is!" Francis shouted. "But where's Earth?"

Of the two planes, Francis was closer to the train, and decided to pick up Jessica, leaving Earth for Jupiter. He lined up the train and shouted to Will. "Lower the rope!"

Will tossed it over the side. The rope danced in the wind as it drew closer and closer. Jessica stretched her arms high, grabbing the end. Francis looked down, making sure she had a firm grip before lifting the plane up into the sky. Francis kept searching for Earth, but he never came.

Jupiter watched Jessica climb the rope. Their eyes met, and Jessica shook her head. *Earth didn't make it,* Jupiter concluded. She rose through the air alongside Francis, who glanced over at her. She sent him a signal to head back to base. He grimly veered away from the train, keeping an eye on Jessica's progress.

Still climbing, Jessica cast a quick glance up to see Will peering over the edge. *I could drop her*, he thought to himself. *But that would raise too many questions, like why didn't I use my powers to help her? No, for now I am stuck, but soon there will be an opportunity to dispose of her. Soon.* After much consideration Will pulled Jessica closer and closer to the plane, until she was safely in the seat with him.

Far below, the train exploded into a fiery cloud of smoke, which began at the center, and spread all the way down, demolishing the engine as well.

All eyes watched the destructive blaze. They completed their mission. Several members of the team did not make it, but those that did had seen it through, and they did not die in vain.

The scientist had been eliminated, the bomb disposed of, and hopefully all evidence of it as well. Yet for some reason, Francis was not satisfied. He kept searching the sky for danger, but the looming feeling of unhappiness distracted his mind. They had stopped everything, so why did he feel this way?

Is it because we could not interrogate the scientist? he wondered, for he was eager to learn more about what The Island's intentions were. *Is it the tension between Jessica and Will?*

He racked his mind endlessly for meaning, and deep down he knew the answer. Over the year and a half of being here, he had changed, and he was not sure if it was a good thing. Francis had seen countless die, many of whom could easily have been him.

And for what?

Francis never truly understood the senselessness of war and the overwhelming loss that came with it, until now. He spent the duration of the flight deep in thought, keeping a watchful eye on the sky.

Nobody spoke the entire time they flew. Jessica and Will squished against each other, uncomfortable and agitated. Jessica wanted to throw Will off, and coincidentally, so did Will. However, neither could bring themselves to do such things. They could bicker once they were on the ground again.

By the time they neared the Western Front, the sky had become pitch black with stars scattered throughout. The moon peeked through a cloud. Francis, along with Jupiter, had been worried that they would have to cross during the day. Travelling into Allied territory bearing German markings would not be a pleasant experience. Fortunately, timing was on their side, and the two planes slid past the front lines unscathed, although several artillery shells had come close.

In short time they approached the base, Neptune had previously arranged a way for them to be recognized by their own people. He launched a bright flare into the air, illuminating their surroundings as it fell to the ground. The Island's defenses were lowered, and as the two planes came in for a landing, they were not harmed.

Once the propeller stopped and it was safe to exit, Jessica jumped out. She felt immediate relief and comfort no longer being confined with Will and with having her feet on solid ground, out of danger. She could return to Monica, and stay with Trevor. The thought warmed her, as she had missed him. A part of her had been in constant fear, for if something happened to her, she would never see him again.

Neptune was assisted out of his seat, and taken directly to their medical wing to tend to his wound. Jupiter and Francis gathered with Jessica and Will. The group was escorted to one of the large meeting rooms, where they would debrief with Wash.

The commander entered, sporting one of his cigars latched in between his teeth. "Why don't we start from the beginning?

What happened out there?"

Jupiter took the lead. "We were able to land in enemy territory and scouted the building our intel led us to. Once we established a plan, we infiltrated it. Before we had a chance to interrogate the man posing as one of us, this young man shot him."

Jupiter gestured to Will. Wash eyed him down. "And who are you?"

"Name's Chris Taylor," Will lied. "I was only following orders. I'm sure your superiors will confirm them. I was told to follow a team to that location and take out the target, which I did."

Wash grunted, unimpressed with the results. "We make it a point not to use real names here, son. Were you able to learn anything at all? Do they still have a weapon? And where's Earth?" Francis shook his head. "That's why we were late on returning, sir. The documents at the mansion told us the weapon was already on a train, with its final destination to be London."

Jessica toyed with the metal cylinder in her jacket pocket, but realized it would be best not to tell anyone of its existence. After all, it was never meant to be here in the first place.

"Earth and I boarded the train," Jessica explained. "The soldiers on board were not a problem. The bomb—that was another matter. Earth was doing a great job defusing it, but the Germans rigged it with a trap. He didn't spot it in time. He told me to get off and that he would take care of it himself. So I did. Earth blew up the train after I had gotten off."

The story left the room in a grim state. A moment of silence was had for Earth. Wash continued leading the debriefing. "Are we sure this threat is over? And were you able to salvage any layouts for that bomb?"

Francis thought about the conversation Neptune had with

the team back at the mansion. "If this bomb is truly capable of leveling an entire city, we should destroy any evidence of it. I don't think any man should have that much power, and I already have my own reservations about those we work for. Therefore, we need to torch the place and any evidence that could aid in the construction of another. Then we destroy the bomb itself. Everyone on the same page?"

The entire team agreed with Neptune. No one should hold that power, and Francis knew very well how much damage and suffering it could cause.

He turned to Wash. "During the infiltration, a fire was started. We assume the Germans were trying to cover up what they were doing. All traces of the bomb were scorched, and Earth took care of the rest. To the best of our knowledge, there is nothing on the bomb left. No papers, no blueprints, and no physical device."

Wash nodded. "I see. That is unfortunate. A weapon of such nature could really turn the tide of this war. At least for now, it is out of German hands."

The room fell silent. Commander Wash took a large puff of his cigar, and tapped the ash out onto a tray. "Is that all there is?"

Francis leaned forward. "Unfortunately it isn't."

"And what other matter is there?"

"Sir, you know my situation and why I am here," he began. "I believe that this is what I was sent to resolve. This issue should fix everything that needed to be fixed. And, with my mission complete, my two companions and I will be leaving."

"A pity," Wash stated. "You were a valuable asset to this team. Are you certain you cannot remain here? We have numerous other tasks that need special attention. Just this week we received information that the Archduke, Franz Ferdinand might have been killed by one of our own—a rogue agent.

Tracking him down will prove rather difficult."

"Tempting," Francis lied, "but I will have to pass. I have other matters that I need to tend to, and this is only delaying the inevitable." Francis stood and saluted both his commander and Jupiter. "It has been a privilege to work with you."

"Dismissed." Wash replied, extending an arm to the door.

Jessica, Will, and Francis filed out of the room. Francis led them to his quarters where they could speak in private. He shut the door behind them and exhaled. "Now that we're all back together, and there is no impending threat, can we talk about what happened?"

"What's there to discuss?" Will asked. "We came, we saw, we stopped The Island."

"What's there to discuss?" Jessica's voice was shrill. "Oh we have plenty to discuss. Like how about you ditching me the moment we got here? Or maybe how we all haven't seen each other in over a year?"

"I'm sorry, Will, but she's right. We need to get this out on the table. And not only that, but figuring out why and how there was an Island scientist here."

"Fine," Will grumbled. "Where do you want to start?"

"The beginning," Francis stated. "I was passed out, and Jessica wanted to stay and wait. You gave her a couple of days and then just left."

"I thought my explanation earlier was enough? I didn't want to sit around cleaning. I wanted to be out there, making a difference. And that's exactly what I did."

Jessica shook her head. "I can't believe you. How do you expect me to? You could have said any of that when you left, but you didn't. You didn't even say goodbye."

Francis watched his two friends bicker, but did not interrupt. He knew better.

"I'm sorry, alright? What's done is done." Will argued. "I can't take it back, and to be honest everything just reminded me of The Island. I wanted to forget about that place and what happened. You were a constant reminder, and I just couldn't. I ran, OK?"

The room went silent. Jessica didn't know what to believe anymore. But deep down, she knew she would never trust him again, and that the young man standing in front of her was not Will. Jessica sat down, knowing there was nothing left for her to argue.

"Well," Francis began, "I think this shouldn't have happened—not with how close we all once were. Regardless, it's time we put it behind us and move forward."

"And how exactly do we do that?" Jessica questioned.

"By going back to where it all began. By taking down The Island."

Jessica laughed. "Are you serious? Really? After everything that's happened, you think we're just going to follow you blindly again? No. No Francis, you know full well that I have a life here—that I'm happy. I'm not saying it's more important than taking down The Island, but after all of this, it's what I want to do."

"What about the others?" Francis looked like a wounded puppy. "What about my promise?"

"That's exactly it, Francis!" Jessica shouted. "It was *your* promise. Not mine. I went along, heart-set on this mission from the start. I was with you, but not after everything that's happened here. I can't just leave Trevor. I can't abandon what I've started to build."

"Who's Trevor?" Will interjected.

"You don't get to ask that question, Will," she hissed.

Francis was hurt. Her words had cut him deep, and he felt

like he had lost his once closest friend. "If…if that's what you want to do, I won't stop you. I know what you mean. Stay. I'll go on. Are you in or out Will?"

Will's lips curved slightly into a grin. "You know I'll take any chance to get a little payback. Count me in."

Jessica fumed inside, but did not let it show. Francis looked at her. He could barely utter the words from his mouth. Each one felt like a dagger in his heart. "Well then, I guess this is goodbye."

"I guess it is," Jessica replied stubbornly. She gestured at Will. "If he goes with you, he will get you killed. You mark my words, Francis. He's not the Will we once knew."

Francis was not sure how to respond. How could she still think that? He wanted to grab her and hold her, but he knew it wouldn't change her mind. It would probably make things worse. Despite his gut, he got to his feet and embraced Jessica in a hug. "I'll miss you."

"I'll miss you too," she said, squeezing tightly. She leaned close to his ear and whispered so only he could hear her. "He'll kill you, Francis. Stop The Island, but do it alone. Please."

"You're wrong about him," Francis whispered back. He pulled away and opened the door for her. "Goodbye, Jess. Have a good life."

Jessica stormed out of the room in frustration. She heard it shut behind her, and slammed her fist into the opposite wall. *He's so stupid and stubborn!* she thought. *Why can't he see it?*

She paced back and forth down the hallway. Her mind was twisted. She knew that if she stayed, he would die, but if she left, she would never see Trevor again. The decision boiled down to the two men: Trevor or Francis?

Whichever one she chose, she'd lose the other. Could she throw away everything that she and Francis had ever been through? Certainly he deserved it after just leaving her just now and not listening to her about Will. *Can I live with myself, knowing Will is going to betray him, just like he did with me?*

But what about Trevor?

Simply thinking his name made her feel warmer and happier. She loved him. She didn't love Francis—not like that. Perhaps things would have been different had they not been separated, but now? Jessica could not pretend that Trevor was anything less than perfect.

Her mind started to bend reality, sending her on a guilt trip. *How could you be so selfish? What about the other orphans? What about all those that will or are suffering by their hands? And you would just throw that away for a man?*

Not for a man, no, but for love? Possibly, she thought. How long had it even been since the last time she saw his face? Jessica knew her mind was beginning to choose a side, and she hated it. The impossible decision between a dear friend, and someone she loved was frustratingly difficult, but she had come to a decision.

Francis and Will were left in the room alone. Will watched Francis mope and rolled his eyes. "Ah, she'll be fine. Don't worry about it."

"I thought she was dead. I tried moving on, and then found her, thinking I wouldn't let her go ever again." Francis mumbled. "Turns out she loves someone else, and I was too late. I thought we'd always be together—the three of us. And now it's just you and me."

"We'll make it work. Now let's get a move on. Island's not going to shut itself down." Will was agitated. He did not want to linger around anymore, especially to give Jessica time to reconsider. She left all on her own, which made his life and goal that much easier.

"I guess you're right."

The door flew open and Jessica stormed in. "Alright, if we're going to do this, we do it my way. First, I don't trust or like you at all," she said to Will. "So don't ever expect me to work with you from here on out—at most, I'll tolerate you. And if you do anything even remotely sketchy, you will be in for a world of hurt. Second, Francis, the moment we are done this, you are taking me back to Trevor. I don't care if I have to drag your butt through all of time itself, it's happening."

She took a deep breath and continued to bark instructions. "Just to be clear, you're making me leave my entire world behind, and the chance for a normal life. The only reason, I'm doing this is because of everything we've been through. I care about you, Francis, but you're so blind to see whatever it is that's going on with Will.

And finally, you're going to give me some time before leaving to write a letter to Trevor, explaining my decision. Once I've sent it, we can go. You good with that?"

Francis was stunned. He had not expected her to return, and after receiving that earful, he felt guilty for her decision. He dropped the subject altogether. Francis had been through too much to be bothered by this. She was capable of choosing her own path, just like he did. If this was her choice, he would not bear its weight.

"Deal," Francis said. "Come back here once you've finished with your letter."

15: HOLLOW

Ypres, Belgium
November 11, 1914
10:45 A.M.

J essica had to ask several people before finally receiving a
paper, envelope, and writing utensil. She found an empty
room where she could be alone with her thoughts. Shortly after
considering what she wanted to say, she began to write.

> My Dearest Trevor,
>
> I don't know exactly how to tell you this, but I won't be
> coming back for a while. You've always been so good at
> understanding and listening, so please, hear me out. You
> know my past, and all the terrible things that happened to
> me. You also know how much I care about my friend,
> Francis. Before you even think it, don't worry that I am
> leaving you to pursue a relationship with Francis. I am
> yours.
>
> I told you of our goal to stop those that put us through all
> those experiments. I'm afraid the situation has changed.
> There were the three of us at the start, but somewhere along
> the way, Will, the one I told you about, changed. He's not
> the same person, and to be honest, he terrifies me.
>
> I can see it, but Francis refuses to look. If I don't keep on
> this journey with them, Francis will be left alone with Will.
> I am certain that Will is going to betray him in some way,
> and I'm having a hard time thinking of how I could live
> with myself if I stay here.
>
> Please understand, Trev, that this is the last thing I want to

do. All I want is a normal life—a life with you after the war. But I wouldn't be me if I stayed here and let them go. It's hard to explain, but I need to do this. I am so sorry. There is a chance that I may never return, but you can bet your life on it that I will claw my way through hell to get back to you. You are my whole world.

I know that if I told you in person, you would insist on coming with me, but you can't. You belong here, and this is not your fight. I love you with all my heart, and I will come back to you. I'll always have your pocket watch to remind me of us. It, and your letters, have been the only thing that's kept me going since we've been apart. This is something that I need to do. Please try and understand.

Yours for all of time,
Jessica

Tears soaked the paper as she wrote. No decision in her entire life was more difficult than this one. She hated herself for needing to save Francis, but she despised herself more for choosing to do so, rather than stay with Trevor.

Jessica struggled to explain and justify the decision, even to herself. She only hoped that Trevor would understand.

As Jessica was sealing her letter, damp with tears, Francis and Will were still in his quarters.

Francis watched Jessica leave, shutting the door behind her. He turned to Will. "You really screwed up. You need to make this right."

Will shrugged. "What do you want me to do? I've already apologized. I've done everything I can think of. She just doesn't trust me anymore."

"Were the things you said to her that bad?"

"Apparently. At the time, I didn't think they were." *And at the time, I never thought I would see either of you again.* "She'll get over it eventually though, right?"

Francis shook his head. "I don't know. But for now I would just be cool. Don't do anything to get her riled up."

"Gee, you think?"

Francis sighed. "That's not the only thing that's bothering me though."

"Oh?"

"What was an Island scientist doing here in the first place?" Francis questioned. "I mean, how? Why?"

"I don't know." Will lied. "Maybe he was like another Nimue that just got sent here."

"I don't think so. Before you shot him, he recognized me. He said, 'It's you.' How would he know me if he had been banished?"

"He said that?" Will kicked himself for not pulling the trigger sooner.

Francis nodded. "He knew who I was."

"Maybe they just sent him away as punishment after we escaped."

"No," Francis said grimly. "I think they are sending people after us."

Will laughed. "You can't be serious? Why go after us? And if he was after us, why would he be working on that bomb?"

"To get our attention?" he suggested. "Look, I don't know, but something's not right. He was clearly an Island scientist, and he knew me. There's got to be something I'm missing."

Francis had an epiphany. "What if all they needed to take control of time was for someone to travel through it?"

"What?"

"Stay with me," Francis insisted. "What if I opened up a path to everywhere we've been, and they are now following us?"

"But that scientist was here before we were," Will pointed out. "So that can't be it."

"That's true." Francis slunk back in his chair. He ran a hand through his hair. "This is just all so confusing."

"How about we just get our answers from them, huh? We'll break into Island headquarters and force them to give us answers," Will suggested.

"I guess that's all we can do. I just finally felt like we could get some answers, you know?"

The door creaked open, and Jessica stepped inside. "They said they would deliver the letter personally. I am ready to go when you are."

"Are you sure?" Francis asked. "Because once we leave, there's no turning back."

"I know. I'm ready," she replied firmly.

Great, Will or rather, Uriel, thought. *It would have been so much easier without her.*

"Alright, but I don't want to deal with the two of you yammering at each other." Francis clarified.

"If he stays out of my way, and is who he says he is, we won't have a problem."

"Fine by me," Will agreed, though he had different intentions.

There was a momentary silence before Jessica worked up the nerve ask one final question. "Where do you think we'll end up this time?"

Francis stared into space. "Let's just hope it's somewhere a little more stable than here and now. We're close though."

Jessica hesitated when Francis reached for her hand. *Was this the right choice?* As if he had read her mind, Francis spoke.

"I'll get you back to him. Promise."

She shook the jitters out of her head and grasped his hand. Francis stood between his friends to ease their discontent. He interlocked his fingers with theirs, clinging tightly to both of them. "Everything's going to be fine."

Those were the last words spoken as Francis focused his mind to trigger his ability. He felt the tingling sensation, the feeling of being sucked forward, and then, nothing.

The three companions were moving through time, though none of their minds could comprehend what was going on. Francis' was entirely lost in a memory.

His parents were fighting. Francis stood in the upstairs hallway, clinging to the staircase railing, which was just as tall as him. The young boy moved from pillar to pillar as if scaling the side of a mountain.

When he reached the top of the stairs, he sat down and gently slid on his bottom, thudding on each step. He was so little that every bump went unnoticed by his mother and father, who shouted in hushed tones in the kitchen below.

The boy stopped the moment he could see the kitchen through the white wooden bars. It was late in the night, so his black Batman pajamas blended in with the shadows. His sister had gone to bed long ago and had not stirred for hours.

Francis listened carefully, watching the silhouettes of his parent's arms waving frantically in the kitchen.

He heard his mother's voice first. "Why are they doing this?"

"I don't know," his father replied. "I'm doing as much digging as I can, but it's dangerous. Several others have gone missing."

"Isn't there a way to get out of it? Why didn't we know this before going in?" Her tone was agitated.

"You know why. When this deal came my way, I could not pass it up. The money gave us our new home, and can put our kids through school."

"You need to get to the bottom of this," she insisted. "If something darker is going on, you need to find out and expose it."

"Don't you think I know that?" he snapped. "If people are disappearing for asking questions, I don't know how I can do anything. And they're not above going after you and the kids—that's what troubles me."

"They wouldn't."

"They would."

"But they're just kids."

"If I can get access to the lower levels, I might be able to find evidence to put them away. But it's incredibly risky. If I get caught, they'll disappear me like they did the others. And I couldn't cope with it if they went after you."

There was a long silence in the kitchen. His mother embraced his father. "So what do we do?"

"I'll see if I can find a way without drawing attention to myself, which won't be easy, seeing how they keep everything under lock and key."

"And what if you do find evidence? What then?"

"I'll have to take it to the news, most likely. I'd need to be careful though. The Island has their claws in everything. It needs to be a broadcast company that they don't own."

"I'm worried about you."

The two figures moved behind a wall so that Francis could not see them any longer, but he could still hear them.

"I know, darling. I've already lost friends on this project. I don't want to lose you, too. I think it will take a long time for me to gain access to where anything incriminating would be."

"Then take your time." He heard his mother's soft voice. "Do it right. Stay low, work your way up, and then bring them down."

"But what if I slip up? The higher I go, the more in danger we are."

"If they are doing what you think they are doing, don't you think the risk is worth it?"

Another stint of silence. "You're right. But if one day I don't come home from work, or there is a random freak accident, get the kids out of town. Stick to back roads, use only cash, and start somewhere new."

His mother agreed, and the two of them emerged from the kitchen. Francis had to move quickly up the stairs to his room in order to not be caught. He crawled into bed, and wondered what his parents were talking about, and then forgetting it had even happened.

EPILOGUE

New York, 1935

The streets of New York bustled with life. Local kids played football in the park with a worn, tattered little ball. Horns honked as a Ford Roadster driver waved hello to a passing Tudor. A young man hollered at passerbys, waving newspapers and exchanging money with pedestrians who were eager for their informative articles.

Down the lane was a busy barbershop. A striped red and white barberpole spun around and around out front. Next door was a local tavern bearing a fancy wooden sign with The Commodore painted neatly in gold lettering. Across the street was an Italian restaurant, Dominique's, which bordered yet another bar, Top Tavern. Still further, on a corner just beside the water was a large plot that had not been developed yet. It was barren and full of dirt, which was used only as a good spot to feed pigeons small flakes of bread.

However, on a cloudy day like this one, there was nobody to feed the cluster of cooing birds. The only person near the plot was on the corner, passed out with a bottle of liquor in his arms.

One moment there were only birds in the lot, and the next, out of thin air, were three bodies. The pigeons, rightfully terrified, took flight, scattering in every direction. They were the only ones to notice the three appear.

Jessica took a hard tumble, smacking her head against the ground. A small scrape formed on her forehead, but blood did not trickle down. Will landed flat on his back, dazed from the sudden impact. Francis remained unconscious and motionless, his mind elsewhere.

Will and Jessica gasped for air, in shock from the jolting trip. While sucking in oxygen, Jessica kept a keen eye on Will. "Where are we?"

Will glanced around, searching for clues until he saw a large statue that he instantly recognized. "Looks like we made it to New York."

"Not quite," Jessica frowned. She observed the buildings, the cars, and the traffic in the water. "Look around, it's New York, but it's not the one we know."

As Will scanned the area, Jessica tried to shake Francis awake. "C'mon Francis. Wake up!"

She checked his pulse when he did not move. He was still breathing. She tried shaking him awake again, but to no avail.

"He alive?" Will asked.

"Yes, but he's not waking up."

"How many days again was he out when we first got to Belgium? He'll come around."

Jessica stared at her unconscious friend. "You'd better wake up soon."

Will watched her lean over Francis. This would be the perfect opportunity to eliminate the two of them, now that he knew where they ended up. He could start over from scratch, more careful this time. Will towered over Jessica and Francis; his eyes darted back and forth wildly. Nobody was watching.

He reached down and thrust his hands around Jessica's neck. She clawed at him, trying to break free, struggling for air. Jessica reacted quickly though, turning invisible, while simultaneously kicking Will in the groin. He collapsed to the ground.

Jessica remained camouflaged and rolled over to Francis,

pushing his body further away. Francis, too, went invisible at Jessica's touch. She caught her breath, chest heaving up and down. Jessica clutched her friend's unconscious body in her arms, praying that Will would not find them.

Will had risen to his feet, angry for losing his prey. "You're quick—I'll give you that!" he called out to the open space. He scanned the area, trying to figure out where she was hiding. "I'm going to find you, Jessica, and when I do…"

He didn't need to finish his sentence. Jessica knew what he was capable of. She tried to remain calm, holding onto Francis, making as little sound as possible.

Her attacker was growing more and more furious. He ran in random directions, throwing rocks and dust anywhere and everywhere.

"Where are you?" he screamed.

Jessica's heart beat faster and faster, terrified of being discovered, knowing if she stayed there, she eventually would be. This is my chance, she thought. The noise Will made from shouting gave her just enough time to push Francis into the water, and dive in after him.

But Will heard the splash and raced to the water's edge. He scoured the liquid, searching for any sign of his victims. Empty-handed, he started to use his powers to ripple the water, hoping to expose them.

Deep under the water, Jessica grabbed Francis, and kicked her way around the corner of the wall. Her lungs felt like they were going to explode, and she could only hope that Francis would be OK.

Safely out of sight from Will, she emerged, careful not to make any ripples. She cradled her friend's head above the surface, angry that she could not do more to see if he was all right. At least for now, gripping a wooden pillar in the cold water, they were hidden. Jessica watched Will search for them and prayed that he did not look their way.

To be continued…